VERSION ZERO

TITLES BY DAVID YOON

Frankly in Love
Super Fake Love Song

VERSION ZERO

DAVID YOON

G. P. PUTNAM'S SONS
New York

PUTNAM
— EST. 1838 —

G. P. Putnam's Sons
Publishers Since 1838
An imprint of Penguin Random House LLC
penguinrandomhouse.com

Library of Congress Cataloging-in-Publication Data

Names: Yoon, David, author.
Title: Version zero / David Yoon.
Description: New York: G. P. Putnam's Sons, [2021] |
Identifiers: LCCN 2020057329 (print) | LCCN 2020057330 (ebook) |
ISBN 9780593190357 (hardcover) | ISBN 9780593190364 (ebook)
Subjects: GSAFD: Suspense fiction.
Classification: LCC PS3625.O534 V47 2021 (print) | LCC PS3625.O534 (ebook) |
DDC 813/.6—dc23
LC record available at https://lccn.loc.gov/2020057329
LC ebook record available at https://lccn.loc.gov/2020057330
ISBN 9780593332641 (export edition)

Printed in the United States of America
1st Printing

Book design by Tiffany Estreicher

For Nicki and Penny, my lights in the dark

Don't be evil.

—INTERNET PROVERB

Move fast and break things.

—INTERNET PROVERB

Say you are writing a new piece of software.

You should give each version of your software a number to keep track of its progress.

Examples: *version 1.5*, *version 3.11*, *version 7.24*.

Version 1.0 means your software is officially ready to be used in a real-world setting.

Version 2.0 means you made significant updates to *version 1.0*.

Same for *version 3.0*, *version 4.0*, and so on.

If your software is still in development and not yet ready for prime time, you should give it a version number less than one, like *version 0.2* or *version 0.7*.

The absolute first version number for any new piece of software is *version 0.1*.

There is no such thing as *version 0.0*.

VERSION ZERO

```
1   const VERSION_NUMBER = 0;
2   const AGENT = "BLACK HALO";
3   const year = 0x2018;
4   const enc = [
5      021, 024, 015, 015,
6      026, -031, 030, 016,
7      034, 027, 021, 034,
8      021, 014, 025, -022,
9      017, 016, 032, 027
10   ];
11   let res = ["You are infinite"];
12   const RANDOM_SEED = 20879976793454946324n;
13   if (VERSION_NUMBER % 2 < 1) res.shift();
```

Max is twenty-eight.

It is sometime in the future. Where is he? Probably alone. No friends. No girlfriend. He could still be in Tokyo, among the brutalist canyons of apartment buildings. Office towers crowding into the blue of the early-morning haze.

Max must read a lot. What else would there be to do these days?

Say he reloads his vaporizer with a fresh cartridge. Say it looks like a tiny vial of blood. He takes his first hit. On the other side of the planet I step out into the helgic light of late afternoon, wishing I could have one, too. But pregnant girls can't smoke. So I hold two fingers to my lips and inhale an invisible cigarette.

He exhales a billowing wisp taller than himself. It dissipates like a cloud from an ukiyo-e painting.

Imagine his apartment. Bookcase after bookcase, all the manga and anime he could ever want. No laptops. No devices. A stack of postcards and an inkwell and fountain pen. A small, tidy apartment. An ocean of pretty Japanese girls to look at.

Do they remind him of me?

I do not want to think about that.

Maybe he is working on something secret. Or is he simply hiding?

I know all about hiding. I hide in plain sight.

From below, the square notes of a crosswalk melody float into Max's hearing. It's an old, warbling tune called "Toryanse." Max has probably studied it like he studies everything. He hears it every day—he must, it's unavoidable—and every time it reminds him of the last time we ever saw each other. I'm sure of it.

Going in is easy / Returning is scary
But while it is scary
You may go in / You may pass through

Japan suits him. Lots of tidy spaces and orderly routine. Being Salvadoran American, Max has hair dark enough, stature compact enough to vanish into crowds with an ease he never knew back in Southern California.

Back in Playa Mesa.

I don't know what he does next. Say he removes his Buddy Holly glasses. He presses the heels of his hands into his eyes until swirls and checkerboards appear. When he opens them we are atop that bright snowy mountain under the impossible deep blue sky where the days last much longer than they should.

How I wanted one final kiss. How childish. There was no time anyway. The door shut and I was launched up into the whirling universe of crystal and snow.

And there was nothing to be done about that.

Max presses his eyes and sees flashes of phantom light. When will he finally be free of this thing? He's traveled all over the world. How much farther will he have to travel to escape it?

But while it is scary
You may go in / You may pass through

0.1

```
14   res.push(enc.map((i, idx) => {
15      return String.fromCharCode(
16         AGENT.charCodeAt(
17            idx % AGENT.length
18         ) - i
19      );
20   }).reduce((i, j) => {
21      return i.toString() + j.toString();
22   }));
23   res.unshift(atob("MzU3NzU1MDM2NTgxMDMzNTg0OTU="));
24   res.push(
25      (8939935261623587079n << 2n).toString()
26   );
27   res.push((RANDOM_SEED & 0x18C445CAC40447832n | 0n).toString());
28   res.push("" + (15184538342417885700989896n / BigInt(year)));
29   let as_json = {
30      coordinates: '{"x": 2, "y": 5}',
31      tolerance: 0.1,
32      subunit: [2 ** 8]
33   };
```

Max was twenty-six.

It was way back in the year 2018. Summer. Remember? Hashtags and don't-text-and-drive and fear-of-missing-out and virtual reality. Selfies and the Troll President and revenge porn. All that.

Max walked in the white Californian sunlight. He walked into a village made of glass. The village was Wren. Wren was the world's largest social network. A *social network* was a computer program where many-many people could share their thoughts/photos/videos and also share other people's thoughts/photos/videos. Then they would talk about it all. Sometimes fight. Mostly fight.

For some reason, this kind of thing was hugely popular in the year 2018.

Wren's only product was Wren itself. It had been started by two college kids who worked hard and pulled themselves up by their bootstraps and exhibited Yankee ingenuity and blah,

blah,

blah.

Everyone used Wren, everyone loved it, everyone hated it. And as strange as it sounds, Wren was everything. People used it for news. For gossip. Social plans. Dining tips. Political views. Dating. Shopping. Driving directions. Blablabla.

As strange as it sounds, three billion people used Wren every day on their smartphones. The people could not stop themselves. They said they were *addicted*.

Back then being addicted to tech was considered a good thing.

Tech meant anything involving computer programs, especially the ones used by many-many people. It was different from *technology*, which meant noncomputer things like building bridges and inventing medicines.

Max wore a hoodie. It gave him entrepreneurial élan. All CEOs in the tech industry wore hoodies as symbols of egalitarianism belying their positions of supreme power. Tech CEOs could probably get everyone on the planet to chew more gum with a simple edit to their news algorithms, if they wished. But they did no such thing. For they were good men.

Wren's number one rule was this: *Don't be evil.*

One day Max wanted to be a CEO of his very own Wren.

Max wanted to put a dent in the universe. But in a good way.

His Benevolence, CEO Maximilian Portillo.

For now, Max was in Product.

He walked across the colossal hexagonal green populated with Wrennies playing volleyball, holding yoga poses, or lying about. Three men—Mexican, maybe—were setting up some kind of epic barbecue. They eyed Max as he walked past.

I am not you, Max wanted to say. I'm supposed to be Salvadoran. But I was born here. My Spanish sucks. So, you know.

Max felt the constant need to explain himself. He felt it now.

He entered a glass building. He passed Maurice, the African American security guard. He waved to Aimee, the ever-smiling Whitewoman at Reception.

He passed through the large bullpen full of brown-skinned programmers from India and Thailand and so on. Max, though brown skinned, was not one of them. Wren put the programmers on the first floor as a show of prowess for visitors. The popular belief was that really good programming could solve all social problems, like housing or racism or bullying or sexism or deceit or greed or loneliness.

Anyway.

Max passed through Marketing with its many Whitewomen and arrived at Product, with its many tall and hale Whitemen. Max was not one of them, either. Max had long given up on being one of anyone. He decided to simply be one of himself.

This meant Max had no tribe to speak of, which Max disliked. But it also exempted him from the expectations and assumptions of a tribe, which Max liked.

So Max chose his own tribe: Product. And despite being the only brown-skinned one there, Max did not feel like a fly in milk. Maybe it was because Max was happily deluded. Maybe it was because Product was Max's play space, a mental sanctuary where he could dream up new Wren features and generally make up his own rules as he went along, as conjurers do. Max was Senior Product, the youngest ever in Wren's ten-year history to achieve such a rank.

"Mister Max," said Justin Richards, a tall and hale Whiteman, Max's boss only in title. Justin Richards, and Wren in general, did not believe in titles. Titles were a big pile of bull. Work was not *work*, either. Work was called *hanging out*.

"Mister Justin," said Max.

They fist-bumped.

"Drop what you're working on," said cool-boss Justin Richards. "The Helix wants you."

0.2

The Helix was a sealed office on the top floor of Wren. It was devoted to secret research and development projects. Being entirely made of glass, the Helix appeared to have no walls or ceiling. Just a square platform floating high above the brown chaparral hills of Southern California.

The Helix was named by Wren CEO Cal Peers after the Helix nebula, a cosmic body whose nickname was *the Eye of God*.

Justin Richards eyed a glowing spot on the glass to open it up, and led Max inside. The sky room had but a quartet of blond chairs surrounding a glass coffee table. Not a desk or computer in sight. Max stole a breath. He had just unlocked a secret level in the game of his life.

Two small behoodied Whitemen greeted Max with slack fist bumps. Brad Nason and Brad Barker. Few ever got to meet the Brads. It was whispered that the Brads met regularly with Cal Peers himself.

"Hey, Mister Max," said Brad.

"Enough of this gay banter," said Max, quoting a beloved comedy sketch. They knew it—all techies in the Republic of California knew it—and laughed.

"So, listen," said Brad.

"Here's this thing," said Brad. "A whole, like, suite of programs. Personality tests, free games, do-it-yourself music videos for the kids."

Brad touched the coffee table to illuminate it, and a dozen documents bloomed upon its surface. Max sifted through them without asking. This was something Justin Richards loved about him.

Mister Max just gets right up on in there, Justin Richards liked to say.

"Sixteen Faces, Inc.?" said Max, sifting and sifting. "YouTunes LLC? Are these third-party partners?"

"They're our companies," said Brad. "We just made them last week."

Max frowned. He pushed his Buddy Holly glasses up and raised his eyebrows. "This is about the plateau, isn't it."

"You were right," said Brad to Justin Richards. "He gets it."

"Like, instantly," said Brad.

Fist bumps all around.

"I get it, too, for sure," said Justin Richards. "But just for the sake of double clarity, could you explain the plateau situation back to me in Luddite's terms?"

Max tented his fingertips. "So you know how Wren users are giving us less and less data these days?"

"Sure," said Justin Richards.

"It's not like back during start-up Wren, when user data submissions grew all hockey stick," said Max. When Max spoke, he made sure to make eye contact with everyone at regular intervals, like a sprinkler head. "Now that we're Wren-Wren, users aren't as eager. We've hit a plateau. Advertisers are all, sure, we can sell to style-conscious professional males aged twenty-four to forty in SoCal who play football video games, but what other intel can you get us? Can you get us more granularity?"

"Granularity," said Justin Richards.

"So I'm guessing, and correct me if I'm wrong," said Max, "that we're using little decoy companies to get people to give us more data in a, um, indirect way."

"Boom goes the dynamite," said Brad.

Brad swept the table clean and brought up some site mock-ups.

"Hooking the decoys up to our master user database is the easy part," said Brad. "We're just short on ideas on how to get people to give up more info."

"More info," said Max.

"Stuff beyond hard knowables like music and movie preferences," said Brad.

"We want the squishy stuff—an emotional profile," said Brad. He counted on his fingers. "Classics like openness to experience, conscientiousness, extraversion, agreeableness, neuroticism."

"Then we want to go beyond the classics," said Brad. "Sexual proclivities. Psychopathy index. Subrace. Patriotism. Attractiveness."

Max realized his brow had become damp. He pushed his glasses up. "Huh."

"We can't just ask outright for that type of data," said Brad. "Users would spook. Or they'd just give a bunch of self-conscious answers, which is useless to us."

"Heisenberg principle, yo," said Brad.

"We need decoy ideas," said Brad. "Fake contests, fake articles, whatever."

"Well, Mister Max can riff all damn day," said Justin Richards. "Right?"

"Huh," said Max again. The table before him glowed with rectangles.

"We're calling this the Soul Project," said Brad. "Work on nothing else; tell no one. Mister Cal wanted to be here, by the way. He had to be at a thing."

Brad struck a pose. "Get that data so's we can get paid, nigga."

0.3

So Max worked on the Soul Project, and nothing else.

He brought his chunky black laptop to the sunlit Helix and set it next to Brad's thin gold laptop, which sat next to Brad's identical thin gold laptop, and did not leave for a week except to eat barbecue (prepared by the Mexicans) and pee in touchless travertine bathrooms (maintained by Mexicans).

The Brads were hardly ever there, leaving Max to work alone in silence.

Max came up with new ways of getting users to give emotional data to Wren without knowing it. This *without knowing it* part was important. For as it grew, Wren had garnered a certain reputation. Words—ominous words—like *Big Brother* and *surveillance capitalism* began being thrown about.

Coming up with ways of getting data was not the hard part for Max. That was the easy part. The hard part was those ominous words.

Max struggled with this hard part. He felt this hard part was the hallmark of his generation. Example: a college friend, not a friend-friend but a Wren-friend, scored a plum gig doing public relations crisis management and brand rehabilitation for a pharmaceutical company caught price gouging, and was able to buy a gorgeous seaside condo as a result. Max saw her post about it on Wren.

It's probably super easy, Max imagined, to let yourself forget about the poor patients priced out of health care while sitting in a gorgeous seaside condo.

All of Max's friends from college had jobs like this. They had studied hard. Things were paying off. Max, it could be easily argued, had a job like this.

The hard part was a contradiction. Abandoning your morals at the office. Abandoning your morals at the mall, where you might moan about the lack of a local mom-and-pop economy while buying nothing but the cheapest stuff made overseas by stone-faced corporations. Or on your smartphone, where you might give up bits of your privacy to avoid paying two dollars for an application.

In our day-to-day, Max thought, when did we actually live by our morals?

Morals: Be kind, be fair, don't steal, don't deceive, don't bully. Share with those in need. Stuff everyone learns as a child.

Besides work and shopping and time spent playing with smartphones, the only time Max could see where morals were given proper attention was at night, in bed, in those few luxurious minutes before succumbing to sleep.

Anyway. Max gave a like to that post about his friend's condo.

Max dealt his like by tapping an icon. Everyone had infinite likes and gave and received them without a thought. Likes were a worthless form of currency.

And yet: a perfect transaction log of these likes were maintained by Wren.

Why?

Max went outside to lie on the great hexagonal green with his eyes closed, resting, not sleeping, thinking about morals and stuff, when he startled at an insect crawling the rim of his nostril. He opened his eyes and saw not a bug but Akiko, inserting a blade of grass into his nose. Max lay there and let her do it.

Max would lie there and let her do anything she wanted, if only he could.

"You haven't been at your desk, duncie," said Akiko.

"Been working up in the Helix with the Brads," said Max. "No big deal."

"Shut up." Akiko smiled and punched his bony shoulder hard. She could punch him again and again if she wanted, as far as Max was concerned. She could punch him all day forever.

Akiko leveled her eyes—eyes that could decimate a cursed horde—and said: "You have to tell me what you're working on."

The world tilted. Max wanted to tell her everything. But this was an impossible kind of want. He wanted, had long wanted, to touch a small smooth crease above her left eye. A small scar. A childhood collision, an epic misadventure.

"No way. The Brads would eat my face," said Max. "Cal Peers would find out who this Max person was and eat my face. Cal motherhugging Peers."

Motherhugging was an old joke of theirs, from a poorly censored movie they had stumbled upon as kids. *Drop the motherhugging gun or I'll shoot.*

"Dude," said Akiko, awestruck.

"Right?" said Max.

"Well," said Akiko, still awestruck. "I guess high five for you."

They high-fived, and Max held her hand for just a moment too long before releasing it. He hoped she hadn't noticed.

Akiko was an elite programmer at Wren. She worked on the first floor, a pillar of focus amid a sea of men all staring at her for the usual reasons. She was the only female elite programmer at the entire company. She and Max had worked there together for three years now, which was equivalent to ten in the real world.

Everyone wanted Akiko on their projects. So she worked on everything, and worked late nights. As did Max, because everyone wanted him on their projects, too. They worked well together. People often said they shared a brain.

But that was not the real reason why Max worked late nights.

Late at night, the office was clean and cool and—if he was lucky—empty but for him and her, huddling over the same screen glowing blue-green. Solving problem after problem, except for the one unsolvable one within Max.

Akiko Hosokawa was Max's beautiful and keen and astute and excellent friend since high school, and the one who got him an interview with Wren in the first place. She had a forever-boyfriend, Shane Satow, who was also Max's excellent friend since high school.

Max, on the other hand, had a modest string of girlfriends come and go through high school, into college, and beyond. He had even taken some of them on double dates with Shane and Akiko on occasion. With every drama, every breakup, Max had turned to Akiko for advice and sympathy. She was in a forever-relationship, after all. She knew the most about love, and how to keep it.

But secretly, Max never wanted Akiko's advice. He would tell Akiko, in fine detail, how each of his relationships was not as robust as hers and Shane's.

Why can't I have what you guys have? he would say.

What he really meant was: *Why can't I have you?*

Akiko, oblivious, would say something like, *One day you'll meet the One.*

But I already did, Max would think.

Back in the Helix. Passing clouds cast socclusing shadows upon Max one after another until the whole sky was billowy and gray. Max was grateful for the cool.

He saved his work—a simple text file—into a secret folder shared by the Brads and Cal Peers.

The file contained ideas with titles like:

Who is your ideal sexual partner? Take the quiz. This is most definitely not safe for work.

Could you do better as president? Click here to play.

Max gave the file the self-deprecating name of "Maxs_shitty_decoy_ideas.txt."

I guess high five for you, Akiko had said. But what exactly were they high-fiving for?

Time to take a break. Max pushed back and stood. Something caught his eye.

At the table next to his, Brad's laptop was ajar. He must have shut it in a hurry and not noticed that it had closed down on a plush key-chain fob—a fat little brown bird, the proverbial Wren—and therefore remained awake.

Max looked about the room. Were there cameras? He pretended to enjoy the view.

No cameras.

People in tech were always prognosticating the next big thing. Self-driving utopias, printable body parts, etc. Most people were slow-witted follow-fashions. Most people were not paid to sit in the Helix and dream up the future. People like the Brads.

Max had his own ideas about where tech should head. Was he as canny as the Brads? If not, would a peek—just a peek—lend him insight?

Or an advantage?

One day, Max would have his own thin gold laptop. He was pretty confident of it. Until then—

Max lifted the laptop lid. The glow of it dawned upon his face.

The screen showed an open spreadsheet titled "accounts_confirmed.nums."

In it were listed the buyers who would be paying millions for the data collected by the Soul Project, buyers like the National Security Agency, the Central Intelligence Agency, the Department of Homeland Security, the Russian Foreign Intelligence Service.

Spooks.

"This is fucked," blurted Max to the room.

He stood. The clouds above deserted him and left him once again alone under the sun and blue sky and brown chaparral hills and nothing else.

He nudged around the trackpad, found his own laptop on the network, and gave himself a copy of the file. He left Brad's computer as he found it. He closed the lid back down on the little brown bird.

Max turned back to his desk. He slapped his chunky black laptop shut, clamped it under his arm, and hurried down from the Helix to knock on the door of Justin Richards.

"Yo," said cool-boss Justin Richards.

"Soul Project is fucked," said Max.

0.4

Close the door," said cool-boss Justin Richards, sensing a Talk.

"So," said Max. "I think I found something I wasn't supposed to see."

"Uh-huh," said Justin Richards.

"It's just, Brad's laptop was open, and I just saw it."

Which was sort of true.

"Hey," said Justin Richards. "You leave your fly open, people are gonna grab your junk. Not your fault. That's on Brad."

"You would grab Brad's junk?"

They chuckled. Max sat, grateful for cool-boss Justin Richards.

Max opened his laptop. "So, dude. Did you see this accounts_confirmed thing?"

"No," said Justin Richards, all eyebrows and question marks.

Max pushed the laptop closer.

"Are we selling out to spooks?" said Max.

"Well," said Justin Richards, scanning the spreadsheet. "To be fair, this is mentioned in the Terms and Conditions that everyone accepts during sign-up."

"Which of course everyone has read from top to bottom," said Max. "Shouldn't users know we're basically building a Big Brother database?"

Justin Richards blinked at the words *Big* and *Brother*.

"Well," said Justin Richards. "To be fair, all our user data is anonymized."

Cool-boss Justin Richards was becoming a little bit douche-boss

Justin Richards, and it made Max nervous. He knew what was coming next. *Wren does not keep any personal identifiers* and blablabla.

"Wren does not keep any personal identifiers like names," said Justin Richards. He clicked around on his laptop to show Max an example. "Just their unique mobile device key. So while we may know that this user, 18800002-3ffe-02dc-w90a-78c44c20016c, is a single non-dating non-car-owning first-generation Salvadoran American male aged 26, with a recommended pricing tier of Premier Full Retail, living near or around 1004 Gullsnest Avenue in Delgado Beach, phone number 323-555-0055, with affinities for computers and internet and entrepreneurship and Japanese manga—did not know that!—and the only child of two immigrant parents with blank port-of-entry dates, we won't ever be able to point a finger at that and say, *That is Maximilian Portillo right there.*"

Max just looked at him.

"Anyway, it's all blended into a big intersectional affinity data set for faceted advertiser audience targeting," said Justin Richards.

Max looked at him some more, enough to make him smile a self-aware smile, and suddenly Justin Richards was cool-boss again.

"It's bullshit, I know, it's bullshit," said Justin Richards finally. He lowered his voice. "This whole Soul Project thing creeped me out from the beginning."

"I just feel like we should say something to someone," said Max. "Maybe even Cal Peers."

"You want time with Cal Peers?"

"Unless you kinda wanna talk to him on my behalf?" tried Max. "Brad can't know I saw his junk all hanging out."

"Eh," said Justin Richards with a wave. "I'll just ask Brad for a copy outright, problem solved. He doesn't know what I have and don't have access to. We could meet with Mister Cal together, if you want."

Max swallowed. "Together."

"It might be good for you," said Justin Richards. "You get to be the hero making sure Wren stays on the up-and-up. Although, fair warning: motherfucker can be one challenging motherfucker."

Max nodded. "I just . . . This whole Soul Project thing. It's getting way far away from *Don't be evil.*"

"I feel you one hundred percent," said Justin Richards. "I'll get something on the calendar. Might be a day or two, which is probably a good thing. Give your thoughts time to rise and firm up."

"Like my dick," said Max.

Justin Richards laughed, which meant Max could finally laugh, too.

0.5

The glass village of Wren headquarters overlooked the hard, glittering Pacific from atop Playa Mesa: a bucolic toe-shaped peninsula, named *mesa* because of its colossal table-like topography. A Masada of tech million- and billionaires.

Back during the war, with all the Whitemen gone to kill kill kill and be killed killed killed, Playa Mesa was once populated by Browns of all stripe. They made bombs and things in sprawling war factories. They leased borrowed homes long enough to fool themselves into thinking they owned them. Things were nice.

But the war stopped, the factories closed, and the Whitemen came back hungry for homes and jobs. The Browns were no longer needed. The Whitemen drew red lines on maps to push them out. The economy shifted away from manufacturing and toward design and information and other vestibularities. So the Browns, newly unqualified, moved out to poorer areas like Hancock or Delgado Beach. They got jobs making coil springs or sewing blue jeans or cleaning offices or driving corporate shuttle buses.

Like the bus Max was sitting in right now.

Real estate values radiated down the sides of Playa Mesa from the epicenter of Wren headquarters, and the winding shuttle bus discharged its passengers by income bracket in descending order as it climbed down: Whitemen Senior Staff first, then the Asian Browns of Programming, then the Whitewomen of Marketing, then the Non-Technical Browns.

Max lived in a sleek, spartan bachelor apartment in between the Whitemen Senior Staff and Asian Browns of Programming levels.

But today was Thursday, so Max did not get off at his usual stop high up on the mesa. Max was the last one to get dropped off—far out in Delgado Beach, in an area known as Playa Mesa Bottom. He could've gotten a ride from Shane, who picked up Akiko every night in the Poolwhip, but Max had spent enough time as a third wheel and was on a break.

"This is you," the bus driver said. He was an old African American man who had seen things that most people in 2018 could not comprehend.

Max gave a chin nod. He stepped out of the freezing air-conditioned bus and into the stifling hot dusk of a ramshackle neighborhood. Three children and their dog stared at him exiting this outrageous luxury van emblazoned with the Wren logo.

It was not a great neighborhood—it was the kind his Whitemen coworkers liked to call *ghetto* or *sketch*—but Max loved it anyway. Every Thursday he stepped out of the Wren shuttle and breathed deep, just like he was breathing now.

Because he was home.

"Flaco," said Dad as Max approached. *Flaco* was a nickname that meant skinny. In English it would be *Slim*. On a crumbling porch of a crumbling stucco house sat Dad, playing an old Spanish étude on his guitar, cigarette between his lips, one leg elevated on a phone book. He worked ten hours a day at a coil spring factory in Hancock; twelve hours if you counted the commute.

"Pizza before five minute," said Max's mom from the kitchen within. Mom worked in a garment factory, sewing together designer blue jeans for ten hours a day.

On the weekends Mom and Dad cleaned tech offices. They woke before Max did. They came home late. Most days, they would call or video-chat before bed. But Max almost never got to see them in person, except for Thursdays.

They made sure to knock off early for pizza night, every Thursday.

Max loved them both with a ferocity that, if tipped just so, could turn into anger. Because they did everything right, according to the American Dream. They worked hard. They paid a mortgage. They showed up every day to jobs they hated and never complained. And what was their reward?

Still more work.

"In this country it's live to work," his dad would explain without bitterness. "Not work to live. I'll take you back one day to the old ranchito in El Salvador. Drink, play music, be with friends. Eat what the land gives us."

But his mom told Max the truth: the ranchito, stolen by the ruling gang; Dad's friend, disappeared one night after curfew; Mom's friend's fifteen-year-old daughter, married off at gunpoint; the land, powder-dry. One betrayal after another.

Paint as rosy a picture as you like, she would say. America has its problems, but at least it's the only country where the picture comes close to matching the real thing.

Dad had no papers, nor did Mom. Max, born on this side, was the only one.

Max saved all he could to afford a lawyer with serious game. The deportations were happening, after all. The great El No Paso wall was being constructed.

After that, Max would decimate the mortgage and set up a retirement fund.

After that, Max would become His Benevolence, CEO Maximilian Portillo.

And Max would make his dad proud.

Being *proud* meant that a parent could look at their child, see them for who they really were, on their terms and their terms alone, and be able to honestly say:

You're pretty damn cool.

Not that Dad would ever use the word *cool*.

Max thought about what his mom had said, about the picture matching the real thing, and began drafting a post in his mind. He would alert users about the Soul Project. He would talk about ideals, and integrity, and other stuff. The post would get a million likes and change everything.

"Wake up, stoner," said Dad, and pinched Max's neck.

Max, lost in thought, did not react. They sat at a tiny octagonal dining table with a wobbly leg that made their drinks slosh. Dad grumbled, knelt down to tighten a hidden wingnut, and gave the table a shake: stable, for now.

"¿Estás bien, m'ijito?" said Mom. Mom gave Max the slice with the most chorizo. She always did this. Max managed a smile.

"I'm fine," said Max. "It's just . . . Wren's being all unethical."

"What, like stealing money?" said Dad.

"Worse than money," said Max. "User data. But the squishy stuff."

"I don't get it," said Dad. He sipped a beer.

"What is esquishy stuff?" said Mom.

"They're trying to trick people into telling Wren, like, their personal feelings and political affinities and all that," explained Max. "But I'm gonna put a stop to it."

"I don't get it," said Dad. "Is Wren making profits yet?"

Then Dad made a sour face: *You kids and your computers.* Whenever Dad did this Max would become defensive about his chosen industry by spewing jargon.

"This year we got cash flow positive," said Max.

"What that means?" said Mom.

"Listen," said Dad. "I don't know computers. I'm too old to learn data and all-go-rhythms and all that stuff. All I know when I use Airlift on my phone, I get a taxi. When I hit BUY on A2Z, it gets delivered. Your boy Shane, he's always talking about making his own app, too, right?"

"YouPool," said Max.

"Use YouPool, people come and clean your pool. Is Wren like that?"

"You so very smart, Flaco," said Mom.

Max gestured with his pizza and spoke carefully. "Wren's not exactly like YouPool. Wren is the world's most popular social media network, empowering millions to keep tabs on friends old and new, share thoughts, keep up with news, unleash creative potential, and foster awareness and understanding," said Max, unconsciously quoting Wren corporate out of sheer habit. "Social media's not a bad thing in theory. But in reality Wren could care less about unleashing creative potential or whatever. They just want to get more users, in order to get as much information on each user as algorithmically possible, in order to get more valuable. To advertisers."

"So Wren sells ads," said Dad.

"It's more complicated than ads," said Max. "It's a platform of APIs that—"

"I hate ads," said Dad. "They pop up and over and they're so annoying."

"Dad," said Max.

"Anyway, so that's the thing-thing," said Dad. "Ads."

"Dad," said Max.

"Papi," said Mom. She touched his forearm, and Dad set his hands back down.

Dad became very gentle. "Listen. My smart boy. Do this for a while, but then next job maybe do something more real. Something that you point at it, and you go, *I made that,* and the people go, *I need that, thank you for making it.* Whatever that is, just do it. You feel me?"

Dad pointed at his can and it dripped with sweat, as if anointed with wisdom.

"Just do something you love, and keep it simple," said Dad. "But don't be like me. Don't get your hands dirty. Okay? Let us take the dirt so you don't have to."

"Then you get married and make the babies ándale," said Mom. Mom and Dad had Max when they were twenty. All their Salvadoran friends had kids when they were twenty. That was their role. The kids in turn would take care of the parents in old age. That was their role. Didn't Max want someone to talk to on his deathbed?

Max was twenty-six. Already six years behind. Not behind the twenty-year-olds at Wren, though. None of those kids were having kids.

Being Salvadoran American, it was hard to tell which set of rules to follow.

"Ha ha ha, marriage and babies, sure," said Max to Mom. Then he spoke into his phone. It was a seven-month-old Quartz Milc 9, already middle-aged by tech standards. "Hey, Milc, find me a soul mate."

"Here's what I found about soul mate on the web," said the Milc.

That night Max lay very still on his vast empty bed in his vast empty bedroom.

Max had a good-luck dollar in his wallet that Dad gave him. On the back was a pyramid with its top cut off—another Masada. Atop the pyramid was a radiant panopticon eye overlooking everything.

Max opened his laptop and began jotting down talking points for his upcoming meeting with Cal Peers in a new note titled "Vision Statement."

How much would you sell your soul for?

0.6

How much money was enough money?

That was what Max woke up thinking.

Max actually knew: four million. After taxes. Invest all of it in something safe, live off the gains, and make work forever optional for himself, for Mom, for Dad.

Four million bucks in 2018 would make any parent proud.

Four million would be enough. And then what? Rest?

Max would not rest, of course. He would start another company, and then another, always striving to live up to that old tech cliché: making money while making the world better. And he would start by changing things at Wren.

Call Max a Pollyanna, but he super-much believed in that old tech cliché.

The shuttle took Max up Playa Mesa, collecting Wrennies by order of income along the way. Max sat in the back and continued with his vision statement.

your rights as an internet citizen should not change with every app update

Cal Peers would be impressed. More than that. Cal Peers would be inspired.

Max crossed the hexagonal green and entered the heart of the glass village. He climbed an invisible staircase and entered a transparent cube that lifted him to the sky room. He eyed a glowing panel on the door that led to the Helix.

The panel turned red: *Try again.*

So Max tried again.

Red.

Hey, bro, got a sec? said Justin Richards on Max's phone.

Yah, said Max.

And Max headed back down to Product and rapped on a glass door.

"Mister Justin," said Max.

"Mister Max," said Justin Richards. They fist-bumped.

"I think something's wrong with the Helix door," said Max.

Justin Richards covered his eyes with his hand, a strange gesture, and spoke:

"How long have you been hanging out at Wren now?"

What? thought Max.

"Just shy of four years," said a woman's voice. "That's a very, very long time."

"Cherry, thanks for taking the time to hang out with us," said Justin Richards.

A slim, older Whitewoman entered. She bore a sad kind of smirk. She held a large tablet to her chest. She gestured for Max to sit, and suddenly all three of them were sitting around a little guest table, something Max had never done before in Justin Richards's office.

The world zoomed out and Max felt very tiny. Had Max made a fatal error when he confessed his doubts about the Soul Project with cool-boss Justin Richards?

"Is this . . . ?" said Max.

"I'm really sorry," said Justin Richards. "But yeah. It is."

Max's eyes felt hot and gigantic. "Did I? Do? Something? Wrong?"

Justin Richards covered his eyes once again, and the Cherry person smirked her smirk.

"Not at all, Maximilian," she said. "You've been nothing but a rock star. I just know you'll have no problem finding your next incredible adventure after today."

"Today?" said Max.

"Right now," said Justin Richards through the hand covering his face.

"But why?"

"Restructuring something blablabla," said the Cherry person, but it was hard to hear because Max was no longer listening. He was handed the large tablet. It was apparently his to keep. It contained documents and unemployment information and severance details. He vaguely remembered giving cool-boss Justin Richards, now ex-cool-boss Justin Richards, a big slapping hug. Was Justin Richards crying?

Was Max?

Now Max descended, through Product, down past Marketing, down past Programming. At some point a hand gripped his elbow, and suddenly Max was staring into the dumbfounded face of Akiko.

"What's going on?" she said.

Max handed her the tablet, and right away she knew.

Max kept walking. Two silhouetted men waited by the blinding wall of glass that led outside: Maurice, the African American security guard, and a tall Whiteman with an immense head and heavy hands.

Wren CEO Cal Peers.

Did Cal Peers look at Max? It was hard to tell from the glare.

As Max approached, he could see that yes, Cal Peers was looking at Max with eyes like an owl's by flashlight. He was neither impressed nor inspired.

He was blank.

Cal Peers turned on a heel and strode away.

"Not gonna be the same here without you, Maxie," said Maurice.

"Yes it will," said Max.

0.7

Max thrust his arms and sent forth a ball of blue flame into the sea.

"Hadouken," Max yelled.

"Let it out," said Shane, bracing himself in the open door of the Poolwhip.

The Poolwhip was Shane's van. It was full of hoses and nets and jugs of chemicals. Shane Satow ran his own business, Satow Pool Service, whose logo sprawled across the side of the vehicle in traditional Californian black letter.

Shane rifled a beer at Max. Max, who was terrible at catching rifled beers, fumbled it. The can exploded open and Max hurried to suck the foam.

Normally Shane would rib Max for committing such a foul, but today he did not.

They were at Point Whittier, overlooking a small cove dotted with late-afternoon surfers.

Point Whittier was where Shane came to think his thoughts. Max figured Shane had brought him here to think about what had happened today.

But what was there to think? Max had tickled the whale from inside and got sneezed out the blowhole.

Akiko draped herself across Shane's outstretched arm. The arm did not tremble or buckle under the strain. Shane had worn shredded tank tops and shredded shorts every day for as long as Max could remember.

He cleaned pools in these clothes, went out in these clothes, lifted weights in these clothes. He called these clothes his casualwear. Shane hated dressing up. Shane would probably wear a shredded tank top and shredded shorts when he got married.

To Akiko, of course.

"I just don't get it, mang," said Shane, shaking his close-cropped head.

"What don't you get, baby?" said Akiko.

Max caught himself staring at her. He looked back at the sea.

"Why'd they fire Max?" said Shane.

"Think about it," said Akiko. "One day he calls bullshit on some scary NSA surveillance package deal, and the next day he's let go."

"Cal Peers gave me stank eye on the way out," said Max into the wind.

"Damn," said Shane. He added, "Who's Cal Peers again?"

"Honey bear, seriously?" said Akiko.

Good old Shane, thought Max. He lived far outside the peculiar orbit of tech and could not possibly know all there was to know about a man like Cal Peers.

Max introduced Akiko to Shane long ago, during high school. He sometimes wondered what would have happened if he hadn't ever done that. It was an absurd thought, and ungenerous: for all the many times he thought it, it had given him nothing.

Besides Akiko, Shane was Max's other best friend.

"It's like I was doomed the second I walked into the Helix," said Max.

"So what are you gonna do?" said Shane.

"Be a rock star somewhere new," said Akiko. "I heard Airlift's looking to expand Product. And Knowned would hire you like that."

"Fully," said Shane, nodding.

Below them a surfer caught a wave, bailed out, and paddled back for more.

"I was just trying to do the right thing," said Max. "But I'm starting to think there is no right thing. Airlift, Knowned, it's all the same."

"I heard the Knowned office is pretty chill," said Akiko.

"I mean, it's all the same stupid game," said Max. "Make an app, get lots of users, to hell with laws or privacy or just basic-ass ethics. Whatever it takes to impress investors so they can valuate the shit out of you. Investors give zero fucks what the actual business is. The thing-thing is never the thing."

"It's a user-based circle jerk," said Akiko.

"Wren's not profitable," said Max. "They've never made a dime."

"Shit," drawled Shane. "Even I'm profitable." He thumped the van.

"I could've gotten good at teaching or medicine or art," said Max. "But no, I had to get good at tech."

"That's 'cause tech is cool," said Shane. "I mean, our phones do everything."

Max took out his Quartz Milc 9 and regarded its black glass. Everyone had a Milc. Max's Milc knew where he was, where he came from, and could guess where he was going. It knew who he was with. It could be taking video or audio right now, for all he knew.

Milcs were made by Quartz, the world's biggest computer and phone maker. Quartz was down the street from Wren. Did they have a Soul Project, too?

Akiko hopped down from the Poolwhip and gave him a quick hug from behind—a shoulder hug, a friend hug—that left Max wanting. He gazed at the setting sun.

"You'll bounce back, duncie," said Akiko. "You got this."

It was nice of her to say. But Max had no idea what she meant by *this*.

0.8

Max did not bounce back.

Over the next few months Max did what Akiko assured him was his due diligence: updated his public resume profile, called a recruiter, and scored choice interviews. Interviews anyone in tech would kill to get. Interviews at four of the Big Five, excluding Wren:

- Quartz, the world's largest computer and phone maker
- Knowned, the world's largest news discussion forum
- A2Z, the world's largest online retail store
- Airlift, the world's largest crowdsourced taxi and hotel service

In the year 2018, the word *crowdsourced* meant *dirt-cheap labor*. Tech companies *crowdsourced* many things, like getting people to drive their own personal cars as taxis, rent their own houses to strangers, provide photos of everything, research and write articles, give product reviews, and so on.

And as strange as it sounds, people—the *crowd*—willingly performed all this labor for a pittance. Or often for absolutely no money at all.

In 2018, this was called the *gig economy*, perhaps inspired by the image of a rock star touring venue after venue. Previous generations had classified this type of work as *minimum wage*.

Max's first interview was at Quartz HQ—a huge edifice that indeed resembled a giant outcrop of crystal growing from a vertical seaside bluff. In its glowing interior, he received his plastic visitor badge that also doubled as a biometrically authenticated nondisclosure agreement, location tracker, and photo identification.

He met with a young Whitewoman (Marketing), a tall Whiteman (Product), and an older Brown (Engineering). On a red table before them sat a black smartphone, the likes of which Max had never seen before, marked with the word BETA.

"We've heard such amazing things about you," said Marketing.

"We need help with our upcoming next big thing, and would love if you could come hang out with us here at Quartz," said Product.

"I would absolutely love to hear more," said Max, nodding and smiling.

"Behold," said Engineering, waving a hand over the black phone.

The screen illuminated, and on it were headshots of Max and his interviewers. The phone screen had almost no bezel; it looked like a rectangle of light superimposed upon reality. Some designer's ideal vision of technology: a window of pure information without anything resembling a body.

Under Max's photo, Max's words had been transcribed:

I would absolutely love to hear more.

The words of his interviewers had been transcribed, too.

Their location was marked. Their job titles were noted. They were automatically connected in the Quartz corporate user database.

"We've acquired and implemented new chip technology with huge potential," said Engineering. "Future iterations of our Milc flagship phone can now feature an extremely low-power active idle state for up to forty-eight hours, even in sleep mode."

"You mean it can hear, transcribe, and upload everything even if it's turned off," said Max. "I bet it captures video, too."

Product looked at Engineering. Engineering looked at Marketing. Marketing looked at Product.

"He gets it," said Product.

And then Max said this: "It'd be cool to sell this kind of ambient data through real-time bidding in a back channel, especially if you opt users in by default."

Why did Max say that?

Max said that out of career habit. He said that to impress them, to get the job. And right after he said it, he became instantly confounded by his own self.

"He really gets it," said Marketing.

"I told you," said Engineering.

"Screw the interview process," said Product, grinning. "Let's just do this."

And Product slid a piece of paper with a number before Max. It was a large sum, with bonuses and instantly vested stock options.

"This is amazing," said Max, smiling and nodding. But all he wanted to do was cinch his hoodie down tight so that only the tip of his nose showed.

I had to get good at tech.

Product's phone buzzed, and when he glanced at it he suddenly became transfixed. Engineering's phone buzzed, too, as well as Marketing's. All three of them studied their phones with increasing concern.

Engineering looked up at Marketing. Marketing looked at Product. Product looked at Engineering. They seemed to make some tacit decision with simple nods of their heads, and stood in unison.

"So great to meet you," said Marketing, and Max found himself in a group hug.

Product took back the sheet of paper with the number on it and folded it into his pocket. Max was confused. Did that mean the deal was done?

They released. "Best of luck," said Engineering.

"Best of luck," said Product.

Best of luck?

The following day Max went along to his next interview.

At Knowned, a rust-brown fortress of a building, Max found himself saying:

"It'd be cool to automatically write news headlines that match what users already know and want. No one actually reads full articles anyway."

"Mister Max gets it," they said.

And then that thing happened again: phones buzzed, the interviewers grew concerned, and the whole thing was cut short with a group hug and a *Best of luck.*

Max wondered what was going on. Could it be? It couldn't be. That would be crazy.

So Max went along again.

At the super-generic cube farm of A2Z, he was in the middle of saying, "It'd be cool to work around the local retail problem by sending shoppers at brick-and-mortar stores cheaper prices for the same goods they're looking at," when the buzzing phones interrupted him and the interview stopped.

It couldn't be. *Could it?*

Max went along, and he went along.

His interview at Airlift HQ—housed in a row of renovated pastel Victorian houses—ended before it even began, in the reception area.

"We are so sorry," said Reception, "but we have to reschedule. We will be in touch."

Airlift never rescheduled.

By the end of the week Max's interviews were all done. He felt like a snail in a salt maze with no exit. He said so from his seat in the Poolwhip. Shane had driven Max to each of his interviews, and each in-van debrief session grew more and more trepidatious.

Finally Max ripped off his hoodie and said: "I'm being blackballed."

"That's kinda paranoid, holmes," said Shane. "You'll find the right company, it's just a matter of time."

"That must be what's happening," said Max. "Cal Peers has the whole world on speed dial."

"You don't know that," said Shane. But when Max looked at him, he could see the wheels turning in his head. He could see him wondering if such a conspiracy could be for real.

Shane wrenched about in his seat. "If this shit winds up being true, what you're saying about this Cal Peers asshole, I'll fucking kick his fucking ass."

Max found this endearing. But kicking the asshole of Cal Peers would be about as easy as putting out the sun with a garden hose.

"I'm okay, everything's okay," said Max, breathing in and out slowly.

Shane watched Max do this five times.

"This is some kind of warning from the universe," said Max finally.

"Fucking fuck with my friend, man," said Shane, shaking his head.

"Because why should I even go for these jobs in the first place?" said Max. "Why work for the forces of evil?"

"Because you're really good at it," said Shane.

"I don't want to be good at being evil," said Max.

"You're just doing what you gotta do to get paid," said Shane. "It can't always be a hundred percent the right thing."

"Everywhere I interviewed," said Max. "Evil."

"Dude, come on," said Shane. He shook Max by the shoulder.

Max sighed as he wobbled under Shane's power. "The user experience design at all those companies is optimized for addiction and surveillance," he said. "Evil."

"Max," said Shane.

Max only continued. "They hook people in with low prices subsidized by private venture capital. It's this bizarre corporate socialistic trickle-down redistribution-of-wealth thing that starves out honest businesses through brute force. Evil."

"I don't entirely get what you're saying?" said Shane with a brilliant smile. "But I'm telling you, you will get in somewhere, I promise."

The fact that Max's ranting was over Shane's head filled him with a guilty pride, because it was exactly the sort of thing that he talked about all the time with Akiko—an Akiko Shane never got to see.

But Max did.

Because Shane never worked late nights at Wren, huddled over a blue-green screen and tossing profundities back and forth like a ball.

"Akiko always did say evil was baked into the tech industry," said Max.

"She did?" said Shane. He glanced at Max, then at the road, then back at Max, as if wondering: *What else do you guys talk about?*

"Baked right in," said Max.

Shane draped a wrist over the steering wheel. "Listen, just find a way to love what you do," he said. "Cleaning pools ain't exactly sexy, but like, for me, I get to work on my tan, I'm not stuck behind a laptop, and plus they ain't nothing evil about pools. There's no Cal Peers in pools."

These straightforward, prebulent truths sounded like Dad talking. Do something you love. Keep it simple. It irked Max, because he would not be happy doing something simple. His desires were complex. His ambitions were complex.

He was incapable of pretending otherwise.

"Like, kids love pools?" said Shane, counting reasons on his fingers. "They're good for exercise? Hot-ass girls in thong bikinis like to lay out by 'em?"

Max finally allowed himself a laugh. "Nice."

The van came to a stop at a red light.

"Get yourself back in the game, and fuckin' get yourself a hot-ass girl, too," said Shane. "Before you know it we're both gonna be chillin' by a pool with our respective hot-ass girls in fuckin' thong bikinis like, *What the fuck were we even stressing about?*"

Max snorted at the comical image of Akiko in a thong bikini—she always wore rash guards to the beach—and grinned at his friend Shane. Shane grinned back, his face bathed in red light. It was the light of the womb, of warmth, of protection. It was the same light Shane had wrapped Akiko in during her Trouble Time, and now he was sharing it with Max.

"Green light," said Max.

More like blue-green, he thought. The light meant it was time to go, to accelerate, to proceed forward. *Blue-green like aqua.* Max was quietly struck with inspiration.

The van moved.

"So, dude," said Max. "You still want to make that YouPool app of yours?"

Max looked at Shane. Shane looked at Max.

"Aw shit," said Shane with a smile.

0.9

They dove in to YouPool.

Pun intended.

"Every tech company you go to," Max had said, "you have to leave your soul at the door. Let's create the first company that lets you keep it."

With Shane's blessing, Max appointed himself His Benevolence, CEO Maximilian Portillo. Shane was COO (chief operating officer). Akiko was CTO (chief technical officer). The YouPool app would let users schedule pool cleanings.

"We're gonna make millions," said Shane, thumping a pec.

"Making millions makes men evil," said Max. "How about we make enough?"

Shane nodded at this, intrigued by Max's concept of Enough.

Max would run YouPool with fairness first. Customers would pay standard prices, but now have convenience, à la carte ordering, and pool cleaner ratings.

On the other side, pool cleaners signed up with YouPool could expect the same rates, but now have higher volume and YouPool's built-in marketing tools.

No one would get undercut.

This would not be about *crowdsourcing*.

Akiko worked early mornings and late nights on top of her regular Wren workday to get version one of the app built. It took her only a week, because Akiko was brilliant like no other. Max stayed with her these late nights over at her and Shane's place. No sound but the sound of her keyboard typing.

It was a magical sound.

In brief flashes, Max would fool himself into thinking this was his apartment. But never for long. Because there was Shane, asleep on the couch. His couch. There was the dresser overflowing with his and her clothing. Hiding amid the clutter atop the dresser was a heavy coffee mug, a relic from the Trouble Time.

It was not his apartment. Max took his leave every night, with a respect neither Shane nor Akiko realized. Which was okay.

While Max and Akiko worked on the tech, Shane rallied pool cleaners out in the field, even though they were technically competitors.

"Tell them a rising tide lifts all boats," said Max.

"I'm gonna say it my way, though," said Shane. And he did, and pool cleaners signed up, because Shane had his strange rough-cut charm.

And for a while, things worked okay. They made some money. People liked the service. But it wasn't quite Enough, and Akiko still had to work at Wren while improving YouPool in the wee hours, and Shane (and now Max) still had to drive around in the Poolwhip to clean pools themselves.

The only way Max could reach the goal of Enough was to hire programmers, a few salespeople, and so on. This meant money. This meant funding.

So Max took Shane and Akiko to all the big tech investors everyone knew, investors with crazy names like Burning Bush and Angels & Devils and Faust.

"So it's pool tables?" they would ask.

"On-demand pool cleaning, like, swimming pools," Max would say.

"Whatever," they would say. "What are your five-year revenue targets?"

"$600,000 per year," Max would say. "That's a $200,000 salary for each of us, which seems pretty damn decent if you ask me."

"$600,000 isn't exactly crushing it," they would say. "We were hoping you would say more like $600,000,000."

"Oh, we're not making millions," Max would say. "We just want a good living."

"I respect that, Mister Max," they would say, and they'd smile weird little smiles.

This was their way of saying, *Max doesn't get it.*

Three months later, Max shut YouPool down. Akiko was burned out from working two jobs. Shane was burned out from trying to clean pools and manage a needy workforce at the same time. And Max had run out of ideas for growth.

Max stood knee-deep in a shallow pool in the sparkling Californian sunlight, waving a pole net around, lost in thought under his big straw sunhat. A cherub pippled water from its tiny concrete penis.

He had told his dad: "YouPool is doing great."

"How much are you making?" said Dad.

"Enough," said Max.

"I heard about this Vietnamese kid down in Spencer who made this app that was some kind of flying bird video game? Made five million dollars in one year."

"That's amazing."

"One year. Five million."

"Good for him."

"How's everything else going, Flaco?"

"Great," said Max. "Doing what I love, just like you said."

The shifting blue-green water made Max think of a pool party back in high school, back before Akiko dated Shane. It was night. Max sat alone with Akiko at the far edge of the pool in its dim aqua glow, both of them the only ones not wearing swimsuits, and he remembered how her pinky finger crept sideways like a tiny creature seeking a tiny cuddle, and then simply stayed there touching his. They stared without a word at their two pinkies laying side by side.

Then two strong arms lifted Akiko from behind and tossed her splashing into the water, clothes and all.

When she surfaced she shot a sexyangry look at a grinning Shane, who, in nothing but his ripped shorts, gave a moon-howl and dove in to retrieve her.

They'd been together ever since.

0.10

How much would you sell your soul for? A million dollars? A thousand? Certainly not free. Certainly not nothing.

Yet that is what we expect from users every time they donate data to the internet: little pieces of their soul, for free. With every post, every like, and every share, the great internet eye in the sky, the iEye, builds a digital model of their very being. Maybe I sound dramatic. But think about it: You would never give such information away to a stranger on the street. Our phones, however, are a different story. They're especially designed to make giving away information as effortless as possible. And then companies like Wren sell that information without the users' knowledge to people who could use that information against them. And we profit from this transaction.

Doesn't feel right to me. Not at all.

Our rights as human beings should not change with every app update or be subject to terms and conditions that no one ever reads. I believe privacy is an inalienable right. Which is why I believe all tech companies, including Wren, must behave responsibly and transparently with user data so that we can make money while still providing people with a healthy, safe experience. I believe that |

Last saved 13 weeks ago

0.11

Akiko Hosokawa's mother had a superpower. Her superpower was to make large men shrink in size. One man in particular: Akiko's father.

Akiko's mother did this slowly at first. Little jabs in private, then only among friends, and finally out in the open, in public.

Wide load, coming through.

When I asked God for a hunk, he thought I meant this bread dough right here.

The food at home ain't doing it so I'm gonna eat out, if you know what I mean.

Before she married Akiko's father, Akiko's mother had been captain of her color guard in high school. She threw parties. She got drunk for the first time at age fourteen, and the boy who nursed her afterward called her beautiful, and the boy after that, and the boy after that. There was never a shortage of boys.

Into adulthood, she worked in sales in order to keep the party going. It did not matter to her what she sold.

Of all the men she met during this brief, manic time, Akiko's father was the strangest. Hair, dark. Stature, compact. Observing the world from behind a pair of heavy acetate Cary Grants. Akiko's father moved about the world very gently, lest he break anything. He was not in sales. He did not *do* people. He was in the relatively new field of *computer programming* and knew languages only machines knew: COBOL, Pascal, assembly language. He was not her mother's type.

But Father loved Mother in a way no other man had done before. Earnestly. Without question. His sturdy loyalty gave the social butterfly a haven in which to rest her wings, and at the age of twenty-nine they were married. It was the happiest day of their lives.

Quite literally, because every day after became worse and worse.

Akiko's father did not party. He liked to stay home. He worked from his den over a dedicated analog connection, a rarity in those days. He had a distrust for society's emphasis on appearance. He *let himself go* while Mother watched in a fresh dress and makeup.

Akiko's mother began to flap wildly about her haven, now become unto a cage. Her first affair happened just months after Akiko arrived into this world; by the time Akiko was six, her mother was on her third.

At the time, Akiko's father called them *Mother's very good colleagues.*

Later, when Akiko was a teenager, he called them *his own personal failures.*

With each failure, Akiko could swear the man shrank a few inches. It turned out the cage was not just for her mother. The cage was for her father, too, and was built of the most unyielding material of all: his own loyalty.

She knew this because he would never defend himself against her mother.

I can't just tell her no, he would say.

And so her mother wouldn't stop. Akiko hated the woman for bringing so much pain into the family. Father absorbed it all, becoming numb. Watching television for hours and hours. Any show would do. It did not matter. He went from being a man of few words to a man of no words.

Except when Akiko took up *computer programming* in junior high. They spoke to each other, not in English but in LISP, in the airless sanctum of her father's den cluttered floor to ceiling with striped accordion printouts from years ago. He taught her object-oriented code. They played something called a *MUD*, or multiuser dungeon, in the *Star Trek*–themed realm. Father taught Akiko the Vulcan mind meld, which to her delight was a real thing that actually worked.

The more father and daughter bonded, the more vicious Mother's attacks became. Flying words became flying objects, flung through the den's doorway, drive-by style. She smashed the computer monitor; he replaced it. She burned the printouts in the backyard; he printed more. Akiko's gray, shapeless wardrobe wound up in the trash—Akiko shared her father's disdain for appearances—and Father simply bought replacements.

In hindsight, by the time the heavy coffee mug struck her above the left eye, Akiko reckoned her mother, the original abandoner, must've felt abandoned by her own daughter and husband and that horrible computer of theirs.

I can't just leave her, Father would say when Akiko urged him to. *She has a good heart in there. We have to help her find it.*

He sank deeper and deeper into his chair, like the thing was unhinging its cushions to swallow him up. The word *weak* flashed in Akiko's mind, and she suddenly had the horrific urge to strike his face.

Disgusted with where she was headed, she chose instead to be home as little as possible.

She taught herself how to go out every evening and not come back until very late. Parties, movies, more parties. Anything would do. It did not matter.

She met a beautiful boy named Shane at a pool party. She called him *Mr. Muscles* behind his beautiful back. She was seventeen, a junior. She let him touch the scar above her left eye as the tourmaline water bobbed and warped around them.

Shane asked about it.

Who the fuck throws shit at their own kid?

From then on, at every party she went to, Shane would happen to be there, too.

One night—the final night—Akiko came home to find Mother wielding a fireplace poker, drunk and smashing every framed photo she could find.

You pick all this shit up, she said. *Look at this goddamned mess.*

This can't go on, said Father. *I think we need to find you someone.*

I already have someone, said Mother.

You could say this was when the Trouble Time officially started. But it had been happening for years already, hadn't it?

Akiko ran far into the void of the night. When she stopped to catch her breath, she found herself in front of an apartment in Delgado Beach.

Shane's apartment.

Shane took her in. He gave her his bed and his food. He gave her all his time, too, canceling his pool clients one by one.

They stayed one night, then the next, then the next. Akiko reckoned they would only have to stay forty-two more before she finally reached eighteen years of age. In America, that was the age when a child became an adult and was no longer beholden to anyone.

So Akiko waited forty-two days.

At Shane's urging, Akiko wrote letters every morning to her father.

I'm having the best time ever with my good friends.

Love you lots and tell Mom I love her, too. Can't wait to be home.

And so on, from a different post office every time, leaving a tidy paper trail in case her parents tried calling child protective services or— worse—a lawyer.

They never did. A desperate, damaged part of Akiko wished they had, even if it put Shane at risk of being accused of kidnapping.

Forty-two days passed without incident.

Shane resumed with his pool clients. One of them, some BSD tech exec with a full-size Olympic, an indoor single-lane endless, and two hot tubs, said he couldn't find good programming talent for shit. Which was how Akiko carried her father's computer programming flame into Wren's engineering department.

BSD stood for big swinging dick.

Forty-two days became a hundred, then a hundred more, then a thousand.

Akiko's father eventually left her mother, sold the house, and retired to a seaside suburb outside Tokyo, effectively deleting any evidence of Akiko's childhood.

But, as Akiko's father would say during their programming sessions, nothing ever really gets deleted. Just flagged as inactive. Then it simply becomes hidden.

0.12

Max saw it while scrolling his feed and froze.

Who is your ideal sexual partner? Take the quiz. This is most definitely not safe for work.

And another: *Could you do better as president? Click here to play.*

His Wren-friends were taking the quizzes and playing the games that he himself had designed. They were sharing their results, which got more Wren-friends to participate and share, which in turn got even more to do the same. Because it was *fun.*

Social media was fun.

Social media was not a bad thing, in theory.

But theory was never reality, was it?

It was Saturday. The Soul Project was live. And it was doing great.

Max wanted a big rock to come out of the sky and crush him.

"I want a big rock to come out of the sky and crush me," said Max to no one.

"What?" said Dad from the other room.

"Nothing."

Max had moved back into his parents' house to save money. He lay on his tiny high school bed before an open laptop.

"Are you working?" said Dad. "You need a break, mijo."

Dad said this with a concerned pride that made Max's heart go sour with guilt. YouPool was dead. He did not run an app for a living. He cleaned pools. He was a pool cleaner. It was not the thing he loved. But Max couldn't tell any of this to Dad.

Max wished he could be like Dad. Dad, who barely spent any time on his ancient phone or ancient computer. Dad, for whom social media meant calling friends on the yellow touch-tone phone.

Max wanted to yell and scream at his Wren-friends, to tell them they were unwittingly building a psychographic profile for government use. That instead of the feds spying on us, we were doing the spy work for them.

But then again, what was the point? Max himself was guilty of giving away personal information to corporations. Like everyone, he skipped the Privacy Policies and Terms and Conditions when signing up for some so-called free video game or whatever. Like everyone, he tagged every photo he took with its location. Like everyone, he scrolled the feeds every day, blithely liking this or sharing that, even though he was aware it was all being tracked and categorized.

If Max didn't care about his own soul, how could he expect others to?

He thought about his vision statement from three months ago. He could imagine publishing it, maybe earning a few likes, and not much else after that.

His room felt hot and stuffy. He requested a taxi and went to Shane and Akiko's place. He had to talk to someone. Not just someone. He had to talk to Akiko.

Max squinted out at the blinding white beach just beyond the bike path, already filling with families setting up barbecue picnics. The faint arpeggios of corrido music floated in on the ocean breeze. The sky had become tea colored, with embrivant views extending to the black silos of the oil refinery and the mountains beyond. Max stifled the urge to post a photo.

Why did he always want to post a photo?

"You want a beer?" said Shane, and rifled a can at him. To Max's surprise, he caught it without even looking.

"Holy shit," said Max.

"Everything okay?" said Akiko, still in her pajamas.

"Yeah," said Max.

"No," said Max.

Finally, Max said, "You know that secret project I worked on at Wren?"

"What about it?" said Akiko slowly.

"It was called the Soul Project." Max explained it. Every detail.

"I don't get it," said Shane, crushing a can and opening another.

"Baby, they're selling to the government—"

"No, I get that," said Shane. "I just don't get why people go along with it."

"I don't, either," said Max. "Even me, just now I wanted to post a picture of the beach. What is wrong with me?"

Like everyone, Shane was registered on Wren. But unlike everyone, Shane never used it. He was a year and a half older than both Max and Akiko. When it came to smartphone culture, he was about as ignorant as Dad.

Old Man Shane.

"You're addicted," said Akiko. "Everyone is. I am, too. We post, we get likes, we get this little rush. The Soul Project gives Wren users a new way of getting fresh new likes. And I work at Wren, yay. I'm part of the problem. So I should just shut up, right?"

"Hey," said Max. "We tried to do our own thing our own way. It just didn't work out."

"It's not that it didn't work out," said Akiko. Her eyes grew cloudy with regret. "It's that there was never any room for YouPool in the first place."

Max looked at Akiko, who sat seiza in a parallelogram of sunlight.

"You're saying it's all go big or go home," said Max.

"Yep," said Shane.

"Or hope to get noticed by one of the big guys and get acquired," said Akiko. "Everything's just an exit strategy. I need a strategy to exit Wren. We should just quit tech altogether."

She stared at the ocean for a moment, growing cloudier and cloudier.

"You know how the more you drink, the more it takes to get you drunk?" she said. "That's Wren. The more you post, the more likes you need to get that rush. So you post more, and so on et cetera infinity. In a vicious cycle I help build every day."

"Baby," said Shane, reaching out to her.

"The internet's this big turd I keep polishing," she said.

They all nodded at this.

"Okay, so, but," said Max. "What if we could fix things instead of quitting it?"

"How?" said Akiko.

"That vicious cycle you're talking about," said Max. "We could break it."

"Wren would never let that happen," said Akiko. "Their whole mother-hugging business model depends on that vicious cycle."

"I'm saying you could do it, technically," said Max.

Akiko and Shane watched Max drink his entire beer in five long gulps.

Akiko smiled. "What are you thinking about?"

"Open your laptop," said Max.

0.13

ere's User Master, the great big user database," said Akiko, her eyes dancing. She typed some commands, rainbow-colored text on black, and waited with two fingers pressed to her lips: a leftover gesture from her smoking days.

Max leaned in. Shane peered from over his shoulder.

"There I am," said Max. "1,449 posts, 2,005 shares, 14,280 likes given, 20,606 likes received, blablabla."

"Affinities: tech, entrepreneurship, politics, immigration," said Akiko.

"Everywhere I've been, all the stuff I've bought on A2Z," said Max. "You're here, too, Shane. We're all here."

"Damn," said Shane.

"Do you think we can do it from here?" said Max.

Akiko typed and typed. "No remote permissions. Gotta go hardline at the office."

Max looked at Akiko. "They'll log your gate entry. You'll get fired."

Akiko touched her lips and thought. "No, we could do it."

"Are you sure?" said Max.

"We could do it," said Akiko, rising. "Bring hats. And let's go buy cigs."

"You're not seriously going to smoke," said Shane.

"Just trust me," said Akiko.

They wore identical black tee shirts and black jeans: the uniform of the Wren programmer. They wore black boonie hats and black caps.

It was night. Late.

They turned off their phones, lest their locations get tracked. They parked a quarter mile from the Wren parking lot. And when they approached the darkened glass village, Akiko led them into a back alley full of grease bins and recycling.

"Mushin no shin," said Max to no one.

"Huh?" said Shane.

"It's Japanese for *courageousness of action*. Let's go."

They entered the alley.

There, Akiko lit three cigarettes, one for each of them, and they stood as the ash burned down. Akiko snuck a drag. A tiny ball of orange glowed before her face.

"Come on, baby," said Shane. "No more smoking ever."

"Couldn't help it," said Akiko, grinning. "This is where coders like to smoke."

Beside her a door began to open. An exhausted Mexican man in kitchen whites emerged with a cigarette in his mouth and fished for a lighter.

"I got you," said Akiko, and she lit it for him. He nodded *Thank you*.

And they stomped out their cigarettes and slipped in through the door.

"There's a workstation here out of camera range," said Akiko, leading them to a conversation booth reserved for private calls. They crammed inside and gathered around a laptop plugged into a wall jack. She logged in under a nameless admin account. In seconds, they once again could see the great big user database.

She smacked a key—and a new screen full of odd commands appeared.

"There we are," she said. She turned to Max. "What first?"

Max thought for a moment, then said: "Let's just do all of it."

"Heck yeah," said Akiko. She actually cackled.

She typed and typed, executing commands in rapid succession.

```
public void asplode(thing) {
    delete from USER_MASTER where thing = *ANY*;
}
```

"Asplode," said Max, laughing. "I like that."

Akiko typed faster now.

```
asplode(LIKES_RECEIVED);
asplode(LIKES_GIVEN);
asplode(COMMENTS_RECEIVED);
asplode(FOLLOWER_CT);
```

And so on.

```
Commit changes? (Y/N) Y
This cannot be undone. Are you sure? (Y/N) Y
Changes merged with master.
May the force be with you.
```

"And also with you," she said.

She cleaned the computer with an alcohol wipe and slapped it shut.

"That's it?" said Shane.

Max and Akiko looked at Shane, then at each other, and laughed.

"What were you expecting?" said Max.

"I don't know, like, a big shutdown noise or something," said Shane.

"Sometimes you have to break a thing in order to fix it," said Max. "Homie, we just broke Wren."

"We did?" said Shane.

Max looked at Shane.

"Sweet," said Shane. "Fuck this place."

"You just saw the biggest hack in Wren's history," said Akiko. "Now let's get the eff out of here."

"Can we do one thing first, super quick?" said Max.

Max removed his black shirt to reveal another shirt, a white one, underneath.

"What are you doing?" said Shane.

"Claiming responsibility," said Max.

0.14

A man becomes his choices, Pilot Markham had read once. One of those word-cum-image aphorisms online, a virtual bit of inspirational needlepoint.

What a lie.

Given the choice to do anything, men will simply choose to do what everyone else is doing. Choice is an illusion. Mankind is a dumb herd.

A boy is born.

His powerful and motivated parents shunt him, the bothersome thing, to nannies and boarding schools from an early age—so early that when they are murdered along with a dozen other conference leaders by a bus bomb in Geneva, all the boy feels is a great distance between him and the world, a distance he only increases by hiding behind a world of computers.

Young Pilot Markham finds this world of computers a comforting fortress of perfect crystal. Later, as the internet is formed, the crystal walls become tinged with the sunset-hued idealism of leftover hippie spirituality. There is talk of a cyberrevolution, and transparency, and communities, and empowerment, and world peace, and blah,

blah,

blah.

No other industry talks like that. Not finance, not real estate, no one.

World peace in an app?

Assholes.

At age twenty-nine, Pilot Markham produces his first million-dollar business, backdoor security keys for the NSA, and then his second, a universal code library for the then-unheard-of internet of things.

Pilot Markham is recognized now. A player. He meets Anna. She follows him along the brunch and cocktail circuit, all silence and grace as Pilot Markham pitches ideas to the powerful Whitemen who can make things happen.

Pilot Markham creates his third, then fourth, then fifth company.

Smartphones arrive, and Pilot Markham launches his sixth and most lucrative company, selling every tilt and movement of these new devices to local law enforcement. He talks the talk. His product empowers people to take back crime-ridden communities through constant monitoring. He begins to believe his own blabbleglug. Because men must believe in something. Otherwise there is only money. And money is morally inert. Money is nothing.

And my God, what if you believed in nothing?

Data is collected and sold. The red lines of real estate are shifted to favor the wealthy. Police eagerly put more Browns in prison.

On monitor 2 in his towering wall of screens, Pilot Markham watched Snowball.

"Why?" Pilot asked Snowball.

On monitor 2, Snowball sniffed and sniffed, as guinea pigs will do, and flounced off frame. Pilot switched cameras and followed it.

Anna, gorgeous Anna, athletic and Asian—how he loved Asians—delivers their first and only daughter. Pilot misses it while at a meeting across town.

One month later his wife's caesarean section scar bursts from infection, his porcelain doll rudely cracked open, and is rushed to the hospital. He misses that, too. It is the day of the IPO. He is across the country, ringing a ridiculous bell in an outrageous room full of men all dressed alike, all shouting for money.

Not money. More.

It occurs to none of them to ask how much money is enough, and so Pilot does not ask, either, and the idea of Enough goes unnoticed.

Given the choice to do anything, men will simply choose to do what everyone else is doing. So Pilot chooses this idea of More.

Meanwhile, at Anna's side sits her best girlfriend and her best girlfriend's stunning and kindly and selfless brother Kent Navy, the soon-to-be film star. A soaring brown Adonis of a man. She deserves him.

She divorces Pilot and takes their daughter with her to London.

Years go by. Pilot promises to do better. Work/life balance, unplug and reconnect, blablabla. But a man becomes his choices, and again and again Pilot chooses to work behind his crystal castle wall of computers. He sells his sixth company and earns enough money to buy a time zone.

But not enough money to buy his daughter back.

Noelle.

Now, at this point in his life—early fifties—Pilot realized he had for years chosen to be an entrepreneur, mogul, leader, billionaire. But not husband. Not father. And now he could only honestly call himself one thing.

One day three years ago he came home alone to his newly bought smart-palace of concrete and steel and walnut and slate and found he was very tired of being Pilot Markham. And he never stepped outside again.

Pilot sighed and turned to monitor 5. Like everyone, he scrolled Wren out of habit and ennui. He skimmed the tedious litany of rage and quotidian ephemera and self-promotion. He did, however, find Wren's livestreaming feature interesting. It was—to use preinternet terms—like having your own personal TV broadcast.

For a moment, Pilot fondly recalled the preinternet days.

But enough nostalgia. Time to begin the test.

Pilot logged in to Wren as a fake user. It was easy to create a fake account and amass fake friends. Wren was designed to be easy, after all.

He tapped BEGIN LIVESTREAM. A few users joined, simply because Wren told them they should join. Then more joined, simply to see what everyone else was seeing. And they were seeing Snowball.

On monitor 2, Snowball found the trap and sniffed and sniffed at it until its alantine jaws snapped shut on his neck, hard enough to immo-bilize him without crushing, and he clawed away at the floor to no avail: tic tic ticticticictic.

The crowd grew to fifty now, all silently watching.

Two viewers had hit the REPORT button. Wren admins would boot Pilot's broadcast soon. He made a note to find a hack around that.

This is wrong, someone said in the chat window.

The poor animal

And yet, they kept watching. Typical.

One viewer was his neighbor, a wealthy teenage Whiteman named Brayden Turnipseed. Pilot secretly kept him on monitor 4. There sat the boy in full view of his networked security camera system—very easy to tap—lounging and watching Pilot's homemade snuff movie with the same nonchalance he reserved for cop shows or video games. He smoked a hash pipe. According to his parents' emails, he had the house to himself for a full summer while they were away on vacation.

Brayden had the whole house to himself, and yet for four days straight he had not stepped outside. He had spent four days almost entirely on his laptop or smartphone, hanging out with invisible friends, smoking weed, masturbating.

Pilot found Brayden fascinating.

Pilot pressed a key to activate the last part of the test. On monitor 2, a bolt clicked open. The snout of a dog pushed open a door: Helen, his golden retriever. She must be crazed with hunger by now. He hadn't fed her in three days.

Helen splayed low and snarled and bit down on the guinea pig, hold-ing still as the life leaked out of it. And then Helen began to eat the way dogs eat.

Fake

Is this for a horror movie or something

Outraged viewers shared the broadcast, calling on authorities to act. In minutes it was taken down from Wren, but in those minutes the video had already been captured, repackaged, remixed, and shared elsewhere.

It was used as animal rights propaganda. Conspiracy theories emerged about its faceless maker. It was picked up by news sites, which earned traffic and advertising revenue from it. A looped version appeared as a visual joke on some of the darker places online.

On monitor 4, Brayden had moved on to his laptop. Pilot squinted closer: porn. Brayden stroked himself twice but got distracted by another window containing his Wren feed, and seemed to forget all about masturbating.

Pilot leaned back. He would talk to this Brayden. The internet was a broken world, and Brayden was growing up inside of it. What kind of boy did that make?

The internet: instant, free, throwaway, permanent, anonymous, bullying, never-ending, lascivious, and so on. Deliberately designed this way by sociopathic Whitemen in thousand-dollar hoodies.

Pilot wanted to gut them all and shit and piss in their open cavities, and then sew them back up.

But he had no right. Because he was one of them. A man becomes his choices, and over his lifetime Pilot had become his, and now he could only honestly call himself one thing:

A monster.

After an hour or so, Pilot's Snowball broadcast went fully *viral*— bizarre 2018 slang for *hugely popular*. But oddly, Pilot noticed that no instance of the video had received a single like anywhere on Wren. The likes it had previously received—which were many—had vanished.

He did a little hacking around to check. His wall of screens filled with rainbow text on black. Confirmed: posts everywhere no longer had any likes whatsoever. Like buttons everywhere on Wren no longer liked when clicked. They no longer did anything.

A few minutes later the video of the man with the Black Halo mask appeared in his feed, and that was when he and the rest of the world first heard about Version Zero.

We broke it to fix it, said the man in the Black Halo mask.

Pilot rubbed his eyes, went up a staircase, and emerged into a hallway. He turned and entered a room that was empty but for sofa cushions arranged on the floor. He had discarded the sofa itself, which he found bulky. He arranged the cushions into a single large rectangle, lay down, and rested in Shavasana pose, the corpse pose, and became motionless.

It was not sleep. He never slept, not these days. He would meditate for one hour. Then he would rise again and continue his research.

And for the first time in his three-year exile, Pilot smiled.

"Who are you?" said Pilot to the man in the Black Halo mask.

0.15

A man wears a white mask marked with a large black circle. He sits in a corporate lobby. Behind him a logotype is visible: Wren. The mask is virtual, superimposed and tracked digitally. His voice has been disguised. The video is a mezzotint, all black and white.

The words VERSION ZERO appear at the bottom of the screen.

BLACK HALO: How much would you sell your soul for? A million dollars? A thousand?

The frame freezes for two seconds. It resumes.

BLACK HALO: How about zero? That is how much you have sold it for in the mirror world.

Freeze.

BLACK HALO: With every like you give, you give Wren a piece of your soul for free. A tiny void is left behind. You give two hundred likes a month on average. Wren remembers them all. It knows what you like better than your best friend. You like, like,

like. The mirror world consumes your likes. And
within you, a void grows.

Freeze.

BLACK HALO: Every like you receive promises to fill
this void. You post. You get liked. You feel good for
a moment—but only a moment. You post again. Your
phone becomes a slot machine that you pull over and
over. The void grows. You will never escape it. The
only way out is to leave. Wren's worst nightmare is
if everyone simply leaves.

Freeze.

BLACK HALO: This is why we broke Wren. We broke it to
fix it. We will keep breaking things until the mirror
world is finally fixed once and for all. Wren takes
your soul and sells it to the NSA, CIA, FBI, and SVR.
You agreed to this without knowing you were agreeing
to this. Follow this link and read for yourself.

*Freeze. A link appears on the screen: quar.tz/
wren-soul-project.pdf*

BLACK HALO: You are infinite.

Freeze.

BLACK HALO: Without you, they become zero.

The day was piercingly hot. Mist rose off the blacktop of the street lined with lush greenery, the picture of a Mediterranean Arcadia stirring from languor.

Pilot found it blinding.

He walked to the house next door—almost a thousand feet away—and rang its doorbell. It was a mansion, really, built in the typical Playa Mesa faux-Spanish style to better disguise its size.

Brayden's millionaire Whitemen parents had founded SnapJobs.com. Brayden was eighteen. He was their only child.

Brayden opened the door and squinted out from the darkness.

"I know you are smoking weed," said Pilot. "I can smell it."

The boy ran a hand through his wild yellow hair. "I have no idea to that which you are referring, sir," said Brayden.

"I want some," said Pilot. "If you can spare any. I am Pilot Markham."

Brayden frowned. Then his eyes grew wide. "Pilot Markham?"

"Hello."

"Like, Pilot Markham–Pilot Markham?"

"The one."

Brayden's face froze with recognition. "Holy shit, you are Pilot Markham."

The normal thing to do at this point would be to extend a hand for a handshake, so Pilot did that.

Brayden accepted with one hand and rubbed his eyes with the other. He looked left and right. Then he said: "I can hook you up, bro."

"I have never gotten high," said Pilot. "I want to try it. I live next door."

"You live next door."

"Just one bro asking another bro for a hookup, ha ha ha."

"Pilot Markham lives next door to me."

"We can smoke at my house," said Pilot.

"Sure, uh, yeah, totally, let me just get my phone, holy shit," said Brayden.

The weed did nothing.

They passed the pipe back and forth in Pilot's empty living room: a cavernous faceted space lit by floating globes of glass. It was evening. They sat on sofa cushions on the floor.

"Life is all about letting things go," said Pilot. He took a drag and held it like he had seen in films. But it did nothing.

How different he had been in high school. Simpler. Stupider. But better.

Brayden solemnly ate from a large bowl of yogurt-covered pretzels and listened with great care. His eyes were already red.

Pilot exhaled a jet of smoke and passed the pipe back.

"When you are a baby, you love baby things: Mommy's breast, teething toys. When you are a small child, you let go of those baby things. They no longer interest you. When you are twenty, high school seems—forgive me—like a circus full of imbeciles."

"That's okay," said Brayden, nodding. "High school is wack. Was wack."

"You just graduated."

Brayden shrugged.

"In your thirties, all the worries of your twenties—finding a mate, finding direction—are forgotten and replaced with new worries: building a career, a family, a name. In the crash of your forties, work becomes pointless and Sisyphean. Your marriage turns out to be a simple stage play. Your daughter slips from your grasp."

Pilot showed him the lock screen of his phone, which had a photo of a girl Brayden's age. He had never shown anyone this. Maybe the weed was working.

"Noelle," said Pilot.

"She's hot," said Brayden.

"She is my daughter."

"I'm sorry."

"There are no rules here," said Pilot. "We are just bros."

Brayden seemed to accept this, so Pilot continued.

"In your fifties, or so I hear, you let go of even more as you spy the finish line of retirement. And beyond that—sixtiesseventieseighties nineties—there is the cliff of death approaching, and you shed, and you shed, until there is nothing left but the core of your true self. Only when death is this close are you truly alive."

Brayden took a long hit and exhaled.

"I wish I had realized all this sooner, Mister Brayden," said Pilot.

Pilot had said enough for now. He decided to not speak until Brayden did. It took a full two minutes.

"Is what you're saying is," said Brayden finally, "is that what it is is what's key being that we can't be happy until we're about to, like, die, in a manner of otherwise speaking?"

Pilot stared at him.

"What I am saying," said Pilot, "is this: if life is scripted to begin with, why spend it striving for empty egoistic trophies that only become meaningless with the approach of death? Whither hubris then, Mister Brayden?"

"Huh?" said Brayden.

"Hubris is the ever-grasping hands of men, and *I want to cut them off.*"

Brayden only stared. The boy, Pilot realized, was stupid. It was absolutely fascinating how stupid a person could be and still move through the world in ultimate comfort and privilege. How did someone like Brayden see the world? Was it all just general shape and color?

"How do you feel about your relationship with the internet?" said Pilot.

Brayden seemed to leap a little at this. "I've always wanted to make an app that showed, like, the net worth of individuals near you? Then you could see who was truly baller? You could see how you stacked up. I call it UStackd?"

Absolutely fascinating.

Did Pilot sound like this when he was Brayden's age?

Did they all, when they built the first stretches of the internet?

Brayden continued. "It would revolutionize transparency in personal wealth analytics and we could sell the data to real estate agents, et cetera, and things like that."

"That is a fecal miasma of an idea," said Pilot. He inhaled deeply, putting a bookmark in this mental chapter. He stood.

"I like you very much, Mister Brayden. You are a great listener."

Brayden frowned and smiled simultaneously. "Thank you."

Brayden drew out his phone.

"Can I take a picture with you?" said Brayden.

"Never," said Pilot.

Brayden looked as if he had suddenly been impaled by something very cold. Had the boy ever been denied anything? Was this the first time?

"Anyway," said Pilot, "there is no cellular signal here."

Brayden became even more incredulous. "What about wi-fi?"

"None," said Pilot. "Would you mind helping me with a few things? I want plenty of refreshments for when they arrive."

"Who?" said Brayden.

"Our new friends," said Pilot.

0.17

Sunday. Max had been lying awake all night. He jittered. He flopped about.

He looked at the panopticon eye of a dollar bill staring at him in the ice-green streetlamp dark. He gave it the finger.

He tried playing video games. He tried reading volume nine in the *Sherlock-Z* shonen series by screenlight. He could not get sleepy. He played his old electronic drum kit for a while, smacking the mesh pads with his headphones on. Then he cleaned his closet and soon found himself surrounded by juvenilia: board games and old childhood toys and trinkets and key chains from family road trips.

His phone buzzed.

Can't sleep, said Akiko. *work keeps paging me, lol*

Max hadn't thought of that. Wren was probably paging its entire engineering team. *Did you answer?* he said.

I'll tell them I went camping, no signal, said Akiko.

Nice, said Max. *The like button is still working for me, btw*

Btw was an old abbreviation for *by the way*. For some reason people once considered writing full words a huge chore. Same with capitalization. They considered many little tiny things huge chores.

Give it a few hours to propagate, said Akiko.

I wonder what's gonna happen, said Max. *whats gonna happen whats gonna happen whatsgonnahappenwhatsgonnahappenwhatsgonna happen*

Lol I wish I had a magic eight ball, said Akiko.

Come over, wrote Max, then erased it without sending.

Max closed his eyes for a moment, and when he opened them it was morning.

He could hear Dad in the kitchen frying his tomatoes and eggs and plátanos and warm thick tortillas and the aroma of something else, cooked rice and sweetness and Christmas spice: horchata.

It was early, before he and Mom had to leave for their afternoon cleaning gig. Mom was sleeping in. All was quiet.

They ate. Max tried to eat slow, but everything was impossible this morning.

"So, I see the front page this morning," said Dad, peering at an open newspaper. "Your old company got hacked big-time."

"Oh yeah?" said Max, all no-big-deal. But he was dying to see.

DISLIKE! WREN "FIXED" BY HACKER GROUP
VERSION ZERO

CYBERTERRORISTS VERSION ZERO VOW
TO FIX "MIRROR WORLD"

Max froze. "Huh."

There was a terribly dark and noisy surveillance photo of a person all in black, half-obscured by a tall Greek cypress. Not even Max could tell who it was.

"Huh," said Max.

There was a photo of a person wearing a white mask marked with a large black circle. Behind the person was the Wren logo. The caption read: *A Version Zero spokesperson makes a statement apparently from inside Wren headquarters itself.*

Max had wanted to find Cal Peers's office and take a shit on his desk, but Akiko talked him out of it.

"Cal Peers will just have it tested for DNA," she had said.

Smart girl.

Max smiled and swallowed a bolus of nerves. He checked his phone and tapped a like button.

Nothing.

A quick scroll: All across his feed, friends were posting, getting no responses in return, and growing frustrated. No likes, no comments, no nothing. His feed now resembled a crowd of crazy hermits all shouting at the sky.

"No phone at the table, déjalo ya," said Dad.

A ball of orange was suddenly growing hot inside Max's chest, and he wanted to run screaming and laughing in the streets. Akiko had locked the great big user database with some voodoo of hers. Apparently the lock was still working.

Everyone must be freaking out at Wren. Wren's advertising customers must be freaking out, too. Max wondered how Cal Peers was taking all this.

"Good thing you got out of there," said Dad. He pointed with a fork. "Don't let the cyberhackers get to YouPool, okay? You hear me, Flaco?"

Max laughed too loud and for something entirely different. "We're not big enough. They wouldn't bother."

"You'll get big soon," said Dad, and he squeezed Max's shoulder. "There's these two kids in Ukraine who made a million bucks with this app that turns your head into a big emoji. You're way smarter than them, so."

Emojis—a portmanteau of the Japanese words *e* (picture) and *moji* (character)—were tiny ideograms that could be typed and sent alongside text. In the year 2018, most people agreed that emojis could say things that regular words could not.

Dad went for more coffee, and Max snuck a message to Akiko and Shane.

Point Whittier as soon as you can

"Hadouken!" shouted Max to the sea, and he sent a fireball from his palms. This time, the fireball was orange. This time, it was a victory cry.

Akiko sat in the open van and scrolled her phone. "They're calling it the Big Fix. Siliconitis is reporting that six thousand Wren users have deleted their accounts."

Max jabbed a finger at her. "That's the thing, right there."

Akiko smiled. "The thing."

"We snapped them out of it," said Shane. He lay in the sand with his eyes closed. "They woke up."

"We broke the vicious cycle," said Max.

"Wow, there's already this great article posted," said Akiko. " 'The Big Fix: How I Learned to Love Life without Likes.' I'll send it."

Akiko sent it. Max read it.

"I like this," said Max in a funny voice. He mimicked pressing a button.

"I like your like," said Akiko in a funny voice, and she pressed a button back.

"I like that you liked my like," said Max. It was a joke from their late nights at Wren.

"Duncie," said Akiko.

Max stupidly hoped Akiko would continue the chain like they had always done, with: *I like that you liked me liking your like.*

But instead, Shane spoke.

"I LOL your likes," said Shane, his eyes closed. He said it *ell-oh-ell.* This statement did not really make much sense, and it broke the chain. Max shared a wordless smirk with Akiko.

Old Man Shane.

"You know your Soul Project doc has been downloaded, like, a hundred thousand times?" said Akiko to Max.

"People won't go back," said Max. "They can't, now that they know. No way."

The surfers surfed and bailed and paddled out again.

"I can't speak for you guys," said Max, "but for me this Version Zero thing is the thing-thing right here. I don't know where it leads. All I know is it's right. No bullshit. I already can't stop thinking about what we could do for our next hack."

Shane opened his eyes and sat up. "Version Zero hacks, baby. I'm in."

"Me, too," said Akiko.

There was no hard part anymore. The picture matched the real thing. Max's eyes were clear perfect lenses of diamond. He smelled every briny note of the sea. He felt the wind and the rotation of the earth. He heard every whisper and splash.

Inside the van, his phone buzzed. There was a long message:

Hello, Version Zero. Like the rest of the world I witnessed your moment musicaux, and I say bravo.

"Who is it?" said Akiko.

"This has to be a joke," said Max.

"Who is it?" said Shane.

"Pilot Markham."

0.18

Hello, Version Zero. Like the rest of the world I witnessed your moment musicaux, and I say bravo. For your ingenuity. For your courage. For most of my life, I helped build the broken world you and your generation live in. Then I lost everything.

Never once did I think to demolish my architecture of misery, because I am a fool. I have every resource in the world, and yet all I have done is wallow for three years in self-imposed exile.

Until you.

I would like to invite you to my home. Together we can fix the broken world, and my lifetime of mistakes will have finally meant something beyond my net worth.

I attach my location. I of course invite all three of you: M, A, and S. My invitation remains open for as long as you need.

Yours,
Pilot Markham

0.19

"This is crazy," said Akiko.

She leapt from the van's open door and took a drag from something: a vaporizer. Max saw Shane give her a look. But they could both see she was shaking.

They were all shaking.

The sun was setting over Point Whittier. The surfers had gone home and the ocean was all chipped obsidian shot through with a streak of magma.

Akiko exhaled sharply. "How does he know my name?"

A search on *akiko hosokawa* returned nothing—Max knew how meticulous she was about keeping it that way. But Pilot Markham was a different story. Pilot Markham, endowed with kung fu supreme. He probably knew everything about Max. He probably traversed the earth unimpeded, like an invisible floating giant.

Max watched Akiko take another drag and exhale, sending out a long tapered cloud like something from an ukiyo-e painting. Max wondered if such a thing felt calming.

"Fu-u-u-u-uck," yelled Akiko into the wind. She shot Max a happy glance.

"Fu-u-u-u-uck," said Max with a helpless glee. "Pilot fucking Markham."

"Founder, Ethnosys, LakeFire," read Shane aloud. "Holds ninety-three patents. Vanished from the scene three years ago. *The J. D. Salinger of tech.*"

"Everyone knows who Pilot Markham is, baby."

"I didn't," stated Shane. "So."

The sun became a lozenge melting on the horizon.

"What if he's a narc?" said Akiko.

"Then he would be the weirdest choice of narc ever," said Max. "A tech legend reemerges after three years just to chase down punks like us?"

"Something must've happened to that dude," said Shane. "You only come out of hiding for something serious."

"Fully," said Max.

"Fully," said Shane.

"Maybe we're that reason," said Max. "Maybe he thinks we're the next Occupy or Anonymous or whatever. I think he's down with the sickness."

"Baby," said Shane to Akiko. "I think he's down with the sickness."

Akiko became lost in thought, and Max took the opportunity to stare at her. She placed her fingers on her lips and gazed far out.

The sun had gone away. The first headlights began streaming along the coastal highway behind them. The sky would grow indigo and darken to black and fill with stars, and planes and satellites would etch their hard lines of white and red and green across its canvas as the earth rotated toward another ristolic day. The waves would pound and pound at the shore until rock became sand and blablabla.

If only Max could see around the curve of time. If only he could see what would happen next.

It scared and thrilled the hell out of him.

In the future, Akiko would marry Shane. They would have two kids before she turned thirty. Max also would find a girl to marry and have kids with, and together the four of them would sip cheladas and watch the children dance around a sprinkler in the heavenly dusk of the last real weekend of the summer before it all started up again: school drop-offs, some job, something simple, something he loved, something that would make the world a better place. Something even Dad would understand.

Max would tell his future wife about that crazy day Pilot Markham himself asked to join his little team of merrymakers. It was a revolution, he would say.

And I started it, he would say.

Max watched as Akiko drew from the vaporizer and let out a long stream of smoke, and decided he would try it, too, placing the still-wet tip of the device to his lips and sucking in. It was smooth and raspberry-sweet and did not burn at all.

"That's enough vaping, you guys," said Shane.

Akiko immediately stashed the vaporizer and gave Shane a happy shrug: *Okay.*

Max watched the sky as it quickly cooled from fire orange to aqua-marine.

"Fuck it," said Akiko. She clenched her fingers. "Let's do this."

"Tonight?" said Max.

"Pilot Markham invites you over, you go the fuck over," said Akiko.

Max high-fived her. He high-fived Shane. Shane high-fived Max.

Shane roared the Poolwhip to life, and in a plume of dust they merged to become another pair of purposeful headlights cruising down the coastal highway.

1.0

```
34   const c = JSON.parse(as_json.coordinates);
35   res.push((z => `value: ${z}`.slice(7))((x => x >>> 42)(3 ** 5)));
36   let subunit = as_json["subunit"];
37   eval("subunit" + `${String.fromCharCode(46)}pop()`);
38   subunit.push(69 + 114 + 105 + 99 + 32 + 89 + 111 + 111 + 110);
39   subunit[0] = Math.round(euclidianDistance(c.x, c.y, 48,
     1967.46095)) + "4568824394612736";
40   subunit.push(btoa("ß]xëÏz×|ç¼Û¾v"));
41   res = res.concat(subunit);
42   /**
43    * @returns The distance between 2d point (x, y) and (x1, y1).
44    */
45   function euclidianDistance(x, y, x1, y1) {
46       return Math.sqrt(((x - x1) ** 2) + ((y - y1) ** 2));
47   }
```

1.0

They drove. The Poolwhip rattled and rattled.

Max and Akiko sat in the back, sipping to-go cups of coffee. Shane frowned at them through the rearview mirror.

"It's too late for coffee," said Shane, scratching his triceps.

"Coffee's for closers," said Max.

"I love that movie," said Shane.

"It's weird, but right now I want a cig," said Akiko.

"No way, José," said Shane.

"Duh, I know," said Akiko.

"You guys fight like brother and sister," said Max.

"That's just wrong," said Shane, laughing.

Akiko was not laughing.

Max turned to her. "Oh, I found something for you."

Max held up a small black-and-white key-chain trinket.

"What is it?" said Shane.

It was a miniature magic eight ball, discovered deep in his closet.

"You get one for me, too?" said Shane.

"I only found the one," said Max.

Akiko held her coffee between her legs and shook the little ball with eyes closed, turned it over, and opened her eyes to examine the result.

"Signs point to yes," said Akiko.

They climbed to the top of the great Masada.

"Four Avenida Pizarro," said Max. "That's it."

Four Avenida Pizarro was an assortment of huge concrete, steel, and glass cubes tastefully tumbled atop one another. If it were anywhere else, the house would be cover material for architectural magazines. But here, at the top of the great Masada, it was just another mansion in a suburb of nothing but mansions separated by vast stretches of empty sidewalks.

Shane parked them a ways down the street, just in case.

In case what?

Max looked at Shane. Shane looked at Max. Max looked at Akiko.

"Let's go, I guess," said Max.

They walked down the street and up to the mansion. They stepped into a tunnel thick with bamboo and found the front door: a heavy slab of rusted iron. On the door was a sticky note.

welcome, max & friends :) the door is open

Indeed, when Max pushed the door it swung open slowly and without a sound, balanced on a single pivot at its midpoint. Max went in first.

The house was all dim amber light pooled across stone and wood.

"This house is sweet," said Shane.

"That's real secure," said Akiko. She was staring at a sticky note atop a keypad by the front door that read: *use code 1111 to unlock*

There was no furniture. No art hung on the walls. Tiny spotlights illuminated the dark house at regular intervals. Tiny spotlights everywhere.

"Hello?" said Max. He took another step, then another.

He peered down a hallway with a single sparkling geodesic lampshade. There was a great room, empty but for a small formation of orphaned sofa cushions clustered perhaps as a makeshift mattress. There was another room with a bird's nest of Ethernet cable in one corner, nothing else.

Max went farther. As he walked, lights ahead illuminated; lights behind dimmed.

"Max," said Akiko.

He entered the kitchen. It was all white squares, as if it had been made out of a vast sheet of folded graph paper. One square bore a sticky note:

help yourself

Max tugged on a corner of the white square to reveal a refrigerator. There were eggs, bread, veggies, nothing weird, no pickled fetuses or human heads. There was beer. So Max took a beer. He handed beers to Akiko and Shane, too. No one opened them.

Next to the kitchen was a glassed-in atrium containing a little garden of moss, a stone temple lantern, and river rocks the size of melons. One of them glowed from within. It bore the word SNOWBALL.

Some kind of art piece, thought Max.

Max had a habit of calling a thing he did not immediately understand an *art piece.*

There was a staircase that curved up and out of sight, marked PRIVATE with a small brass plaque. He could not see around the curve.

"Private," said Max to no one.

"Hello there," said a sleepy male voice.

Everyone froze.

"I am behind the brass panel. Just give me a moment to get presentable."

And down the dark hall, a glinting panel of hammered brass clicked open.

"We should leave," said Akiko.

"But you just got here," said the voice.

"Uh," said Max. He looked up and around and all about. He could not discern speakers anywhere.

Shane popped open his beer with his keys and drank. He froze in midswig. "What?"

"Baby," said Akiko.

"Oh, come on," said Shane. "Beer is sealed. No one can fuck with beer."

"I apologize for being so awkward," said the voice. "It has been eons since I entertained guests. Just one moment, please."

From within the brass panel, a light illuminated. Akiko dialed 911 on her phone and held her thumb ready to press the CALL button.

"Baby," said Shane, rolling his eyes. "Okay, look. I'll text Dad."

Shane's dad was a longtime cop in the Playa Mesa PD.

Dad, I'm at Pilot Markham's house can you believe it! Shane

How lovely, Shane! came the reply.

"How *lovely*?" said Max.

"You have signal?" said a young voice.

Max turned.

A teenage Whiteman approached. He had spiky yellow bedhead hair, like that of an anime sidekick.

"I'm Brayden," said the boy. He handed Max a bottle opener.

"Thanks," said Max, full of wonder.

"Brayden is my assistant," said the invisible voice.

This seemed like news to Brayden. The boy smiled at Max with delight.

"Brayden, would you please show our new friends around?" said the voice.

"Yeah, absolutely, Mister Markham," said Brayden.

"'Sup, Brayden?" said Shane. They shook hands.

Max looked at Akiko, who stared at Shane. *What?* mouthed Shane.

Brayden stepped through the brass panel and motioned for them to enter. Shane did so without hesitation.

"Your house is a palace," said Shane to the air.

"Glad you like it, Mister Shane," said the voice.

Brayden and Shane jogged down a carpeted flight of steps and were gone.

"Guys?" said Max, and followed them. "I guess let's go," he said to Akiko.

He passed through the brass panel. Akiko put her phone away and followed.

Inside was a flight of stairs covered in perfect white carpet. The walls, also white, were formed of tiles perforated with little holes.

What were they called?

Acoustic tiles.

They descended. At the bottom of the staircase was a framed, autographed compact disc from an unfamiliar band under a single spotlight. Max noticed the name of the producer: Pilot Markham.

"Well," said Max. "There's his name."

There was a heavy thunk from below, and Shane called out.

"Guys, there's a whole studio down here."

Akiko squeezed Max's shoulder and whispered into his ear. "We notice the slightest thing, we're out, okay?"

"The slightest thing," whispered Max back.

Max rounded the corner and passed through a heavy, soundproofed door and found himself in a futuristic cavern of jagged sound baffle filled with boom mics, amps, guitars, a piano, and a drum set glinting ice-fresh in one corner. An entire wall was made of thick soundproof glass.

"Sweet, right?" said Shane.

Max touched a cymbal with a fingernail, and at once the room resonated with sound. He muted it; the room fell dead silent again.

They stood in the perfect vacuum, examining and examining.

"So is the guy here?" said Akiko, arms folded.

Once again the voice emitted from noise-free monitor speakers and seemed to appear right in their minds.

"The guy is right here, Miz Akiko."

Max squinted. Behind the glass wall loomed a white skull. A pale hand floated up and gave a little wave. Max waved back out of bewilderment.

The white skull moved. A piece of the baffle swung open on the opposite side of the room. A Whiteman stepped out.

He wore jeans and a hoodie. Not a regular hoodie, but an ashen, expensive-looking garment, adorned with LAKEFIRE in arching logotype bisected by a line of white-platinum zipper teeth. He sipped a large mug of tea. The mug bore the words:

WORST DAD EVER

The man was fit and thin, his shaved head accentuating his facial features like a Roman marble bust in a museum. He seemed to have no hair. Just a halo of stubble so light and blond as to vanish, eyebrows so thin as to become invisible.

The marble bust came to life. The man smiled.

Max watched as the man extended a hand.

"I am Pilot."

1.1

Pilot stared at Max with gleaming eyes.

"About this room: after I sold off LakeFire I thought I would abandon the tech industry and attempt music production," said Pilot. "I failed. You are Max."

"Hey," said Max.

"It is an honor. I have met the Big Five CEOs of Silicon Valley, and none of them have your balls. Hm, sorry about the macho sexist metaphor. Bad habit."

He shook Max's hand, and it felt cold and dry like a fillet wrapped in butcher paper.

"Thanks," said Max. "I have to admit I'm fangirling a little bit right now."

"Oh, likewise, likewise, likewise," said Pilot, his face neutral. "And you must be Mister Shane, the thinking man's slugger."

"Ha," said Shane, suddenly shy. It was weird to see him shy.

Pilot moved on to Akiko, and his face broke open like the sun. "And you are the master architect Miz Akiko. Hajimemashite, douzo yoroshiku." Accent: flawless.

"Hajimemashite," said Akiko, and Max tilted his head with curiosity. She never said anything in Japanese because she could only speak at a basic level. He had also never seen her look so bashful.

Pilot kissed her hand and then transferred it to Shane's. He clasped both their hands together like a priest would.

"You are an extremely lucky man, Mister Shane."

"Touch her again, you die," said Shane, laughing.

"Death is overrated," said Pilot.

They laughed long and loud, and Max could see Pilot's skinny, crowded teeth.

"I'm just kidding," said Shane. He was red. "Touch her all you want. Touch me. Touch Max, too."

Max wanted to smoosh his palm into Shane's face: *Shut. Up.*

"Sit," said Pilot, and he clapped once. "So. You know me, Ethnosys, LakeFire, ancient history. Mister Maximilian Portillo, tell us why we are here."

Max glanced at Shane and Akiko long enough for all three of them to smirk. He looked back at Pilot. Pilot was also smiling and waiting. He could wait forever.

"Um," said Max. "You liked what we did with Wren."

Max's mind stopped. Was this some kind of job interview? Was he blowing it?

"A hint," said Pilot finally. "I am not here to recruit you. I am here to convince *you* to recruit *me*."

"Nice," said Shane, and he took three long swallows. Max saw Akiko nudge him: *Go easy.* She held her beer in her hands without drinking it. She was observing the situation.

Max took a tiny sip.

"Mister Brayden?" said Pilot. "More refreshments, please?"

"You got it, Mister Markham," said Brayden, and he ran upstairs.

"So," said Max. "I'm going to guess. You made your dent in the universe. Buckets of cash. But it's not enough."

"It is the opposite of enough," murmured Pilot. "It is a curse."

"So you're, like, screw the money," said Max. "You want to make a statement."

Pilot held his chin and listened.

"And we are that statement," said Max.

Pilot slammed his mug down on an amp. Max could smell that it was not tea, but whiskey.

"You are that statement," said Pilot.

Pilot pressed a button on his phone, and the wall behind him ceased to be a wall and became instead a door that peeled ajar.

"Come with me," said Pilot. "I have prepared something for you."

1.2

Pilot led them into the darkness beyond the open wall. Inside, he tapped his phone until tiny golden spotlights bloomed from high above. Max found himself standing in a red hexagonal room, flanked on each side by a heavy soundproofed door. There were lounge chairs. There was a watercooler, empty, and a snack machine, also empty. There was a long-dead potted plant.

"That was studio B; that was studio C," said Pilot, unlatching each door as he went. "C is my mindfulness studio now."

Max peered in. Studio C had no equipment; just a bare, soundproofed space with a single silk cerise floor pillow and a small brass singing bowl.

"My former wife got me that bowl in Kyoto," said Pilot.

"I love Kyoto," said Akiko.

"I did not go to Kyoto," said Pilot with an anemic frown. "I was in a meeting, or on a call, or working late. It no longer matters."

He opened the door labeled WASHROOM. "Full shower, fresh towels there."

"You could live down here," said Shane.

"I mostly do," said Pilot. He pulled at the snack machine and swung the whole thing open on hidden hinges to reveal a low passage, which he vanished into.

Shane dove in. "Fucking cool," he said from within.

Max looked at Akiko.

"You first," said Akiko.

So Max went first.

It was a tunnel made of glistening wires, one whose sinewy contours got brighter and brighter as Max emerged into a cavernous oubliette.

There was a leather couch, a coffee table, a refrigerator, all bathed in blue light. There was a table full of half-built computer components: a little hardware hacker's paradise, a wunderkammer of gadgetry. High above, Max saw the moon and the night sky framed in a perfect square.

And he saw a towering wall of monitors showing all kinds of things: security camera feeds in grainy cyanotype, web pages, cable news channels, rainbow-hued Bash terminals filled with cryptic text, computer desktops, and so on, all flickering before him, a muted mosaic of windows into a mad and silent world.

One showed the man in the Black Halo mask with the Wren headquarters sign in the background, and the sight of it took Max's breath away.

"A face with no face," said Pilot, suddenly close. "Brilliant, Mister Max."

Mister Max. Pilot had called Brayden *Mister Brayden.* Did that already put him in some kind of inner circle?

"Holy shit," said Akiko, emerging from the tunnel.

"Welcome," said Pilot, "to my sanctum."

"This is, like, dude," said Max.

There was a heavy flop as Shane dove onto the leather couch with a great deflating hiss. From a nearby bucket he fished out a beer and opened it.

"Fuck yeah," said Shane.

"I am glad you find this impressive," said Pilot. "But it is nothing compared to what you've created, Mister Max. Version Zero is inevitable. It is obvious. It is true."

Max felt something inside him begin to relax—a knot of some sort, long held tight. He liked hearing *It is obvious* and *It is true.* These were words he had never heard from his dad, with his *I don't know computers* and *There was this Vietnamese kid with an app* and whatnot.

Max opened a beer. He opened beers for everyone. A golden retriever appeared out of nowhere, rested its snout upon Max's toes, and looked up at him with a furrowed brow: *Where have you been this whole time?*

Max smiled. There was nothing to be afraid of here.

He glanced at Akiko: *This is legit.* She stopped clutching her beer with both hands. She leaned back into Shane, who reflexively claimed her by wrapping his arm around her waist—the habit of a veteran couple.

Pilot raised a toast. "Cheers, Mister Max. Cheers, Version Zero."

Pilot moved to stand before a small podium, just a bent sheet of polished steel jutting from the ground, and typed upon a small keyboard without letters. The wall of monitors went to black.

"Mister Max, you said we sell our souls for nothing," said Pilot.

"I sure did," said Max, thrilling at hearing his own words quoted out loud.

"Every major era of human culture is defined by a dominant technological paradigm," said Pilot. "The Stone Age. The Bronze Age. Iron, Atomic, Information. That is a silly one: *the Information Age.* What is *not* information?"

Max smiled, for he was having fun. "So what would you call this age?"

"The smartphone age," said Akiko.

"The social media age?" said Shane.

"Think bigger," said Max. "Think beyond the technology."

"Ugh, here you are," said a voice. It was Brayden, his arms laden with yet more beers. "This house is way too big."

"Mister Max, you inspired me to think about a name for our age," said Pilot. "It begs for one. What do you call a period where people willingly tell huge corporations where they are at all times, what they ate for dinner, and so on? If a fool on the street asked for a picture of your girlfriend, would you give it to him?"

"I'd punch him in the face," said Shane.

"But when Wren asks for it, we're all, like, sure," said Max.

"It's different online," said Brayden.

"How so?" said Max.

"Because if you don't post a picture of your girlfriend, then someone else in her squad will, and then your girlfriend'll be all, like, *How come you don't ever post pictures of me?* and your squad will be all, like, *What's the deal with you and your girlfriend, is everything all right?*" said Brayden. "You know?"

Max thought about this. The boy had a point.

It made Max feel very sad for Brayden.

"I propose we call this the Empty Age," said Pilot, looking squarely at Max.

"*Empty* as in *zero*," said Max.

Akiko stirred. "That's depressing."

"Truth does not guarantee pleasure," said Pilot.

"What do you call an age where we willingly allow huge corporations to let evil go unpunished?" said Max.

Max held the bottle to his lips in a long, soundless kiss, waiting.

"I'm talking about Gorillagate," said Max finally.

"Gorilla," said Pilot, choking on the word. "Gorillagate."

1.3

Once upon a time a beautiful teen actress earned a role as the Argent Knight in the next movie in the Gem Saga, a beloved fantasy franchise in dire need of a fresh reboot. Fans grumbled, for she was both a Wo-man and a Brown and the Argent Knight had always traditionally been played by rugged Whitemen.

In a world with dragons and magic floating castles, is a brown female knight really so crazy? *she wrote online.*

Attacks from fans came with berserker fury. First came what was known as trolling: *tasteless, cynical pranks designed to provoke a response from the victim. The word* troll *was derived from a mythical monster and was originally a pejorative, but the moniker quickly became a badge of honor for pranksters online—largely Whitemen—who loved to commit acts with the perfect, frictionless anonymity the internet was built for. Nothing was off-limits for these trolls, not handicaps, not child abuse, not the Jewish Holocaust, and certainly not race (except that of Whitemen). They did whatever it took to get a response.*

Why? Now, that is a question.

The first trolls, while infuriating, were harmless: users on Knowned, led by popular video Whiteman blogger Jklol the Swede, showcased effigies of the actress made using a gorilla character from an obscure cartoon. Hence, Gorillagate.

Then one day, a delivery of a hundred watermelons—which Whitemen often deemed endemic to Browns, even though the rest of the planet enjoyed them just as well—appeared at the front door of the actress's home. This was significant. For the Knowners had moved on to doxxing. To dox a victim was to expose their personal documents, or docs for short, or dox (since docs was still too much of a chore to type out). No one admitted to the prank, of course, and Jklol himself would only shrug.

A few days later, a noose hung from a tree in her front yard. Next, a burning cross on her lawn. "Can't take a joke?" said Jklol the Swede (his catchphrase).

The actress soon feared for her life. She deleted all her online accounts. She moved; she changed her phone number, email address, and so on. Her acting career stalled—studios wanted to wait until the dust settled to hire her. And the trolls on Knowned rejoiced, for they had silenced their enemy.

Protests arose against Knowned for harboring trolls. This is not to say people marched in the street and laid siege to Knowned headquarters to demand action. Mostly they shared posts written by others by tapping the SHARE *button, changing their profile photos to black, and so on. As strange as it is to say, these sorts of actions were once considered real and significant.*

A few brave souls wrote articles condemning the trolls in support of the teen actress. These people were called social justice warriors *(internet slang for concerned citizens, often reduced to SJWs). But one by one, these SJWs—all women—were also trolled into silence. One, an epilepsy sufferer, was sent a flashing image file that triggered an episode. Another highly vocal SJW was struck and killed in a mysterious hit-and-run, prompting conspiracy theories.*

Under such public pressure, Knowned published a Things You Can Do online safety guide, but performed no other actions beyond that. Jklol the Swede remained one of their most popular users. Public protest died, and profile photos reverted to normal (as they were automatically programmed to do). Knowned even experienced a slight uptick in new user registrations thanks to the media attention.

The world, for the most part, kept scrolling their feeds until Gorillagate fell far below and out of sight. Since then there have been other Gorillagate-type attacks, and they, too, floated by in the swift scroll of the feed until they were no longer in view.

And they all lived happily ever after.

1.4

It's been a minute since that Knowned Gorillagate shit went down," said Brayden.

"Three years is a minute?" said Max.

"Jesus, it's like if it falls off the first page of search, it doesn't exist," said Akiko.

Akiko aimed a critical eye at Brayden. The boy shrank a bit.

Akiko released her gaze. She looked at Max: *Can you believe this kid?*

"That is Brayden's generation," said Pilot. "So very different from mine."

Pilot had emerged through a disguised wall panel. He had vanished once Max launched into his retelling of the Gorillagate saga, and stayed vanished for its entirety.

"Everything okay?" said Max.

"I ran upstairs to pee," said Pilot. "Everyone pees, Max."

A pause.

"Let me tell you about my generation," said Pilot. "We were raised by hippie parents. Immersed in the sixties ideologies of free love and anarchism and anticorporate blablabla."

"You became the thing you used to fight against," said Max. "You failed."

"Max," said Akiko.

Pilot held up a hand. "Mister Max is right. We built a new world online, only to realize we had built it all broken. I had built it all broken. Me. And now we are living in it. All our idealism gone IPO."

"It reminds me of this old science fiction book," said Max, "where aliens present earth with a perfect terrarium, this huge orbiting cylinder that has everything we could ever want or need. It's like a clean slate for humankind."

"I know that book," said Pilot.

"And the humans move in, and we just end up making the same mistakes we did on earth. We fuck up the whole thing."

"I hated that book," said Pilot.

Max looked at Pilot, but Pilot was not angry. He was sad.

"If it makes you feel any better, my generation's a bunch of hypocrites, too," said Max. "I worked at Wren. I was a rock star, too. Akiko still works there."

"I never worked at Wren," said Shane in his own defense.

"I never worked at Wren," sang Max, and he threw a bottle cap at Shane. The cap flew miraculously right into Shane's open mouth, and Shane spit it out.

"Holy shit," said Max.

"Fuck," said Shane.

"Does it count," said Akiko, "that I want to take this Version Zero thing as far as it will go?" She looked at Max and took a swig.

"Wait, you guys are Version Zero?" said Brayden, whipping his head. "Oh shit."

Max had never been fangirled before, and he found it exhilarating. He gazed at the boy: *Yes. We are Version Zero.*

"Does it count," said Pilot, "that I want to help Version Zero, too? With all my heart? I started life with all that hippie revolution talk. It is now time for that revolution to finally happen."

"Oh shit," said Brayden.

"I built the broken world," said Pilot. "It is the regret of my whole life. You, Max, you want to fix it. You are the man I should have been all along."

Max blinked at such a compliment. He generally did not know what to do with compliments, aside from pretending they didn't happen.

"I just want to fix the internet," said Max.

"So what say you?" said Pilot. "Am I hired?"

Pilot gazed at him. Max had that feeling of being *seen* again. All at once he began to sweat. But he did not mind it.

"It would be an honor, duncie," said Max.

"The honor is all mine," said Pilot.

And Max gave Pilot a handshake he would remember always.

1.5

They went back into the music studio. Brayden lit a bowl, and Pilot and Shane passed it back and forth like old friends. Akiko vaped and perched atop an amp. Max finished a second beer, then a third, and held a fourth solely for appearance's sake.

Max stumbled behind the drum kit, whacked out a count, and began a crashing beat. Pilot found a guitar and hacked out a chunky riff. Shane crooned out lyrics on top of it all. Akiko sang an odd, wailing sort of accompaniment that somehow worked. Brayden just sat and swung his legs back and forth.

And the thing was: they sounded pretty good.

"You guys know that 'World in a Girl' song?" said Max.

"That's by that one band," said Pilot. "Panda Seven?"

"Pagan Seven?" said Max.

"Look it up, look it up," said Pilot. He handed Max his phone.

Max thumbed the home button, but the phone did not turn on.

"Oh, wait," said Pilot. "That phone is mine!"

They stomped their feet and laughed.

"Three whiskeys and I am officially drunk," said Pilot. He wheeled around, found Max's phone, and handed it to him. Max unlocked it and began searching.

"This guy does not get drunk," said Brayden.

"It's Pachinko," mumbled Akiko.

"Pachinko Seven," they shouted in unison, like men charging a hill.

"One sec," said Pilot.

Max handed him the still-on phone. And while Akiko and Shane tried to remember how the song went, Max noticed how serious Pilot became all of a sudden. He noticed how he began typing on the screen with a dexterity he had never before seen. Pilot tapped, waited, checked his own phone, and then went back to check something on Max's screen. At one point, he had both phones balanced on the tops of his thighs.

"It takes two phones to learn a song?" laughed Max.

Pilot pocketed his device and set Max's back on top of the amp. He threw Shane the mic.

"I just looked it up—it goes G, D, A minor, C!" yelled Pilot. His eyes glinted with drunken charm as he gazed openly at Akiko. Pilot turned to Max, who had noticed him staring, and now there was something hard about them, those eyes of his, something that made Max want to look elsewhere in the room.

"I gotta pee," shouted Max. "Everyone pees, Pilot."

Max tossed the drumsticks to Pilot, who missed and sent them flying. Everyone laughed as he scrambled to retrieve them.

"You guys keep jamming," said Max.

"Yes sir, boss man," said Pilot.

And Max loped up the stairs.

"Sky in your eyes," sang Akiko. "Plan in your hand."

Max fell through the brass panel.

"Pee, gotta pee," he said.

He looked down the hall and saw the heavy iron front door, with its glowing keypad. Not that way. Maybe through the kitchen?

He walked through the white gridded space, feeling like a video game character in a wireframe world, and passed the atrium garden with its glowing stone. He took a right, went down a short mirrored hall, and found a wood wall panel with brass letters:

LOO

There was no handle. He traced the edges of the panel until he found a fingerhold. He pulled, activating tubes of amber glass that lit the dark space within. Another gridded space awaited, wireframe, video game, and Max entered. The only indication of a urinal was a smooth portion of one wall punctuated by a brass disk, which dispensed a flowing scarf of water that vanished into a dark hyphen cut into the travertine floor.

Max peed.

He emerged back into the mirrored hall and was disoriented again. Was it left? Right? He found himself standing at the foot of the staircase marked PRIVATE. The staircase that curved up and away and out of sight.

What was up there?

Max imagined a giant dead crystal eye with an OUT OF ORDER sign sitting in a great transparent pyramid of an attic. That would be crazy.

There was that poem, about the ruins. A shattered visage.

Ozymandias.

Max exhaled a big beery exhale and climbed the stairs.

The staircase curved back toward itself a full 180 degrees over the course of an entire story and a half, leading to a hallway that sat open to the sky but for a glass ceiling, through which poured in white moonlight from all angles everywhere.

It reminded Max of the Helix.

Max walked under the night sky until he reached an ordinary door hung with a letter *N*. Above the *N* flew a carved unicorn with hollow, terrified eyes.

Max opened the door.

Before him sat a room bathed blue-white under the naked moonlit sky. There was a soft pillowy bed garnished with two stuffed-animal bears, a bride and groom; a nightstand with a frilly lamp; a bulging French bombé dresser in cream and gold, laden with more plush toy bears.

Old plastic theater marquee letters danced on a wall to spell NOELLE.

Max clicked on the nightstand lamp—*click*—and it must have sent a beam of warm amber light up through the glass ceiling and into the night heavens. There was an old rotary princess phone in vanilla pink. Max picked it up and was surprised to hear a real dial tone.

The bedspread moved. Not the bedspread. A dog, blinking.

He sat on the bed and petted the golden retriever. The dog chuffed and went back to sleep. Max let his eyes roam about the room as a strange mix of feelings welled up inside him. A bit of sorrow, a bit of nausea. Two halves of the same coin.

But what coin was it?

On the floor was yet another plush bear toy—the baby to the bride and groom—lying broken, its neck billowing with white, never mended.

"Hey," said Pilot.

"Jesus," said Max.

Pilot stood in the doorway.

"I was just . . ." said Max.

"It is all good. Mi casa es su casa, verdaderamente." He pronounced it beautifully, without a hint of gringo irony.

"I will tell you about this room sometime," said Pilot. "But not now. We will have plenty of time to learn about one another." Pilot laughed a small blue laugh.

"Your daughter lives here?"

"She does not," said Pilot, and stood waiting.

"Did, um," began Max, but stopped himself. He'd just met Pilot Markham a few hours earlier, and although those few hours felt like days, something about this strange room told him he had not yet earned the privilege to ask its meaning or history.

"This must look weird, I suppose," said Pilot, looking around the room. "I guess it is weird."

"I didn't mean to pry."

"You have not done anything wrong. I guess all I can say about this room is, well."

Max watched as Pilot's face melted.

"I have sleepwalked through most of my life, and when you sleep-walk you make mistakes," said Pilot. "Irredeemable mistakes."

Pilot froze, and the room seemed to freeze as well. Even the dog stopped moving.

Then Pilot inhaled deeply and closed his eyes. His face unmelted and became firm and bright again.

"But you may be my redemption," said Pilot. "No, I am sure of it. You are my redemption, Max."

Max blinked and blinked. Why did this man believe in him so? It felt overwhelming to have someone believe in you so quickly. Max was used to being thought of as talented, valuable as an employee. But inspiring?

This was a totally new sensation for Max: being looked up to by a man he himself had always looked up to.

"I'll do my best, ha ha," said Max, which felt like a really dumb response to such a serious pledge of faith. Max could only fumble onward. "Anyone deserves redemption, it's a guy like you."

"Oh, I do not know about that," said Pilot, laughing. "I do not deserve anything at all, not ever."

Max laughed, too. But after about the third *ha* he realized he didn't know what he was laughing about. So he petted the stuffed animals on the bed, just for something to do.

"She likes bears," said Max.

"She did," said Pilot. "Not anymore."

Pilot moved to leave. Max did the same. Pilot put his hand on the light switch.

"She is dead," said Pilot.

Click.

1.6

There was a place Max had read about once, called the Stonehenge of America. It was a colossal structure, five sixteen-foot-tall slabs of granite arranged with astronomical precision in a star formation atop a grassy Georgia hilltop farm in the 1980s. Eyeholes drilled here and there let people find Polaris or glean the day of the year as the sun cast a mark upon a calibrated central column.

Carved into each slab were instructions in eight languages. *Be fair. Be just. Seek beauty and love.*

Basically: *Don't be evil.*

They were called the Georgia Guidestones, and their polished faces glinted in the sunlight. They were revered, feared, derided, vandalized, and worshipped. Wind and rain lashed them. Through it all the slabs stood fast, all 130 tons of them.

The man who created them never explained their purpose. People filled this void with whatever they wanted. Home-brew pagan philosophies. Antichrist conspiracies. Neo-Nazi prophecies. Hope for a post-Armageddon paradise.

When pressed, the man simply said this:

Mysteries work this way. If you want to keep people interested, you can let them know only so much.

And then he did the coolest thing Max could think of.

He vanished.

1.7

Max looked up and saw clouds. A vee of pelicans sailed by. Only once he put on his Buddy Hollys could he then see the glass ceiling and its truss supports.

He sat up—too quickly—and held his throbbing temples. He was halfway on a bed in nothing but his briefs. One testicle hung out for all the world to see. Max tucked it back in.

There was a nightstand made of glass hexaprisms, and upon it stood a glass dodecahedron of water beside two headache pills the color of baloney. Max took the pills, drank the water, and began the herculean task of pulling on his pants.

He looked around. It was not the Noelle room, and for that he was grateful. Because few things were creepier than passing out in a ghost girl's room.

He checked his phone—something he did first thing in the morning, a bad habit—and saw an entire text message conversation between himself and Dad.

Dad I'm staying at my mentor's house tonight, remember? From B school?
I dont remember him.
He's a great friend . . . Shane and Akiko are here too
Ok have fun very b careful mijo

He had no memory of texting that. Jesus.

He rose—slowly—and ventured into the silent skywalk. The morning sun threw tessellated shadows across the walls. He passed a room in which a body lay.

Shane.

Max froze. Shane gave a single sharp fart and turned in his sleep. Akiko lay there, too, and Max stared at them for a moment with wonder.

I think that Shane guy likes you, Max had said that night at the pool party.

I've seen Mr. Muscles, said Akiko. *He's, like, a senior.*

Would you go out with a senior? said Max. They were juniors.

I don't know, Akiko said. *Maybe for fun.*

Not me, Max said. *I would date someone in my same grade.*

Someone in our class? Who is it? Who? Tell me, duncie.

That night, in the dark, when their pinkies had snuggled up to one another.

Max walked down the skywalk and descended the curved staircase. He felt memories of last night trickling back into his braincase.

Pilot had led him out of Noelle's room and back into the basement, where they jammed some more. Slower, more emotional songs this time. Then Akiko fell asleep, and Shane carried her up and away, and then Pilot called it a night, and after that it was just Max and Brayden scratching out a big noisy shit salad with their instruments. Then Brayden abruptly said bye and went home to sleep.

Max remembered sneaking into Pilot's office and teetering before the wall of monitors and noticing something weird on one of the screens:

How lovely, Shane!

Had he really seen that?

After that he woke up to see a vee of pelicans sailing by in the sky above.

He wandered the house, through the great room with its floor cushions, past the garden atrium with the glowing SNOWBALL stone.

He heard a wind chime. So he followed the sound.

He turned the corner to find a wide blue rectangle of light that led down a corridor of extruded glass. The glass opened to reveal a deck of perfect lines of pale walnut surrounding an asymmetrical aquamarine rhombus—a pool, unlike any pool Max had ever seen—and a crisp white table elaborately set for brunch: eggs, bacon, asparagus, juice and coffee and bread and tea and so on. Max felt his stomach stir.

At the table sat Pilot, staring at a laptop. "He lives," said Pilot.

Brass bells swayed on a web of twine and made distant gamelan music.

"Bloody Mary?" said Pilot, offering a pitcher of red. "Hair of the dog."

"Yes, please," said a voice behind Max. Akiko emerged into the sunlight.

"I'll just have a dry bagel," said Max.

Pilot squinted at him with small eyes. "I have artisanal hand-cut bacon and you want a dry bagel."

"Sorry."

"I am just playing. Mi casa es su casa."

"Sorry."

"Enough with the sorries."

"I'm still drunk," said Max, assembling a plate with care. "I don't even remember texting my parents."

Pilot started giggling. It was a strange sight.

"What?" said Max.

"That was me," said Pilot finally. "I figured you would need the assist."

"Wait, did I hand you my phone?"

"I did it from my workstation. You were very fucked up."

"You—"

"During your times of trial and suffering, when you saw two of everything before thee, it was then that I carried you. Down the hall. To the guest room." And Pilot gave him a crushing side embrace.

Max stared at a vague spot on the table and remembered Pilot with both phones on his knees. Taking forever to look up the chords to that Pachinko Seven song. It was one thing to know about surveillance. But it was another to meet the person doing the surveilling. What was the difference?

Consent. The difference was consent.

"Mister Max?" said Pilot. "Mister Max?"

Max stared and stared.

"Oh no," said Pilot. "You are freaking out because of my phone access."

"A little," said Max.

"I am so sorry," said Pilot. "I just assumed we were a team now. With transparency. Let me make it up to you. I will give you all my creds. I am so stupid."

Pilot slapped himself hard in the face with both hands, twice.

"Hey," said Max. "Hey, stop."

"Hypocrite," said Pilot, slapping himself. "Hypocrite. Hypocrite."

"Jesus, Pilot," said Max. "Stop hitting yourself."

Pilot stopped all at once. He held Max's eyes for a moment. "I truly apologize, Mister Max."

"We're good, we're good," said Max, and he gave a reassuring pat on the back to one of the most powerful tech legends in history. At his house. Hanging out by his pool.

Total insanity.

Pilot had impossibly long smoke tentacles straight out of the *Soft Ghost Edition Black* manga. He could reach anywhere. He could do anything. Spy on a neighbor, hack text messages. And now Max could call upon that power, too.

For what?

For the next hack, of course.

"Oh Jesus, save me," said a voice. It was Shane, pushing back the sunlight.

Akiko cocked her neck. "It's your own fault, duncie."

She sprang up, kissed him, and gave him a plate. Max watched in horror as Shane piled it high. For Shane was a food-piler: eggs atop bacon atop melon atop whatever the fuck else. Max's plate, by contrast, was a neat study in object isolation.

"Fire and ice," whispered Max.

"What?" said Shane, his mouth full.

"So, Mister Max," said Pilot. "How would you like to proceed?"

"You mean our next hack," said Max, chewing. "Let's brainstorm."

At the far end of the yard a cypress tree rustled. Everyone stopped. For a moment Max imagined agents in windbreakers marked FBI emerging from the greenery. But instead of feds, it was Brayden.

"Mister Markham," called Brayden. "Did you know you had a backdoor in your wall this whole time? I just discovered it from my side."

"I knew," said Pilot to himself. Max looked at him. But Pilot only winked.

"What?" said Brayden.

"I had no idea," said Pilot to Brayden.

"God, it's so hot," said Brayden. "My phone says it's not supposed to be this hot."

"And yet," said Pilot.

Brayden broke into a lazy flailing jog.

"I have to show you guys something," said Brayden.

Brayden grabbed Pilot's laptop, but was soon flummoxed. "What is this?"

"My custom operating system," said Pilot.

"Looks like a Minotaur OS base," said Akiko.

"Look at you, Miz Akiko," said Pilot, impressed. "I threw lots of home-brew stuff on top. I like to keep all my interfaces as a single pane of glass."

"Very nice," said Akiko, and she fist-bumped the tech legend.

"I'll just use my phone," said Brayden. He went to his Wren feed. "So, the like buttons aren't working here—Version Zero, Big Fix in effect, right? But watch."

He found a post, copied its link, and switched to a web browser showing a purple-hued site. He pasted the link into a field. He tapped a button. A clone of the post appeared—this time with fully functioning like buttons.

"All my friends are using it," said Brayden.

Max squinted at the screen. "Man, that was quick."

"What is it?" said Shane.

"Someone made a workaround," said Max. "UnfixTheFix.com."

1.8

Within a half hour, it was on the news.

WANT YOUR LIKES BACK? HERE'S HOW

"When did this drop?" said Max.

"It's, like, already been fifteen hours," said Brayden.

"Don't you mean *only* been fifteen hours?" said Akiko.

"Tempus fugit," said Pilot.

"¿No comprendo?" said Brayden.

"What does the article say?" said Max.

"I don't know," said Brayden.

"Ah, look at this," said Pilot, clicking around. "Wren is temporarily partnering with UnfixTheFix while they work on undoing Akiko's handiwork. And people are signing back up to Wren. All it takes is one click. See?" Pilot showed them a page on Wren with a single button labeled COME BACK, PILOT MARKHAM.

"Man, that was quick," said Max again in disbelief. "We need to come up with a stronger hack."

"How can your name be on that button?" said Brayden. "Didn't you delete your Wren?"

Akiko laughed, and Pilot joined her.

"What?" said Brayden.

"Nothing ever gets deleted," said Akiko. "At Wren we just flag stuff as inactive. But it's all still there in the database. Every photo or post or anything you've ever shared. Everyone in tech keeps everything."

Brayden grew uneasy. "But what about temporary pix?" He was referring to a type of service popular in 2018 that promised to store photos for only twenty-four hours and then delete them, so that users could safely share explicit or "off-brand" photos without fear of soiling their permanent online record.

Akiko laughed again, and Pilot joined her again.

"But that means," said Brayden, "that means that all the shit I posted under different accounts, all that shit is still on a computer somewhere?"

"You mean, like, under pseudonyms?" said Max. "What kind of shit?"

"Nothing," shouted Brayden.

"Wait a sec," said Shane. "So you're saying my old pix I posted way back in the day like on MyFace.com are still out there?"

"Well," said Max. "MyFace got acquired by Yello, which got acquired by Wren, so yeah, I bet Akiko could dig them up if she wanted to."

"I could, honey bear," said Akiko, drilling a fingertip between Shane's ribs.

Shane folded his arms. "But I used different usernames, so."

"But you used the same physical location, didn't you," said Akiko. "But you've had the same internet company forever, haven't you."

"IP lookup," said Pilot and Akiko, as if it were some fun catchphrase.

"What is I pee look up?" said Shane.

"Wait," said Max, looking up as if a star had just appeared in the sky. "Brayden, Shane, you just came up with our next hack."

We have to go beyond the typical hack," said Max. "The typical hack just doesn't last."

The sun had become microwave-hot, so they now sat under a sail canopy at the end of the pool, dangling their legs in the vitreous bottomless blue.

"As in hacks get patched over, à la UnfixTheFix?" said Pilot.

"As in people forget hacks, like, *bam*," said Max, snapping his fingers. "That Gorillagate actress gets hacked, gets destroyed, everyone gets mad for a minute—and then they go right back to normal."

Akiko nodded. "The Russians hacked our democracy, for fuck's sake."

Akiko was referring to a presidential election in the year 2016, where agents from the country of Russia manipulated public opinion through social media, hacked into opposition emails, and blackmailed politicians with lurid surveillance sex tapes to successfully engineer the election of a puppet president in the country of the United States of America.

"True," said Pilot. "And the people reacted with—"

"Nothing," said Brayden.

Max pointed: bingo.

"I guess everyone did just go back to normal pretty quick," said Shane.

"So what do we want people to do?" said Brayden.

Max realized he had never stated an explicit goal before this moment. He pushed up his glasses.

"Did you know that if everyone in SoCal stopped driving their cars for one day, the smog would clear up instantly?"

"No way."

"Yahweh," said Max.

Everyone waited for Max to deliver his punch line.

"Here's the weird thing about all the problems of our world," said Max. "They need upkeep. Global warming needs that regular stream of greenhouse gases we make when we drive. Income inequality needs One-Percenters to keep hoarding their money. Evil is a habit. Drop the habit, and the problems of the world just lose momentum and stop."

Akiko laughed weird, because she tended to laugh weird when Max got serious and fired up, and Max loved it. He kept going.

"Imagine if just for one day everyone stopped using the internet. No posts. No scrolling. No notifications. The tap goes dry."

"Advertisers would freak," said Akiko. "Then investors would freak."

"The Mister Cals of the world would freak," said Pilot.

"Data is lifeblood for our tech bro overlords," said Max. "As long as we feed them, they can continue their habit of being evil. If we deprive them, suddenly we're able to demand things change for the better. Or we could just build our own thing, call it Wren 2.0 or whatever, and build it right the next time around."

"The next time around," said Pilot, still with that dry sickly smile. It was an odd smile. Max observed it for an extra second, then another, because it was a smile that said:

I know something you do not.

It occurred to Max that Pilot might have reasons of his own for joining Version Zero. The first thing he could imagine was some sort of side business that would profit from an enlightened user base, rejecting the broken old internet and eager for a better alternative.

If anyone could have a better alternative ready to launch in his back pocket, it would be Pilot.

Max's mind immediately erupted with fantasies of being appointed

Chief Design Officer (or something) of an imminent Internet 2 (or something).

He caught himself. *Silly me.*

"So what's our next move?" said Akiko. She sculled water with one foot and made Max's slack legs dance.

"We have to get personal this time," said Max. "A social eruption in your face."

"Ew," said Akiko.

Pilot leaned in. "What are you thinking?"

"Yo, Brayden," said Max.

"Yo," said Brayden, his face a scramble of water-light.

"If your friends somehow saw all the weird shit you posted under pseudonyms back in the day, how would you feel?" said Max.

Brayden froze in midtoe. "Wait, what?"

"It's just a what-if, dude," said Max.

Brayden spoke without hesitation. "I would deny everything. Then I'd delete, like, all my accounts. Just deadass rage-quit the internet."

"I like where this is going," said Pilot. "I like this very much."

"Now flip the script," said Max. "What if you could see all the secret anonymous shit posted by a close buddy? And the shit was all evil?"

"I mean, to my buddy I'd be, like, *What the fuck*," said Brayden. "But also I'd be, like, *Is it true? But also I'd be, like, What is true, even? Did I really know my buddy at all in the first place?*"

Max shared a nod with Pilot.

"Anyway, then I would rage-quit the internet," said Brayden, laughing.

Max laughed, too, and imagined people fleeing as little volcanoes erupted all over the feeds like lights in the dark.

"Why are we even really online?" said Max. "I mean really-really?"

"Pictures of friends' kids and shit," said Shane.

"Fear of missing out," said Pilot.

"It's funny you ask why," said Brayden. "For my generation, there is no why. Asking *Why are you online* is like asking *Why do you breathe air.* You can't not be online. You're online because everyone's online."

Max and Pilot looked at one another with astonishment at this concept.

"If I'm applying for a job," said Brayden, "and I have, like, zero personal brand presence? Employers'll be, like, *What the fuck's wrong with this guy?*"

Brayden frowned, then continued.

"Or like dating. If you don't have any other shit online, people will think you're a fake ghost account. So you gotta keep up the act."

Max raised his eyebrows, frowned. Poor kid.

Brayden sighed. "Real talk? It all just gets really tiring."

Max and Pilot looked at each other, then at Brayden, this boy who grew up behind a phone.

"How about you, Miz Akiko?" said Pilot. "Why are you online?"

"Shh," said Akiko. She held two fingers to her lips. "I'm thinking."

"About why?" said Pilot.

"About our next hack," said Akiko.

Brayden sat up. "We're gonna hit Wren again?"

"Not just Wren," said Akiko. She knitted her fingers together. "Wren *and* Knowned."

1.10

Knowned is the world's No. 1 trusted guardian of free speech where we can Discover Wonderful Things Together.™ But as in any environment there are safety tips to remember to keep your discussions and sharing safe and fun. Here are some simple things you can do if a troll starts giving you grief.

Learn to identify trolls. Is someone constantly interrupting normal, rational discourse with abnormal, irrational insults or threats of violence or death? You got yourself a troll.

Realize not every jerk is a troll. Plenty of people like to joke around to get a rise out of people. They could be anyone. That's just the internet! It doesn't mean they are a genuine troll with malicious intent. Learn to spot the difference.

Don't feed the trolls. Trolls crave attention. Don't be their bait! The best policy is to ignore them. Eventually, they will just go away on their own and move on to the next victim.

Name the trolls. Trolls love the power their anonymity brings, but once they're "outed" that power miraculously vanishes. Some trolls use the same username, profile picture, or catch-phrase elsewhere on the internet. A careful search will usually lead to their legitimate blog or work profile. Let them know you know who they are! Repeat this process for the next troll(s).

See something, say something. Knowned has Report Abuse buttons everywhere for a reason. It's up to you to hit that button anytime you feel threatened. Our team will investigate and respond, usually within 72 to 96 hours.

Upgrade to premium. A premium Knowned membership shows your commitment to free speech, and we show our appreciation with faster response times, advanced abuse filtering, and more. Upgrade today.

1.11

The Wren-Knowned hack would take place in two phases.

For phase one, team Version Zero sat before Pilot's wall of screens.

On monitors 4 and 5 Max could see two security camera shots of the interior of a café. On monitor 6 Max could see a laptop camera view of Shane. On monitor 7 he could see the café ceiling—the view from Shane's smartphone front camera—and on monitor 8 he could see blackness: the view from the phone's back camera.

Pilot had set up all these cameras with disturbing ease.

Earlier Pilot had handed Max a sticky note.

U: THEGREATMAZE

P: NOELLEPHANT

I TRUST YOU COMPLETELY

The note felt like a mostly empty gesture, for what was Max to do with this? Open Pilot's strange laptop and begin helping himself? *Noellephant.* Would he discover the secret of Pilot's daughter?

Regardless. The sticky note felt as scary as nuclear codes, so Max committed the creds to memory, ripped the paper to confetti, and flushed it down a toilet.

"Microphone check, one, two," sang Max into the mic.

On monitor 6, Shane touched his ear. "And you don't stop."

"You nervous?" said Max.

Shane just smiled and shrugged: *Nervous about what?*

Shane had dressed up for this occasion: actual pants—with shoes!—and a button-down tee shirt: something called a trim-fit, according to Akiko. Pilot ordered them for same-day delivery from A2Z. Shane wore them bursting at the seams like a male exotic dancer in an office worker costume.

Max looked over at the café interior footage. There sat a few afternoon types: old men, students, moms on taxi break.

Akiko jabbed a finger. "There she comes."

A Whitewoman in expensive, tight-fitting yoga clothes entered, sat, and flipped open a laptop. She reached beneath her chair and plugged in a power adapter to an outlet there.

Shane waited ten seconds. He moved to the table next to her, holding up his own power adapter in explanation.

"Mind if I plug in?" he said, all baritone.

Akiko giggled at his voice. "Oh my God."

And the Whitewoman, suddenly gazed upon by a man like Shane, looked him up and down, tucked a ribbon of hair behind her ear, and said, "Not at all."

Max and Akiko and Pilot stomped their feet and clapped.

"Girls like Shane," said Pilot.

"Girls like muscles," said Max.

"They do," said Akiko with a smirking shrug.

A stream of text appeared on a nearby monitor.

"And Team Vee-Zero is in," said Pilot. "Good job, Muscles."

The Whitewoman was Cherry Lacroix. Cherry Lacroix was an Executive Senior Vice President of People Operations at Wren. She was thirty-seven, single, not religious, slightly libertarian in her political views. She liked Doozy and shows on Filmbot and social athletic pursuits like beach volleyball and yoga. She had a younger brother named Brett and two retired parents living in Boca Raton, Florida.

Pilot had compiled all this information over the course of thirty seconds.

She was also the woman who laid off Max from Wren, so many weeks ago.

Every Wednesday Cherry Lacroix posted a photo of the artful cappuccino foam from this café, with the hashtag #WFC, which stood for *working from café*.

A *hashtag* was a special character (#) that prioritized its attached word or phrase in search results. This allowed users to find #cappuccinofoam photos, for example, or people living the #wrenlife. People used these hashtags constantly, because—strange as it is to say—it was once considered very important to be noticed by as many strangers as possible. Hashtags became so prevalent people even used them in spoken, face-to-face conversation for an ironic effect, as in:

I'm never going to that party, hashtag nope dot com.

Cherry Lacroix maintained her weekly café ritual despite increased security policies at Wren caused by the Big Fix hack, because she was Senior, doted upon by an infatuated boss, and used to having whatever she wanted. This was according to Akiko, to whom Cherry Lacroix liked confessing things for some reason.

Not for some reason. The reason was Akiko was Non-White. Which meant she sat outside the tribal expectations of Whitewomen, which meant she was a safe, nonpartisan sidekick to confide in.

Akiko never saw Cherry Lacroix outside work.

Cherry Lacroix's laptop was protected by a virtual private network and other security bogglagons, none of which mattered once Shane plugged in his power adapter. For he also replaced Cherry Lacroix's power adapter with one of Pilot's—a custom item built at his workshop table back in the oubliette—and hid her original adapter aside.

So when Pilot said, *Good job, Muscles*, it meant he and Max and Akiko could now see Cherry Lacroix's computer desktop on monitor 9.

"Muscles," said Max. "Do your dance."

Shane looked lost.

"Shane's gonna dance?" said Brayden from the couch where he lay.

Without hesitation, Shane did the following:

- Raised his sinewy arms to display them in a long, luxuriant stretch.
- Moaned.
- Shifted in his seat with a slight thrust of the hips.

Once again Cherry Lacroix glanced over and tucked a ribbon of hair behind an ear. Shane leaned in to deliver his killer line:

"Is your wi-fi working?"

And just like that, he had turned his laptop toward her and her hands upon his keyboard. There they were now, huddled close together on the laptop camera on monitor 6.

"Password should be CAPFOAM," she said. "Huh, your F key is stuck."

They both reached for it at the same time.

"Dang, girl, your hands are cold," said Shane, laughing.

"They keep it freezing in here," said Cherry Lacroix, not moving her hand.

"Thirty-something skank," said Akiko.

"Fingerprint acquired, everyone," said Pilot. "Miz Akiko?"

On monitor 6, Shane and Cherry Lacroix were now giggling about something with their faces just inches apart. Cherry Lacroix snuck a long look at him.

"I will cut a bitch," said Akiko.

"Fight, fight," said Brayden from the couch.

"Akiko Minnie Hosokawa," said Max. "Now, if it's not too much trouble?"

Akiko pounded away. She angry-typed. On Cherry Lacroix's screen, black windows bloomed and closed. Four progress bars shot to completion in quick succession, and then Akiko restored the desktop to its original state. Not a trace.

"Got you," said Akiko, flinging her fingers at the screen. "I *am* you."

For indeed, Akiko could now control Cherry Lacroix's laptop from anywhere in the world, even while it was in sleep mode, as if she were right on Wren's internal secure network.

"Good job, duncie," said Max to Akiko. Then to the mic: "Muscles, get out of there."

On monitor 6, Shane checked his watch and made an excuse to leave. Cherry Lacroix literally frowned a sad-face frown. She gave him her number on a café napkin. He slipped it into his pocket like a waiter receiving a tip. Then he wrote down his phone number on her napkin in return.

"I'd say let's get coffee sometime, but I guess we kinda just did that already," said Shane with a wink.

"Gehehyeah huh," said Cherry Lacroix.

"Time for phase two," said Max.

Max remembered an old black-and-white television episode in which five characters found themselves trapped in an oubliette in search of an exit, with no idea of how they got there. In the show, the characters had been:

- A clown
- A hobo
- A ballet dancer
- A bagpiper
- An army major

In Max's oubliette, however, the characters would be the tech Big Five:

- Cal Peers, CEO of the social network Wren, 3 billion users
- River Askew, CEO of the taxi and lodging service Airlift, 250 million users
- Linda Belinda, CEO of the discussion forum Knowned, 300 million users
- Jonas Friend, CEO of the computer giant Quartz, 600 million users
- Hunter Mole, CEO of the retailer A2Z, 400 million users

Five people with data on almost half the world's population.

The show never said how the characters got in that oubliette, or why, but Max now knew. They were brought there by impossibly long smoke tentacles that plucked them up and dragged them across the world in the dead of night.

Max had liked that vision. He typed it into a sticky note on his phone where he kept all his Version Zero ideas. Call it a hit list. Call it a dream journal.

Call it both.

1.13

When Shane returned, Akiko threw a cushion at him.

"You gave her your number?" she said.

Shane was back in his shredded tank top and shredded shorts. He caught the flying cushion, no-look, with one hand. "You really think I would do that, baby?"

"So what did you write down on that napkin?"

Max waited for Shane to answer. He looked around and saw Pilot and Brayden waiting, too.

"Cal Peers's cell," said Shane with a chrome-bright smile.

The room exploded with hoots and applause. Max kicked a chair across the room on silent casters. Akiko savored a smile and a slow clap.

"Up top," said Max, holding up a hand, and Shane delivered a high five of great robustness.

Pilot laughed, too, but then his face fell flat. Pilot's smile could stop on a dime. "Max?" he said.

Max nodded. He turned to Akiko. "Let's start phase two."

By now it was early evening, which meant everyone at Wren headquarters had gone home for the day but for the security detail, which no doubt had been upped since Max's Black Halo speech in the lobby. Akiko typed. She woke Cherry Lacroix's laptop, quickly accessed the Wren master user database, and then opened up another window:

Knowned.

She held out a hand to Pilot. "Creds, please?"

Pilot handed her a sticky note.

Akiko did not sign in to the regular Knowned site. She signed in to an austere-looking administrative view, nothing at all like the bright front-of-the-house version regular users were familiar with.

"Where'd you manage to get admin creds, by the way?" said Max.

"I was once on the board at Knowned," said Pilot. "Until."

Pilot stopped. It was as if someone cut off his power.

"Until what?" said Max.

"Until I quit," said Pilot, resuming.

Max nodded. "Why did you—"

"Because it was a festering sore fuckhole of a place full of shit-breathing trolls," said Pilot in a single breath.

Everyone looked at Pilot. He had been shouting.

Pilot lowered his voice. "What is fundamental to human civilization?"

Silence. Brayden raised his hand. "Tools and buildings?"

Pilot winced at the boy's facile answer. Brayden put his hand back down.

"It's trust," said Max.

"Mister Max gets it," said Pilot. "No trust, no civilization. What happens when you construct a social space devoid of trust?"

Max laughed. "You get the internet."

"Because you can post shit all anonymous," said Brayden.

Max nodded. "Shit you'd never post under your real name. There goes trust, flying right out the window. No trust? People's instincts default to *mistrust*. Mistrust makes men mean as motherfuckers."

"Usernames versus real names," said Akiko. "You and I have talked about this, like, a million times."

"You have?" said Shane.

Max and Akiko talked about a great many things, often over text messages, often at night. *We been friends for so long,* Akiko would say. *I can really talk to you.*

An ugly thought flitted by: *I am a better match for Akiko because I am smarter than Shane.*

Max buried it. It was a ridiculous thought. Max knew Shane had leapt into the flaming wreck of her home life to save Akiko, and there were details of that daring rescue that Max would never be privy to.

Details forged by fire into steel bonds, hidden from view.

Shane is a better match for Akiko because she entrusted him with her life, and he has honored that trust ever since.

Here was Max, talking about trust and calling Shane stupid at the same time.

Overcome with sudden guilt, Max said, "Not a million times. Just work chitchat, ha ha."

Max explained. "We're matching everyone's usernames—including all their fake ones—with their real name."

"Well, technically it's more involved than that," said Akiko.

"Okay, nerd," said Max, smiling. Akiko smiled back.

"Okay, nerd," tried Shane, too, but Akiko was already busy typing again.

Akiko had reached some sort of complicated search interface full of checkboxes and pull-downs and runes and cryptograms and other arcana.

She scrolled through an infinite list of user posts and zeroed in on one. "Here's a lovely comment: *Jew stink, jew should go take a gas shower,* posted by some guy named BloodySoil."

"How do you know it's a guy?" said Brayden.

"Oh, please," said Akiko.

Everyone looked at Brayden.

"Four thousand Knowners liked BloodySoil's comment. Just lovely."

Akiko revealed the myriad data attached to the comment.

```
USER DEVICE: Quartz Milc 8.0
CLIENT: Knowned app v5.2.9
DEVICE ID: 109JJFM09R3IR09QEP093V
INTERNET ADDRESS: 128.242.240.244
GEOLOCATION: lat 38.029353, long -78.479607
```

And so on.

"And now we tries," she sang, "to de-anonymize."

"Is it enough to work with?" said Max.

She cross-referenced that Knowned post data with the Wren master user database and soon found a single 99.4 percent data match: a user named Fred Mould.

"It's more than enough," said Akiko. "Here is Fred Mould of Heather, Virginia, otherwise known as BloodySoil."

"Quite the *nom de douchebag*," said Pilot.

"So you just copy and paste BloodySoil's hate comment from Knowned onto Fred Mould's Wren feed for everyone to see?" said Shane.

"Copypasta," said Brayden.

"His friends will love what he's been shitposting," said Akiko.

"Script that shit up," said Max. "Let it run automatically all night across everything on Knowned since the day that motherhugger launched."

"Fucking A," said Akiko. Pilot prepped a code window for her, and she began.

```
public void trollout() {
```

1.14

Fred Mould (1 day ago): Why did the mathematician divide sin by tan? Just cos! Hahaha
12 PEOPLE LIKED THIS.

Karen Mould (20h ago): you are such a geek i love you

Peyton Ching (18h ago): hi mr. mould!!!

Fred Mould via Newsish—What Galaxy Prime Character Are You? Take the Quiz! (12h ago): I got Leaf Man . . . how predictable
8 PEOPLE LIKED THIS.

Jarvis Means (11h ago): I got Captain Polk

Peter Campos (11h ago): leaf man too

Kylee Kapoor (10h ago): empress pyra!!!

Fred Mould via Newsish—Five Female Math Pioneers You May Have Never Heard Of (8h ago): So inspiring! Shout out to all the girls in my classes!
27 PEOPLE LIKED THIS.

Peyton Ching (8h ago): love!

Fred Mould, as "BloodySoil" on Knowned (3wks ago): Jew stink, jew should go take a gas shower
0 PEOPLE LIKED THIS. (4,062 PEOPLE ON KNOWNED LIKED THIS.)

Version Zero (3h ago): #trollout

Fred Mould (3h ago): I don't know what this is, everyone, my Wren account got hacked I think, please disregard!!

Karen Mould (3h ago): honey what is this

Peyton Ching (3h ago): wow

Peyton Ching (3h ago): is this a thing **NewsDay Breaking: Trolls Reportedly Outed Publicly by Cyberterrorist Group Version Zero**

Peyton Ching (3h ago): what the actual f is going on **NewsDay Breaking: My Boyfriend Was Secretly a Nazi. Yours Could Be Too**

Fred Mould, as "BloodySoil" on Knowned (2wks ago): JEW$ died from starvation just like every other concentration camp POW everywhere else, show me the official "final solution" policy docs and I'll be the first to shut up!!! #hollowcaust
0 PEOPLE LIKED THIS. (188 PEOPLE ON KNOWNED LIKED THIS.)

Peyton Ching (3h ago): Mr. Mould

Fred Mould, as "BloodySoil" on Knowned (1wk ago): Never bothered to read Anne Frank diary, not a fan of FICTION
0 PEOPLE LIKED THIS. (2,502 PEOPLE ON KNOWNED LIKED THIS.)

Fred Mould (just now): I have been HACKED everyone!

Fred Mould (just now): Something is seriously wrong with Wren. I cannot delete or edit anything. They need to fix their cybersecurity measures ASAP!!

Fred Mould (just now): Wren are you listening . . . you are ruining peoples lives with lies posted by CYBERHACKERS. You're going down mark my words

Fred Mould (just now): Please everybody you have to know this is not me

Fred Mould (just now): Please everybody

1.15

All morning Max had been checking his phone. He had texted Dad early:

Still hanging with my B-school teacher and Shane and Akiko, todo bien

Ok, Dad simply replied.

Ok, and nothing else.

What did Max want? What else could Max expect? Could he write

Dad, did you see the Trollout hack on the news?

or

Dad, I'm Version Zero, what do you think of that?

Even if he could explain to Dad what he was doing, would Dad even understand? How would such a conversation go?

"I'm fixing the internet by exposing its inherent biases toward sociopathy."

"Is that computers, Flaco?"

"We've exposed over thirty thousand toxic users so far."

"Is this an app? How many did you sell?"

Max got dressed and left his room, walked the skywalk, and descended the curved staircase. He passed through the brass panel and the sound studio (giving the crystal drums a tap) and through the nexus. He opened the vending machine with an easy flip of a finger and entered the twisting black tunnel of wires.

When he reached the wall of screens, Akiko was already there with a mug of black coffee waiting for him.

"You're up early," said Max.

"I didn't sleep much," said Akiko. "I had to see how Trollout was doing."

"Where's Shane?"

"You know that boy can't get up before ten."

Max chuffed. "Oh yeah?"

"He's so high school." Akiko brought up some screens. "Come sit."

Max sat. He took his coffee. It was hot.

"So this is—" Akiko began.

"Account deletions," said Max. "Dang, it's a lot."

"And growing," said Akiko. "At both Wren and Knowned, see?"

Max pushed up his glasses and glanced at all the charts. "News mentions up, social mentions up, hashtags multiplying, and oh shit, broadcast video mentions, too? TV?" He looked at her with a raised brow.

"We're trending," said Akiko. She smiled. This was, Max realized, some kind of perfect moment. A perfect version of the best night from their many late nights at Wren: their bodies close, their minds sprinting along in perfect sync on a flat beach that stretched to infinity.

She was staring at him. It was hard for Max when Akiko looked right at him, and normally he would have turned to his shoes for solace. But this time he held her gaze, and quietly thrilled inside.

She removed his Buddy Holly glasses and gently dug at his left eye with her pinky nail.

"You have an eye booger," she said.

"Keep it," said Max.

Akiko tucked the invisible speck into her shirt pocket and gave it a little pat. A thought seemed to occur to her; she blinked it away. She pinched his nose and shook it.

"We're trending, duncie," she said, and sipped her coffee.

Max's nose tingled for a while after she released it. Shane could take his time sleeping. Everyone could take their time this morning. Above, a white-hot triangle of sunlight stretched down the wall of the oubliette.

Akiko typed and typed, bringing up more charts, and Max could feel her moving because their shoulders were touching and neither he nor she seemed to mind.

"What if," Max said, "what if Version Zero works?"

Akiko paused. "What do you mean by *works*?"

"I don't know," said Max, and he meant it. It occurred to him that he had never really thought beyond their current hack. "Say Trollout or some other hack does the trick, and everyone is just, like, fuck Wren, fuck Knowned, and bails."

"That would be amazing," said Akiko.

"It would open the door for us to make something better," said Max. He backslapped his open palm. "Better than what we have now."

"Hm," said Akiko. She glanced at each screen, one by one.

"We literally have unlimited resources," said Max.

"Unlimited resources," said Akiko with an odd smirk.

Max sweetly furrowed his brow. "What?"

"It's just funny," said Akiko. She took a sip of coffee and admired her mug. "Here is a mug. It's made from this ingenious material called ceramic. Ceramic is easy to clean, durable, and can hold hot liquids. Ceramic solves a specific problem."

Max clinked his mug to hers and waited for her to continue. He loved when she talked like this.

"It's just funny, because the smartphone wasn't invented to solve any existing problem," said Akiko. "We just made it to see if we could, and it wound up creating all these new problems. TV didn't solve any specific problem, either."

"Or soda water," said Max, right on time like he was lobbing a ball back to Akiko in a relaxing rhetorical rally. "Or cigarettes."

"God, I wish cigarettes were good for you," said Akiko.

On-screen, the numbers twitched higher.

Akiko turned to Max with a sudden intensity that made his heart shiver. "What would you do if you had unlimited resources?" she said.

"I mean, we do," said Max. He nodded at the screen. "So I'd do what I'm doing right now."

Akiko undid her question with a wave of her hand. "Say we fix the internet, yay for us. Then what would you want?"

Don't ask me what I want, thought Max.

"Move on to the next problem," said Max with a shrug. "Solve it, try not to create any new ones in the process."

Max noticed he and Akiko had slightly different levels of coffee in their mugs, and took a sip to catch up.

"Why, what would *you* want?" said Max, avoiding her eyes.

He could hear Akiko think, begin to say something, then catch herself. Finally she spoke.

"I would get away from computers," she said. "I think I would hide away from everything for a while. I would travel."

"Where?" said Max.

"I would go in a straight line and keep following it until I crisscrossed every place on earth," said Akiko. Her eyes glinted at the idea. "Yeah."

Max pictured the planet as a big ball of red yarn being drawn by a tiny Akiko.

"Don't forget to visit me," said Max with a laugh.

"You're welcome to come with," said Akiko. "Or go your own way, or whatever, just catch me when we loop around."

Blue yarn now laced in with the red to create a lovely knitwork.

"High five in midair," said Max.

"Like hi-bye," said Akiko, raising her hand. They slapped palms, spilling coffee in the process.

"Shit," laughed Max.

There were footsteps, and Shane stepped into the oubliette disheveled from oversleep.

"Are we winning, babe?" said Shane.

Akiko palmed her forehead. "It depends on what you mean by winning."

Shane dove onto the hissing leather couch. "Come here," he said, stretching out his arms. "Honey bear needs some snuggle time."

His words instantly softened Akiko like magic collapsing a curtain. She pushed away from the wall of screens and into Shane's embrace, leaving Max staring.

1.16

As Shane and Akiko canoodled on the couch, Max sat. He checked his phone. No new messages from Dad. Why would there be?

Pilot now walked into the oubliette.

"Thirty thousand Wren users have deleted their accounts," he said, and wrestled Max by his shoulders. "Up from twenty-eight in a single hour, Mister Max. Version Zero is working."

What do you mean by working? Max wanted to ask. But the praise felt good, and this was tech legend Pilot Markham here with his hands on Max's shoulders, and Max wanted to enjoy the moment.

If it were his dad, he would have to explain why thirty thousand account deletions was a good thing.

"Do you get their money, the people that quit Wren?"

"No, Dad, it's a mass awakening."

"Is this something to do with the biasing for sociopathy?"

With Pilot, Max did not need to explain *biases toward sociopathy.* Pilot already knew what Max was doing. Pilot hand-signaled a three and a zero with all the enthusiasm of a sports fan—*thirty* thousand— and Max felt it like high praise.

As far as Max knew, Pilot only ever had the one child: daughter Noelle. He never had a son. Max found himself wondering what it would have been like to have Pilot as a father.

Max shook off the thought.

Brayden entered, holding a basket of snacks.

"Go to NewsDay's front page," said Brayden.

They did, and there sat the immense golem head of Cal Peers, speaking in silent captions. *We value your privacy* this and *We are hard at work to fix our systems* that. He seemed to fight back vomit with each word. Max had never really studied Cal Peers's face, and he noticed how his orbits had been carved simply from a column of pink wax as if with a spoon, leaving his forehead and nose on the same cylindrical plane like that of a totem.

"They brought out the CEO," said Shane through Akiko's hair. "Whenever there's CEO airtime you know things are bad. Entrepreneurship 101."

"Cal Peers is shitting bricks out of his ass hole," said Pilot, pronouncing it as two words. "I bet we break fifty thousand account deletions by dinnertime."

"Is it all trolls quitting?" said Brayden.

"It's a good mix," said Akiko. "Trolls, but also friends of trolls, and probably a bunch of people scared of being outed as trolls themselves."

"Good," said Max. "Let's make a statement. Something along the lines of *Version Zero is draining the swamp.*"

Akiko winced. "Maybe not *draining the swamp.*"

"Right."

"What's wrong with *draining the swamp*?" said Shane.

"I'll think of something else, something else," said Max. "Is there a good place to shoot video?"

"How about right here?" said Pilot. He tapped around on his phone, and every screen in his wall of screens turned into digital snow. He aimed the phone's camera lens at Max. Akiko and Shane backed out of the frame.

Max straightened. "Is the Black Halo mask up?"

Pilot tapped, and a mask appeared over Max's face on the screen. "Mask is up. Rolling."

Max cleared his throat.

"Yesterday we brought the trolls into the sunlight. They have been living right under your floorboards. They are your friends, your husbands, your boyfriends."

As Max spoke he could see Akiko gazing at him, her face dazzled with light.

"The mirror world showed its false reflection. We have shattered it."

Max saw Pilot nodding.

"There is only one way to be your true self," said Max. "And that is to turn away from the mirror world to face the real. To—"

"Hold up," said Brayden. "I'm sorry, guys."

Pilot stopped recording and lowered his phone. "What is it?"

Brayden held up his phone. "Is this bad? This seems bad."

Max squinted. He read the headline.

MATH TEACHER SUICIDE: "VERSION ZERO KILLED ME"

1.17

What's the rest of the article say?" said Max.

"I never read the articles," said Brayden.

Max read the article.

Fred Mould, a high school math teacher in Virginia, was found hanging in a closet in his apartment. He was discovered when he failed to show up to teach his class. He was beloved by his students. He was divorced. He had one grown son.

Max wondered what math class would have been like had Fred Mould shown up. He scrolled the dead man's feed. Surely Fred Mould's students must have seen what he had been posting. Surely they would have hit him with questions, starting with a few timid inquiries, then a steady pelting, then a sideways torrent.

Max frowned. Max pictured Fred Mould's face growing pink, then red, then shiny with sweat. Maybe it was this inquisition Fred Mould had been scared of. Why else would he hang himself?

But this was just detective cop stuff. Max frowned for a different reason.

"Did we just kill someone?" said Max.

The room froze. Brayden put down his phone as if it were suddenly hot.

"No," said Akiko slowly.

Shane nodded. "No."

"Mister Max," said Pilot. "Are you okay?"

Max took off his glasses, and the room went gray. He spoke to the fog.

"Trolls dox their victims. Is that what we just did? Did we just dox someone to death?"

"Are you saying we're trolls?" said Brayden.

"No," said Akiko.

"We should think about this," said Max. "We should really think about what we're really doing here."

Pilot pointed at the screens. "Thirty thousand people have left Wren because of Trollout. That is what we are really doing. Fred Mould was just chickens coming home to roost."

"Yeah, but the dude didn't have to die," said Shane.

Brayden lit a joint out of exasperation. "I kinda agree, guys. Trolls are bad and all, but most of them are dudes just pulling jokes to get a rise out of people."

He offered Pilot the joint. Pilot doused it in Max's coffee cup, now gone cold.

"Jokes?" said Pilot. "To get a rise out of people?"

Brayden began to shrink. "Yeah, like ha ha, a joke? So what if this Fred Mould was secretly a Holocaust denier? It's not like the dude was a child molester. He wasn't actually physically hurting anyone. Trolling is, like, this internet free speech release valve for all the bad shit you think but are afraid to say."

Max hung his head while Brayden dug himself deeper.

"Me and my friends troll all the time," said the boy. "One time we changed the high school sign to say GRADUATING   ASS."

Shane laughed, but Akiko stopped him.

"We're all trolls to some degree," said Brayden.

"I hope you die, Mister Brayden," said Pilot, aiming his lower jaw.

Brayden blinked.

"I hope your parents get their throats slit while you watch," said Pilot. "I hope all the rich little Whitemen like you get rounded up and shot in the back of the head."

The words *back of the head* floated up and out of the oubliette, and the room fell silent. Brayden frowned small and trembling with growing bewilderment, as if everyone in the room had suddenly changed faces and became strangers.

"Mister Pilot," said Max.

Pilot exploded with a smile. "Just a joke! Just a joke." He slammed Brayden's shoulder with a fist.

Pilot's smile turned to stone. "I am just trolling you."

"That's fucked up, man," said Brayden. He lit another joint and hid behind the glow of his phone. "That's fucked up."

"Trolls drive people to fear and depression and even suicide," said Pilot. "State-run troll farms incite citizens, right in their Wren feeds, to kill whole ethnic groups. And Wren does nothing to stop it."

"I get it," said Brayden, exhaling. "God."

"We troll the trolls," said Pilot. "That is how you purge the system."

"I don't know," said Max. "Maybe we should kill the Trollout script. Lay low. We made our point, but a dead body is a dead body."

"Frankly, I am surprised there is only one dead troll," said Pilot, all cool blue. "I was expecting dozens of dead trolls. Hundreds."

"Expecting or hoping for?" said Brayden.

"You are in my house, boy," said Pilot.

"Ease up," said Shane.

"Max is right, we should kill the script," said Akiko.

"Let it run, please, Miz Akiko," said Pilot. "Let the system be purged."

This was turning into a goddamn Greek chorus, and Max hated Greek choruses. Max clapped hard one time to reset the room.

"Hey, team," said Max. "I say we kill the script. Okay? We lay low."

Pilot bored his gaze into Max's mind. The triangle of sunlight caught his pate and turned him ghostly white.

It occurred to Max that he had only known Pilot for three days, including today.

"You have an opportunity here to do what is right," said Pilot, almost pleading. "I once had that opportunity. I missed it. I lost my daughter as a result."

"What happened to you?" wondered Max.

Max stared at Pilot. Pilot stared at Max. Pilot could outstare the centuries.

"Story for another time," said Pilot quietly.

Max opened his mouth to speak, but Pilot stopped him with his mind. This was not a business venture for Pilot, thought Max. It was atonement.

Max remembered Noelle's room. A time capsule with an old landline phone and no computers in sight. A shrine to the past, and Pilot's forlorn desire to recapture it.

Brayden clutched his crazy blond anime hair. Shane sat next to him, one knee bouncing, watching the two men. Akiko sat ready to strike her keyboard.

"What is going on with you two?" she said slowly.

"We're killing the script," said Max. "At best, Trollout is gonna bring a backlash. At best. I just know it. Don't get me wrong—personally, I think the Fred Moulds of the world are responsible for their own suicides. But Trollout might lose us hearts and minds, is what I'm saying."

"If you believe that is the right thing to do, then so do I," said Pilot.

The triangle of light had drifted away, and Pilot looked normal again.

"I take back what I said about hundreds of dead trolls," said Pilot. "That was crass. From now on, no more dead bodies."

"Ugh, stop talking about dead bodies," said Max.

"I am sorry, Max. You are right. I hear you. Kill the script."

Pilot placed a warm, dry hand on Max's shoulder, and Max found himself thinking of Dad. Dad, whom he loved, but with whom he spoke usually in parallel, with the lines rarely meeting. Dad was not the kind of dad to say things like *I hear you*, and Max realized he had been starved to hear those words for years.

Max nodded at Akiko. She struck a key. Trollout stopped.

"Final count: forty-one thousand account deletions," said Akiko. "And one suicide."

No one spoke for a moment, as if to memorialize Fred Mould.

"You know what?" said Pilot, suddenly happy as a daisy. "I think we could use a change of scenery. I mean, here we are stuck in this dark room for days. Everyone, head home, pack a bag, and come on back here. We'll fly out to Glass Island, get some air in our lungs."

Shane's knee stopped. "Glass Island?"

"I have a place there," said Pilot. "It will be our first retreat as Team Version Zero. Max, what do you say?"

"Fucking nice," said Shane before Max could answer. He rubbed his fists together.

"How about we meet back here in an hour?" said Pilot. "The door will be unlocked for you."

Shane looked at Max with big, eager eyes. He looked at Akiko, too.

"See you in an hour," said Max.

1.18

Shane and Akiko drove home in the Poolwhip to get their stuff for the trip.

Brayden walked home.

Pilot gave Max a ride in his car. It was an ordinary Proton hybrid on the outside, but on the inside things were different. Pilot set a course on the car's single large screen, swiveled his chair away from the twitching steering wheel, and offered Max coffee from its center console in a little paper cup.

Pilot leaned back. He did not bother with a seat belt. "If I die, I die," he said.

Max clicked his seat belt. He took a ginger sip. "This coffee's super great," he said.

Max faked a smile, and Pilot caught it.

"Are you okay?" said Pilot.

"That suicide freaked me out," said Max.

"I insist it is not the fault of anyone but Fred Mould," said Pilot.

"I don't know where there is for Version Zero to go next," said Max.

"Turn off your brain, Mister Max. Get your things. Glass Island is a good place to relax. Let the answers come to you."

"Sounds like some mindfulness shit," said Max.

"Fuck that mindfulness shit," said Pilot with a hissing grin. "I am talking about beer and bocce ball by the sea."

The Proton accelerated and turned and braked with a grace no human could ever match. Max stared at the screen and watched its sensors detect every detail of the passing landscape and make adjustments accordingly.

"When I was your age," said Pilot, "this was the most futuristic thing anyone could ever imagine. A car that could drive itself while its passengers enjoyed refreshments."

"It is pretty damn cool."

Pilot beamed. Max could see he had a good smile. A kind smile. Maybe Pilot had been too kind for the tech scene. Maybe that was why he dropped out.

Max dipped his head. That was not why he dropped out.

"Eh, you get used to it after about a week," said Pilot. "Traffic is still traffic. I do like that it drives safer than most humans can."

"Because humans suck," said Max.

"Oh, no," said Pilot, tsking. "Do not say that. You sound like cynical old me when I was your age."

"When Ah wuz yer age," croaked Max.

They laughed.

"Fred Mould was a human who sucked," said Max. "Rest in peace."

"Fred Mould was simply an inevitable product of a system where humans had been removed from the equation. There could be no Fred Mould without the internet."

"Explain," said Max.

"A delusional racist like Fred Mould would normally have no one to talk to. Maybe he would keep a horrible private diary. Maybe he would scribble on his basement walls at night. He would never stand on a street corner and shout his racist Holocaust denier nonsense in public. But along comes the internet."

"Along comes the internet," said Max.

"And Fred Mould can do whatever he wants without showing his face. Without consequence. He finds other faceless men. They encourage one another. The internet is the world's biggest men's bathroom graffiti wall. A perfect and frictionless outlet for insanity."

This reminded Max of a study conducted at his old school comparing graffiti in men's and women's bathrooms. The men's walls were full of rape jokes, dick doodles, and gay bashing. The women's bathrooms were spotless. It was a confounding study, because there was literally nothing to compare. Max wanted to run around campus, shake everyone he met, and ask: *Why?*

"Why is there even a need for an outlet like that in the first place?" said Max.

"Right?" said Pilot.

"What kind of man even wants to say shit like *jew stink*?" Max said.

"You're asking why men insist on dehumanizing other men."

"Fuck if I know."

"Indeed," said Pilot. "Fuck if any man knows."

The car took a bounce, and Max steadied his cup.

Pilot drained his coffee and exhaled. "There has always been this habit among men," he said, "to take humans out of the equation. The internet is the epitome of that habit."

"Dehumanized systems are efficient, I guess," said Max.

"I used to believe humans were the problem," said Pilot. "We all did. I thought tech could do everything humans could do, but faster and safer and cheaper. Need a cab? Use your phone. Need a fridge, need a therapist, need a soul mate? Use your phone, no need to talk to a soul. It has become the way of doing things. Investors ask, *Will it scale?* and the only answer is *Yes, once we remove the humans from the equation.*"

They both gazed at the car's sensor screen, which missed nothing.

"Then I had a satori," said Pilot. "A realization."

"You realized you were a big robot nerd with social issues?" said Max.

"Thanks for reducing a life epiphany to a joke," said Pilot, and laughed. For a moment Max thought he had insulted the man; but Pilot's laughter was warm and steady as rain, and his eyes danced as if counting the years floating by.

"I realized," said Pilot, "that the future I imagined as a child turned out nothing like my dreams. My science-fictional futures still had people at the controls. The Fred Moulds of the world stayed hidden deep in the closet. But no, the future we got was the one where Airlift drivers can kill their fares with impunity."

"That shit was so fucked up," said Max, and they shared a moment of silence.

They were talking about a series of nine recent murders where Airlift drivers killed the customers they picked up. The drivers were never caught because they all used fake profiles. They all might have been the same person.

In response, Airlift CEO River Askew released a Things You Can Do online safety guide, while still allowing the creation of fake profiles.

"Humans are messy as fuck," said Max. "But they still do the important stuff better than an algorithm."

Pilot toasted to that. "I wish I had realized that when I was your age."

"When Ah wuz yer age," said Max.

A pause.

"I am continually grateful we met," said Pilot. "Am I . . . ?"

Pilot hesitated. Max leaned in.

"Are you what?" said Max.

"I was hoping I could be a mentor to someone like you. Am I being a good mentor?"

"People would kill for a mentor like you," said Max. "You're the best."

"Whatever comes after this Empty Age," said Pilot, "you will be there to bring people back into the equation. You will do great things. I know it."

"Shut the fuck up, duncie," said Max, and Pilot shone bright in return.

I just called Pilot Markham a duncie.

Max saw the Stonehenge of America and its carved words: *Be fair. Be just. Seek beauty and love.*

The Proton's dashboard chimed: they were nearing their destination. Max looked up, and through the heavily tinted windows he saw his parents' street—and spotted a van parked near their house, an outrageous luxury van emblazoned with the Wren logo.

"Shit, stop the car," said Max.

"What is it?"

"Stopstopstop," said Max.

Pilot stopped the car. He looked where Max was looking.

Pilot smiled at Max. "It looks like Cal Peers may be trying to smoke out that inconsiderate asshole who leaked his Soul Project."

Max swallowed a dry lump. "He can't know it's me."

"Of course not." Pilot patted Max's shoulder. "Theoretically, dozens and dozens of people had access to those documents. I suspect his vans are deployed everywhere at this point, a dragnet of surveillance and intimidation."

"You think he called the FBI or Homeland Security or whatever?"

"That would be stooping down to the government for help," said Pilot. "He probably treats his hunt for Version Zero like he does everything: an engineering problem to be solved with technology. But he can't know it was you. He doesn't even know of my involvement."

Max squinted at the van. "You and I can't be seen together."

"Mhm."

"Can you show me how to do something?" Max drew out his phone.

"Of course."

"How do I check in to some place I'm not?"

"May I?" said Pilot.

Pilot was asking for consent, and Max gave it.

Pilot tapped on Max's phone and went to a strange internet address, where he downloaded a system-level file Max did not recognize. Once installed, Max found he was now able to set his geographic location manually to anywhere in the world.

"Dude," said Max.

"Check in wherever you want," said Pilot. "That café seems good."

Max did. They waited. The car ticked under the heat of the caroline sun. Moments later the Wren van started up and drove away.

"Motherfuckers," said Max.

"They will get theirs," said Pilot, patting Max on the shoulder.

"Motherfuckers," said Max.

1.19

P ilot," said Max. "This is Dad."

Dad stood thunderstruck. "You are Pilot Markham."

"Nice to meet you," said Pilot.

"This is the friend I told you about before," said Max. It was a ridiculous thing to say, because even most normal, nontech people knew who Pilot Markham was.

"Hello," said Dad. Then he screamed into the house: "Honey! Max has a guest!"

He pronounced it *ho-knee*. He never called Mom *honey*, except in the presence of gringos.

Dad turned back to Pilot. "Please, come in."

They sat at the tiny octagonal dining table. Mom brought a clinking pitcher of iced soursop fresco and set it on the table, which wobbled. Dad knelt to tighten the wingnut. He chuffed with effort. He groaned back into his chair before yanking the table to test it: stable.

It was hot. Dad was sweating lightly. Dad, Max realized, was getting old.

"Wow," he said. "It's an honor to have the great Pilot Markham in my house."

Dad looked at Max with this gleeful sort of incredulity: *How . . . ?*

"Well," said Pilot in a voice so warm as to be almost baritone, "it really is an honor to be working side by side with a brilliant young man like Mister Max. Your son is brilliant, you know, Mister . . . ?"

"Ulises," said Dad. "This is my wife, Penelope."

Pilot raised his eyebrows. "Ulysses and Penelope? That's incredible."

"It was written," said Dad, and he gave Mom's hand a squeeze. Mom, ever the traditionalist, smiled and went to the living room to let the men do their talking.

"We just came by to pick up a few things for an overnight," said Max.

"I am flying Mister Max and the team out to Glass Island for a retreat," said Pilot.

Dad's eyes flashed big, one time. He was impressed. Bewildered, but impressed. Max felt himself wanting to cry. There was the golden glow of pride in Dad's eyes—a big pride, the pride of a lifetime's work: *America, my son, coil spring factory, Pilot Markham.*

"Can I ask what you are working on?" said Dad with jazz hands, a gesture he saved for when he was nervous. "Or is it top secret?"

Max smiled into his soursop and cast Pilot a sidelong glance.

"Uh," said Max.

"Mister Max is making the world a better place," said Pilot. "The entire planet will feel his impact. That is unfortunately all I can say for now. He is defining a new era."

I am? thought Max. *I guess I am.*

"A new era," said Dad.

Pilot's phone buzzed. It was a strange buzz, more like the sound of knuckles cracking, as if the device contained cartilage.

"This is our flight calling," said Pilot. "Excuse me."

With Pilot in the hall murmuring to his phone, Max and Dad had the room to themselves. Dad leaned in over his drink and whispered.

"God in heaven, Flaco, how did you meet up with the world's richest man?"

"Dad, he's not the richest."

"Well, almost."

"I guess."

"How much are you getting?"

"Dad."

"A man like him, it has to be a lot."

"Dad, we haven't talked money or anything. It's not about the money."

"Well, talk to him. Don't forget. Don't be afraid to ask for a lot."

"Dad."

"What, it's a huge opportunity. It could mean a ranchito for us three, Flaco."

Max really wanted to cry now. Dad was being impossible, but he was also right. Max had read something once about immigrants, how they come wanting a better life and how their kids wind up taking that better life for granted, and lo, a generation gap is born. Here Max was trying to tell Dad that money did not matter; here was Dad trying to tell Max that money was everything: money meant security and freedom and rest for weary bodies that had seen too much toil and violence.

Max felt the heavy commingled surge of guilt and gratitude and irritation that all children of immigrants feel, and he also saw the fantasy those same children see from time to time: the fantasy of handing a set of brand-new house keys to parents screaming with joy.

A ranchito on the top floor of the great Masada of Playa Mesa would be a thing for sure. It would be the biggest thing-thing ever.

The glass of soursop smelled so sweet and cold, citrusy fresh with the faintest dusty hint of freezer burn from ice cubes left unused for too long.

"I'll talk to him about money," said Max.

"Promise, Flaco."

"I promise."

Hands clasped his, and Max looked up to see Dad's face crinkled with open hope. He wasn't being cautious, or coy, or anything. Just bearing all his hope for Max to see.

Footsteps approached, and Dad's hands sprang away.

"We are good for takeoff," said Pilot, reappearing.

He looked at Max and Dad with a thin gray smile.

"Max is lucky to have parents like you," said Pilot. "I wish I had a dad like you."

Dad smiled. "I'm sure your parents did a great job."

"Eh, they got blown up by a bomb."

Dad's smile went slack. "Oh."

Mom had come just in time to hear the words *blown up by a bomb* and froze.

"Shall we?" said Pilot to Max.

Max packed a backpack, and the four of them now stood on the front porch in the blinding afternoon light.

"Have fun," said Dad.

"Very be careful," said Mom.

The three of them hugged. Max sensed the awkwardness of Pilot fidgeting nearby. So Max said:

"Come on, Mister Pilot, get in here."

Pilot joined them, and the four of them hugged and laughed at how funny and exciting this situation was.

Max and Pilot took their leave. Mom and Dad tended to wave all the way until their guests were out of sight, so Max and Pilot waved and waved back at them, and Mom and Dad waved and waved and smiled big smiles until Max and his mentor Pilot reached a far corner.

"Very be careful," shouted Mom.

1.20

Our hearts go out to all the loved ones affected by the tragic recent losses involving our innocent ridership. Safety is our top concern at Airlift, and we would like to take this opportunity to communicate simple things you can do to ensure your safety when using an Airlift-provided taxi or lodging.

1. Make sure your phone is always charged and transmitting your GPS location at all times.

2. In a car, never sit next to the driver; sit in the opposite rear seat in case you need to make a quick exit. Make sure child lock is not turned on. If it is, ask the driver to turn it off.

3. Before you enter a car, take pictures of the license plate, the driver, and the make and model and send them to your friends.

4. Text, call, and post with friends on your phone during a car ride to let the driver know you are not alone.

5. If the driver starts acting in a disturbing manner, exit the car at the next intersection, preferably one with lots of people around.

6. Upon arrival at a lodging, knock on the door first and watch from a distance for ten minutes before entering.

7. Begin shooting video as you enter a lodging. A livestream to your friends is even better, if local bandwidth allows.

8. With one hand, hold out pepper spray or a similar personal defense weapon and sweep every room in the lodging. With the other hand, have 911 (or local equivalent, if available) pre-dialed and ready to call.

9. Take pictures of every room in the lodging and send them to friends.

10. Shout "Hello?" (or local equivalent) repeatedly. This lets everyone around you know you are there.

1.21

They met back at the house and drove out in separate cars: Akiko and Shane in the Poolwhip, led by Pilot and Max and Brayden in the Proton.

"Self-driving?" said Brayden, examining the car's interior. "Nice."

"I spend three years building this prototype," said Pilot, "and all I get is *nice*."

"A hundred people die every day from cars," said Brayden. "Cars are the number one cause of death for kids. People don't deserve the privilege. Car ownership is debt pwnership anyway. That's what I meant by *nice*."

Max and Pilot shared an impressed look. Neither of them was expecting such an outburst of insight from the boy.

Pwnership was early 2000s slang derived from *pwned*, a typo of *owned*, which meant to be dominated by someone. People typed fast and furious in the early 2000s, often using just their thumbs, and typos were the norm.

The road ahead cut through tall grasses turning gold and copper in the afternoon light. There was a single low hill. Upon it rested a single tree in silhouette against a diagonal orange sun. It struck Max as a good place to rest, and Max realized how noisy his brain had become and how nice a rest would be.

"In a thousand feet, you will arrive at your destination," said the car.

There was now a chain-link fence a mile long, and not much else.

"Arrived," said the car.

They approached a hangar, and a small jet, and a uniformed pilot, beckoning.

"Check out this private jet bullshit," said Max.

"It is obscene," said Pilot, all sheepish. "But so much faster than flying commercial."

They pulled up and stood on the breezy tarmac. The plane gleamed. Its door sat open in two toothed semicircles, ready to ingest passengers. Shane and Akiko parked the Poolwhip and joined them.

"Fucking sweet-ass shit," hooted Shane through his fingers.

Pilot shook hands with the pilot. "Mister Cody, good to see you."

"How do, Mister Markham," said Cody. "You see that Arcs game?"

"I still hate sports, Mister Cody."

"A man can change." He said *can* like *kin*. He gave the gang a wink.

"Everyone, this is Mister Cody," said Pilot.

"How do, folks," said Cody. "Y'all climb on in, we're number one for takeoff."

There were no seat belt lights here, thought Max. No FAA-regulated safety instructions. None of this you-may-now-move-freely-about-the-cabin. The interior looked more like a lavish hotel conference room than a plane.

Cody—or someone—had left them a rainbow-colored sushi spread and bottles of sake chilling in ice. A stack of little bamboo cube cups stood nearby.

Shane, being Shane, began piling a plate with sushi atop sushi. Akiko bit her nigiri in half, an odd habit. Brayden removed the fish slices, dipped them in soy sauce, and put them back into place. Everyone with their own way of doing things.

Pilot did not eat.

Before long they were cruising in the sky, and Max was buzzing from the sake. Akiko offered him another cup. Akiko was a pusher, because as long as others were drinking, it gave her permission to drink, too. A person like Akiko with a mother like hers needed permission.

Akiko got giggly when she drank. It made Max feel like the funniest man alive.

Akiko turned red when she drank. Once, Max pressed her forearm and saw the white mark his finger made before the red came flooding back in to reclaim the spot.

Akiko this, Akiko that.

Her skin looked flushed and hot and Max wanted to touch it. Max decided he should do something else. So he turned to Brayden.

"Mister Brayden," said Max.

"Yo, Mister Max."

"Give us the latest."

"On it," cried Brayden. He thumbed his phone quickly, then slowly. Then he stopped. "I don't know how to say this."

Max set his cup down. "Use your mouth?"

Brayden showed his screen. Akiko began reading, then snatched it out of his hand for a closer look. Now she was frowning. Now she was *fuming.*

She flopped her arms and flung the phone away. "I give up."

"Hey," said Brayden.

"What is it?" said Max.

Akiko looked at Max with her eyes closed. "Account deletions have stopped."

"What?" said Max.

Akiko opened her eyes. "People are reactivating their accounts."

"I don't get it," said Shane.

"Because it doesn't fucking make any kind of logical sense," said Akiko.

Max blinked and blinked. Was he drunk? "I genuinely don't understand what you're saying to me right now."

Max held his hand out, and when Brayden handed him his phone he scrolled rapidly left, right, up, and down through tables of live data.

"We just had forty-one thousand deletions," said Max. "This can't be right."

"What's it at now?" said Shane.

"Half that," said Max. "And falling. It's been less than twelve hours."

"Wull," murmured Brayden, "it *is* March Madness right now."

Max cocked his arm and aimed it at the back of the plane.

"Please don't throw my phone," said Brayden.

"So people return to Wren and Knowned," said Pilot, fascinated. "Even knowing now what they are."

"It's like nothing will make people change," said Max. "Is the internet like smoking? Just like smokers know it's bad for them but they're too addicted to stop?"

"Is it a surprise?" said Akiko. "Think about all the evil shit we normalize in our lives. Like: I know these shoes were made by child labor but they're so cheap and cu-u-u-ute. I know my 401(k) is managed by evil empire bankers investing in evil empire Big Pharma, but the forms are just so confu-u-u-using to tweak myself. How is the internet any different?"

"Damn, baby," said Shane. "You get so serious."

"For me personally I would have a hard time quitting Wren," said Brayden. "The FOMO would get to be a lot."

FOMO was short for *fear of missing out* and was pronounced *foam-oh.*

"People want to bet on brackets with their friends," said Brayden. "Wren is where you bet on brackets."

"Yeah, but you agree the internet is a deeply broken place, right?" said Max.

"I agree," said Brayden.

"Everyone knows the internet fucks with our shit every day, right?"

"Agree."

"Everyone knows the internet can't just keep going the way it's going, right?"

"Half my team went on a social media fast a while back," said Akiko. "These are super-savvy, supersmart Wren employees I'm talking about."

Akiko paused. Max knew why. It was impossible to imagine her going back to work at Wren after all this. She would have to quit. And then what?

"Certain technologies hijack the primitive brain to thwart our better selves," said Pilot. "Cars make us fiercely territorial. Television holds our orienting response hostage. Phones trap us in a vicious oscillation between social reward and rejection."

"I just say FOMO," said Brayden.

Max let his hands flop onto the buttery leather of his chair. "So what are we doing here?" he said. "If people keep coming back despite themselves, how are we supposed to fix the internet? Can we just blow the whole thing up?"

"If only that were technically possible," murmured Pilot to his fingernails.

"The only time people change is when something super heinous happens," said Shane, sitting up now. "My grandma used to tell me about how so much shit changed in Japan after Hiroshima. Everyone started looking inward, you know? They stopped trying to conquer China or whatever. A fucking A-bomb will do that."

Max closed his eyes and leaned his head back. He recalled a graphic novel, one of his all-time favorites, where a misguided genius launches a fake alien attack on earth to unite nations through tragedy—even at the catastrophic expense of innocent millions. Version Zero needed something like that.

Without the millions dead, of course.

"We gotta come up with our A-bomb," said Max. "Because hacks don't last."

"Death does," said Brayden, and he held up a photo of Fred Mould and a headline.

RIGHT-WING WHITE SUPREMACISTS FIND MARTYR IN MOULD

"What's the rest of the article say?" said Shane.

"I don't read the articles," said Brayden.

Akiko squeezed Max's shoulder. Max thought about her team back at Wren. She must be on some kind of official shit list by now, after such an unexplained absence. Max wondered if there was a Wren van parked in front of their place in Delgado Beach, too.

Where was there for Version Zero to go? Were Max and his friends and his strange new mentor simply playing at being revolutionaries in this outrageous private jet?

Max drummed his fingers. "What exactly are we doing?"

Pilot answered. "We are going to Glass Island to relinquish all our preconceived notions of reality so that the answers may come flowing forth."

Pilot stood with his hands clasped for a long moment. Then he burst out laughing.

"That was cheesy as fuck, eh?" he brayed.

Everyone else laughed, and Max joined in. It was true what they said about laughter. So many dumb, simple things were true. It made all the rest of it infuriating.

Max's phone buzzed. It was a text. Max stared.

"Who is it?" said Pilot.

The plane tilted. Ovals of light crept down the walls. Max had to sit, lest he lose his balance. He could no longer see the horizon.

"Final descent," said Cody over the intercom. "Glass Island, y'all."

1.22

Max, please inform Akiko Hosokawa that her employment with Wren has been terminated.

—Cal Peers

1.23

It seemed to Max that they would descend into nothing but the ocean itself. But at the last moment a coastline appeared, and a small runway, and at the end of it stood an old man waving from a long electric golf cart festooned with streamers and glittery orbs.

They were Christmas ornaments.

"Heyo," said the old man as they exited.

"Grandpa," said Pilot.

Max looked at Shane. Shane looked at Akiko.

"I thought, that ain't no single-prop coming in, and I knew right away it could only be you," said the old man, hobbling over for a hug. He wore a rifle across his chest. The turbines were still whining to a halt. Max guessed a man like Cody, working for a man like Pilot, could just park his plane anyplace he wanted.

"He looks like one of Santa's elves," whispered Max to Akiko.

"Grandpa?" she said.

"No idea," said Max. "Maybe a nickname?"

"What were you looking at on your phone earlier?"

Max hesitated. Cal Peers must be casting about his suspicions; Akiko was officially among them. Normally, Max would've been terrified into hiding by such a message.

But Max had Pilot. Pilot could body-slam Cal Peers into a skyscraper like a giant mech-warrior if he wanted to. If he were purely driven by animal rage, and not any kind of higher vision.

Max put his phone away. There was no point in worrying Akiko.

"Just spam," said Max.

Max turned to gaze at the perfect green hills and long grassy chales massaged by gusts from the endlessly repeating ocean—a miniature emerald isle straight out of a video game.

"Grandpa, these are my good friends and business partners: Max, Akiko, and Shane. And this is Brayden."

"Well, konnichiwa and hajimemashite. Oh," he said, looking at Max, "um, mucho gusto. Am I right?"

"Mucho gusto," said Max. "And what's your heritage?"

"Oh, I'm just generic standard-issue White," said Grandpa. He then held Pilot's arm aloft as if inspecting him. "My lord, this man never ages. He's got a portrait in his basement that does it for him."

"You got me," said Pilot.

The old man grew earnest. "You holding up okay?"

Pilot shrugged. "Eh."

"You're a fighter," said the old man.

They regarded a nearby orange cone like two men before a grave marker.

"You still make llama burgers?" said Pilot.

Grandpa grinned. Max had read that in the great emotional graph of life, happiness in old age soared and even surpassed that of youth. This old man looked drunk on bliss.

"Climb in, one and all," he said.

Glass Island was a pair of mountainous islands connected by the Isthmus of Nosebridge, located twenty miles southwest of Playa Mesa in the Pacific Ocean. It was originally called Pimu by native Tongvans, then renamed to San Solanus by Spaniards who killed the Tongvans, then renamed to Glass Island by the oil mogul Henry Hutchinson, who appropriated it from the bankrupt Spaniards, and blablabla.

Max had come to Glass Island only once on an elementary school field trip, and his class didn't venture any farther than the tide pools they were tasked with studying. Max never imagined people actually lived here full-time. But of course they did. Where else had their hot lunches come from that day? Who else were all those people driving around in electric golf carts?

Grandpa's cart trundled them down a narrow sidewalk marked with miniature street signs no bigger than dinner plates, passing house after house made of scrap, tin, hubcaps, and drums: a junker's paradise, a first-world Whiteman's utopian vision of third-world charm meticulously crafted into tiki-torched reality.

Max was struck with the urge to never leave this place. They waved at every person they passed. They traveled no faster than fifteen miles an hour, and only on downhills. There was a barbecue pit made out of a dismantled truck bed, and an old Whiteman in an aloha shirt raised his ceramic hash pipe from underneath his straw sombrero in greeting.

"Sammy Sauce, I love you," said Grandpa.

"I love you more, Grandpa," said Sammy Sauce.

The place struck Max as a kind of do-over: their careers done, their money made, the residents of Glass Island had all the time in their remaining lives to make whatever society they wanted. And they chose this—lo-fi, junky, funky, slow as it comes. Max could see himself reading on a breezy bluff surrounded by manga.

If everyone could recalibrate their expectations so, would all the world look like this?

Or was such recalibration a luxury that only cloistered retirees could afford, and only after a lifetime of wealth amassed through unscrupulous exploitation?

Did there need to be losers in order for there to be winners?

The golf cart trundled over an unpaved wash leading to an open gate marked with a plywood cutout of a llama.

"Llamas," said Shane. He pointed.

There was a leaning barn house with a deck draped in fluttering tinsel and a picnic table and a rickety fence beyond. And beyond that fence: llamas.

"Garararararrarara," said the llamas.

"There's a bucket of beer by the picnic table," said Grandpa. "Be right back with some grub." He unslung his rifle and set it with effort against a fence post. Then he vanished.

Pilot fished out beers for all.

"Always meant to come out here more," he said. "It has been years."

Max paced with Pilot while the rest of Team Version Zero followed. Pilot walked slow here. He seemed at ease.

"This place feels really special," said Max finally.

"No cell signal. No internet. All you can do here is just be."

Max looked at his phone. He showed Pilot the text message.

Max, please inform Akiko Hosokawa that her employment with Wren has been terminated.

Pilot was unconcerned. "It is natural that he should suspect you and Akiko. She has been AWOL for a week, after all, coinciding with the Big Fix."

"Has it been a week already?" said Max. Again he imagined a Wren van parked in front of her place in Delgado Beach. "We should lay low."

"Do not let this Cal Peers motherfucker bother you," said Pilot. "We will take care of him."

"What do you mean?" said Max, hoping for a glimpse into Pilot's inner heart. Because—good God—who knew what kind of history he had with a man like Cal Peers? Had something happened between them?

But Pilot said nothing. He smiled and waved to passersby, lazily, as if on a parade float.

Max turned off his phone and pocketed it. The wind drew ornate curlicues all around them. It felt good to be offline, unmarked,

unnoticed,

a blank spot in the endless data continuum.

"How do you know Grandpa?" said Max.

"He and Grandma are very good friends of friends. They are technically Noelle's godparents. Were. Grandpa worked for Polk Chemical during the war. He invented napalm, you know."

"Huh," said Max. He took a swig of the lightest, chilliest beer ever.

They sat.

Pilot gazed at the rickety llama fence and grew still as a statue. "Last time I was here was with Anna and Noelle," he said. "A dozen or so years ago."

He stared at the fence, seeing something no one else could see.

"You really loved her," said Max.

Pilot sniffed and blinked his eyes. "Do you want to see?"

Pilot pulled out his phone: a customized, no-brand device wrapped with tape and foil. The rest of the team caught up, and they all leaned in.

"What are we looking at?" said Shane.

"Noelle," said Max.

"Oh," said Akiko. Max saw her instinctively draw closer to Shane.

Pilot swiped through a surreal collection of photos.

A grainy security camera screenshot of Max leaving Wren.

"Whoa," said Max.

A webcam view of Akiko. Shane unloading his van, from a distance. Brayden dancing in his underwear in front of a massive television.

"Uh," said Brayden.

"Not these," said Pilot, swiping.

The man in the Black Halo mask.

A man in a demon mask in a vast server room, giving two thumbs-up.

A futuristic ski lodge sitting atop a pristine snowy mountain range.

"Not these, not these," he said, swiping.

He finally reached a video of a young girl—ten or eleven—standing on the rickety llama fence. The girl performed clumsy split leaps from the top beam. Max watched Pilot's face closely as the video played. He saw Pilot's eyes soften and grow full of wonder and regret and, just once, flash with nausea.

Noelle missed a leap. She fell. She began crying, which struck Max as odd for a girl her age. Anna Chiang rushed into the frame to help.

"Honey, come help me," said Anna.

Pilot turned the phone off. "That is the last video I have of her."

"She was beautiful," said Akiko.

"She really was," said Shane, and he squeezed Akiko's hand. Max guessed he was fast-forwarding his mind to the day when they would have children of their own.

Max was suddenly struck with the real possibility of remaining alone for his whole life, unless he changed certain things. So he decided to change things, starting from this moment forward.

In a valley turning purple with dusk, Max saw a bird cloud moving in tight formation, creating a living blob that shifted and stretched as a single unit. In his mind he took a photo—*chakee*—and sent it to Akiko sitting just a few feet away.

Do you see the things I see? thought Max. Do you see them how I do? I know you do.

The bird cloud dissipated.

"Noelle was twenty-one when she died," said Pilot. "She died hating me."

"That can't be true," said Akiko, and pressed closer into Shane.

"No, she was right to hate me. I hate me."

Pilot said it perfectly plain. Perhaps his tear ducts had dried up long ago.

"It was only afterward when I learned how brave she had been," said Pilot. "Writing and writing and writing, about only the good things. Was she ever mine?"

"Of course she was," said Akiko. She seemed affected by this news. Akiko loved her own father very much, so Max imagined it was impossible for her to grasp the concept of a daughter hating her father.

"She wrote against Gorillagate," said Pilot. His voice hitched, and he cleared it with a growl. "She stood up for the actress, someone she did not even know, without fear. And for that, she was attacked online, forced to escape from her home in a cab in the middle of the night to a rental in a new city, with new furniture, a new life, a new haircut. One day she went for a morning run—that must have been a new thing, too—and they ran her over. The police always say if you want to kill someone with total impunity, a hit-and-run is a terrific option."

Now Pilot was laughing and crying, those dry tear ducts springing to life, and he said, "It was impossible for her to hide, for she left a trail. All they had to do was follow it. She was doomed from the moment she spoke her mind."

Max opened his mouth to speak, but stopped. He shot a glance at Akiko, who was already looking at him, thinking the same thing: Noelle had been that SJW, or the social justice warrior, murdered at the height of Gorillagate.

"I was asleep when they killed her," said Pilot. "I was asleep my whole life. I will never sleep again until I am dead."

Brayden picked at a big splinter in the fence. Shane watched him. No one really knew where to look or what to say.

"I am so sorry," said Akiko finally.

Max threw an arm around Pilot, and he could tell he loved the gesture. It struck Max that Pilot probably had had almost no physical contact for years.

Max read about a study once. Monkeys were split into two groups: one with physical contact, one without. Those without slowly grew insane. They stopped eating. They destroyed everything in their habitats. They sat in their own feces.

"My little Noellephant," said Pilot. He laughed through his tears.

"But how—" said Akiko. "How did her name stay hidden from the press? I never knew that poor girl was your daughter. No one did."

Pilot stared at nothing. "I could have deleted those troll cowards out of existence before they learned her location. I could have built a castle to protect her in a single day. But I was too busy working. I was too late. So all there was left to do was to try to protect her memory. She would not turn into some meme joke. So I scraped all of it into the trash. Every mention of her name, every photo, every news article."

Pilot took a drink while everyone watched.

"How'd you pull that off?" said Brayden.

Pilot suddenly gave his chest a dry, fierce thump.

"How?" said Pilot Markham. "I am Pilot fucking Markham. That is how."

Ahead, a triangle sounded.

"Boys and girl," hollered a woman from a pair of weathered saloon doors at one end of the porch. "Food."

Max could see a table with a neat stack of burgers.

Max and Pilot and Shane and Akiko rose and ambled over.

"Hope you guys like a lotta llama," said the old woman. She gave Pilot a hug. "Sweetheart, how are you holding up?"

"He's a fighter," said Max.

1.25

Hello world! Noelle Chiang here. But you may call me Noellephant, for I trumpet thru the jungle and stomp all the baddies doing wrong in the world. Mom likes the name. She says Dad likes it too. (She's like his assistant.) You may know Mom from those NEXT institute videos. Is it nerdy that I still think my own mom is cool?

Dad makes apps, but you already knew that. Dad is cool too. Wherever he is.

. . .

Here's a funny thing I realized . . . people never stop being babies. Babies cry when they need attention, right? Adults are the same. Everyone needs attention. Everyone needs to hear: you are real! You matter! Without that stuff, we cry and cry.

Except adults don't cry. Their pain builds and builds until it pops out in strange ways. They do drugs. They do graffiti. They shoot up a school. Me, I used to cut.

I still wear shorts to the beach. And that's all I'm going to say about that.

. . .

Mom and Dad separated. Fat separates from cold soup. Pulp separates from orange juice. She said: think of it as Dad being on another long business trip . . . that he never comes back from lol. Still I'll probably get emails or karps or "shapters" (wtf are those) from him. Or whatever they come up with next. They keep making new stuff. Everybody ditches the old stuff and runs to the new stuff.

. . .

The feeds scare me. But I can't stop reading them. It's awful. It's hilarious. It's everything and nothing. One big nonstop cry for attention and validation, like I said before with the babies, but everywhere all over the world.

The feeds are an addiction masquerading as therapy.

They are the worst therapy I can imagine. I understand the addiction. I pity us all. Because socially—politically—you cannot afford to not be on the feeds.

I think about the trolls. How they think what they do is one big joke in search of a big reaction. How is that different from a baby's cry?

Here's how it's different: babies never bully.

The trolls try to punish me for everything I say. I realize I am becoming a kind of activist. And I won't stop saying what needs to be said. So I troll the trolls back.

In a way, the trolls are making a troll out of me. But what can I do? Be silenced?

Hell no.

. . .

Sorry to get all absent-dad on you . . . BIG NEWS! Got articles published on The Hunt (3), Kraken (2), Poliwonka (4!). Top articles so far: Rape Culture in VR Gaming and How to Be a Woman Online and The Internet Needs a Mother.

Top compliments: Heroine, Nut-twister, Wonderwoman.

Top epithets: c*nt, b*tch, slut, whore, fat, feminazi, lesbian (?), c*mdump, f*ckhole, f*ckskull, gash, blood wound, c*ckchoker, and too many others to list here.

Anyway. Broke 10k followers (don't know how many are trolls). Traffic to Strugglettes off the charts. Making decent ad money. Onward!

. . .

This last month has been hell. Someone phished my personal emails. There is an insane narrative forming now, that, apparently, I was an underage prostitute coached by Dad in secret. Started on Knowned, got upvoted by the boy brigade on NewsWar, now it's on National News Edition. Now it's like fact.

Hope NNE got a lot of clicks out of me. Not linking to them here.

There's a meme photo too. I never asked for that kind of famous.

Spending more time policing/cleaning up/defending myself against bullsh*t coming from all sides than actually writing.

Pain makes you stronger? I hope?

Even wrote to you-know-who for advice, is how desperate I am, but no response. Asked journalist buddies but they have no clue where he is. Ghost dad, lol.

. . .

The good news: gave a talk with my kickass mom in Switzerland last week. Audience of thousands, got to wear the fancy headset and get livecast globally. Our title was How to Include Women in Tech in One Easy Step. Uber-empowering. I told them to invite you-know-who to come, but he's still being the "J. D. Salinger of Tech."

The bad news: got doxxed on Knowned. I tried writing to Linda Belinda, no response. My personal info is now everywhere: my haunts, my habits, all my desire lines. If I move, they win. If I quit my favorite café, they win. Paralyzed . . .

. . .

I have to shut down Noellephant. From now on please directly email me or, even better, mail an old-skool letter. Something safer. I'm taking a break from writing publicly, but please please please do not lose touch. I need you more than ever.

Reason why: yesterday a man showed up at my favorite café with a shotgun and screamed my name before firing four times into the ceiling. Was arrested. No one hurt. I was not there at the time.

I begin looking for a new place tomorrow. Not sure how I will sleep tonight.

I will miss this place. It made me, it loved me, it betrayed me, it broke me.

Farewell, internet.

1.26

Max turned off the tablet. It was a strange home-brew device, with a removable battery held with gaffer tape and no options for any sort of connectivity whatsoever. On it Pilot had written in white ink:

NOELLE

"Jesus," said Akiko. She held the tablet with care for the sacred object it was.

They had walked down a short hill to this spot, marveling at the way the dry sand responded to each step with a little squeaky bark, until they reached the shore where the little waves wiped the wet sand perfectly flat and perfectly clean over and over again into an infinite slab of the most luscious, most flawlessly poured concrete in the world.

Max, wrote Max into this perfect sand, and the waves wiped it clean.

Aki, wrote Akiko, and the waves wiped it clean, too.

Now the two of them huddled beneath a heavy poncho around the screen, reading and reading as the temperature around them fell. The blog entries and articles and letters all ended as abruptly as they had begun, which, Max figured, was pretty much how life worked.

1. Life began out of nowhere.
2. Things happened.
3. Life ended without warning.

Out of the three, only step two was of any importance. It was also the most mysterious.

"She'd been bullied publicly for months," said Max. "I mean, where was Pilot?"

"So fucked up," said Akiko.

It had been the four of them reading the tablet, Max and Akiko and Shane and Brayden, but Shane had grown tired of reading and Brayden got distracted by the discovery of a ball court nearby. Some country club game Max had never heard of called *pétanque*, French for bocce ball. Shane and Brayden sauntered over a small ridge to play, perhaps to make the best use of the falling daylight.

While those two whooped and cantered, Max found himself alone with Akiko in a hidden pocket of tall grass. Grandma had given them the heavy poncho.

Akiko's hair smelled musky and sleepy, like it hadn't been washed in a while. Like her pillowcase, probably, back in the Delgado Beach apartment.

Before them the sun had already set. The ocean surrounding this bluff atop Glass Island had grown still and steely and cold. The sky the color of tea.

"In the real world," said Max, "if you see someone bullying someone, you stop it. You don't let it get all the way to murder. Right?"

"Yeah, but you know Online," said Akiko. "Online is all, *We are not responsible for our users' content*. It's bullshit."

"Isn't that what the CEO of Knowned said? Linda Belinda?"

"She just wants users at any cost."

"Wait, wasn't Pilot a cofounder of Knowned?" said Max.

Akiko frowned, thinking. "What do you think Pilot really wants out of all this?"

"Something big," said Max. "Something only a guy like him could imagine."

She laughed. "I'm not getting arrested for anything, I'll tell you that right now."

"I won't tell if you won't," said Max. The words felt clever to say, but they didn't make a whole lot of sense.

Indigo began to seep into the tea sky from the cosmos above. Max thought about Dad. Dad made coil springs. He got paid. The coil springs were sold for money. They were used in useful machines. They were the thing-thing. Simple. There was no data-tracked freemium crowdsourced business model in coil springs.

Maybe Dad was right.

Maybe Dad was right about everything, and Max and Pilot and everyone of this generation were fools. The world—correction: Max's world—felt like an absurd wonderland with plenty of seats at the Mad Hatter's tea party, but still no room for anyone.

Max began to feel stupider and stupider by the second.

"There was life before the internet, you know," said Max. "I think I remember some stuff from when I was real little."

"Yay, and there was life before cars and the telephone and running water."

"Dang, bite my head off."

"Nom nom nom."

Akiko folded in close under the poncho. This was the Akiko Max grew up with—more a sister than a friend, with all the easy dumb jokes that came with.

Max did not want a sister.

"I just remember the internet was supposed to be this awesome place that would bring the world together," said Akiko.

"It did, but not always in a good way." Max frowned, realizing something. "You ever read the Declaration of the Independence of Cyberspace?"

"Never read it," said Akiko.

"Well, it exists. And come to think of it, the whole thing amounts to a huge dick move."

"Well, now I'm never going to read it."

"Mostly the declaration is about hey, government, fuck you, we don't need you," said Max. "Also, physical bodies are outdated and stupid. And Cyberspace is this whole new parallel world that doesn't need to play by any rules of humanity. Shit: the internet was fully antisocial to begin with."

"That's such a nerd thing to declare. That's such a *boy* thing to declare. If you guys had to menstruate you wouldn't say stupid shit like *bodies are outdated*."

"I would menstruate if I could," said Max.

"That literally makes no sense, what you just said."

They laughed. Max could smell her hair again.

"If you could fix the internet," said Max, "how would you—"

"Two-way links," said Akiko.

"Two-way links."

"Hyperlinks are one-way. You know how we're all supposedly inter-connected in this big global conversation? Conversations are two-way. Links are not. So I call bullshit."

"Because I could link to you without you even knowing about it."

"Mhm. You could troll me, too, and I could never find you. Email me without letting me email you back. Dox me and never show your face. That's not a conversation. There's no purpose to this kind of setup. It's fundamentally anonymous, it's fundamentally *anti*purpose. Just pot-shots in the dark."

"You mean antisocial," said Max.

"I do?"

"You said *antipurpose*. I think you mean antisocial."

"Isn't that the same thing?"

"Six of one."

Akiko shifted and threw the poncho higher to stay warm.

"Anyway," said Akiko. "Two-way links. Not that anyone would ap-prove that kind of core-level change. Entire business models depend on potshots in the dark."

"So then what?"

She shrugged and grinned. "So we're fucked."

It was a dark joke, and Max laughed, because laughter was the best medicine and blablabla. He was having fun. He was having the most fun he had had in a while, and he was having it with his favorite person in the world.

I wish it had been me who got to rescue you, he thought.

Max thought a few sentences, but did not dare say them. They all sounded wrong anyway, absurd lead-ins like *Remember when we first met?* or *How long have we been friends now?* Max set these aside.

"You're saying the system can't change," said Max. "So what if, for our next hack, we make things really personal?"

"I thought Trollout was pretty personal," said Akiko mournfully.

"I'm not talking about hacking users," said Max. "I'm talking about the gatekeepers. I say we hit the CEOs."

"Max," said Akiko.

"And we hit Cal Peers first."

1.27

HOST: So you think they don't have any idea who Version Zero is-slash-are.

GUEST 1: I think he might suspect someone, but he'll never be able to prove anything.

HOST: Cal Peers.

GUEST 1: Cal Peers.

HOST: Think he could win a case against these Version Zero guys in court?

GUEST 1: Maybe for stolen documents, if he can even find a single fingerprint.

HOST: Had to be an inside job. That narrows the field.

GUEST 2: I've said it before—not only is ISIS homegrown, they've also gone white collar, and this proves it.

HOST: ISIS hasn't claimed responsibility.

GUEST 2: Then the Russians!

HOST: The Russians use Wren for psyops, not to stir up ideas about an internet revolution.

GUEST 1: Whoever Version Zero is, what matters is Wren is starting to lose some credibility in the court of public opinion after years of questionable business practices.

GUEST 2: You're on their side.

GUEST 1: I'm not on anyone's side. I'm just saying what's happening.

GUEST 2: One confirmed Trollgate suicide, plus two more suspected and currently under investigation, and you're saying everything's okay.

GUEST 1: I'm saying as of this morning, something like eighty thousand people have deleted Wren, and Knowned is losing users as well—that's awareness, for good or bad.

HOST: Cal Peers issued a sort of apology.

GUEST 1: Sort of is right.

GUEST 2: There is absolutely no proof that the Big Fix documents were real, and there's absolutely no proof that this Trollout thing has any credibility whatsoever in its, its, automated, algorithmized witch-hunt accusations.

HOST: I think the point is—

GUEST 2: Whatever you think might be true—

GUEST 1: What is your point?

HOST: Listen: We use these black boxes. Our phones. We don't know how they work the way they do. Or why they work the way they do. My point is, if we did know how the sausage was made, maybe we'd think twice about signing up for the next big app or whatever. And maybe that's a good thing.

GUEST 2: But in terms of the value of intellectual property—

HOST: Thank you, boys and girls. You know I love the applause, but we've got guests at the table.

GUEST 2: In definitive legal terms—

GUEST 1: I think the Version Zero activists—

GUEST 2: Bullies.

GUEST 1: I think the Version Zero group is the inevitable reaction you get when you spy on a bunch of people in the dark for a bunch of years and then lie about it. I don't think Version Zero's even close to being done yet, not with more and more people paying attention, and especially not with us sitting here on TV talking about it.

GUEST 2: So, more suicides.

GUEST 1: More truth. Don't put words in my mouth. More truth.

GUEST 2: There is no proof—oh, go ahead, clap for the terrorists, yay, terrorists.

HOST: And we're not close to being done yet, either, because coming up next after the break we have viewer live comments, so don't go anywhere.

1.28

No way," said Akiko. "Cal Peers is untouchable."

"Listen—I mean we just fuck with his shit a little," said Max. "Enough to let him know he's touchable, using the same systems he designed."

"How?"

"We do another document leak like we did with the Soul Project, but this time we take it up a level. We get Cal Peers's personal emails. Text messages. Really raw, incriminating stuff. Let Wren users know exactly what he thinks of them. Like, you've been watching us, but now we're watching you, too. Then we move on to Linda Belinda at Knowned, and so on."

"Max, how?"

"Let Pilot figure that part out," cried Max with glee. "What do you think?"

"I think it's a badass concept," said Akiko. "Tough to pull off, unless."

Akiko touched her lips and became lost in thought, transfixed by this challenge. Max watched her think and think. It was a spectacular sight.

Behind the poncho were the click and thud of steel pétanque balls striking the earth. Max could hear Brayden's and Shane's voices struggling against the strengthening evening breeze.

"How about best eleven out of nineteen?" said a triumphant Brayden.

"Fuck you, bro," cried Shane. "Let's go again."

"Looks like Shane's getting his ass kicked," said Max finally.

Akiko turned to Max suddenly, as if he had sneezed. She gave him a hard look.

"I really love talking with you, Maxie," she said.

"I love it, too," said Max.

"I never get to talk about this stuff. Just, like, try to make sense of shit."

"Well, you're good at it."

"You're good at it, too."

"Mutual admiration society," said Max.

"I mean, I love talking to Shane, too," said Akiko, like a question.

"Shane's the man, what can you say."

"But, like, you and me, we've been friends for how long now?"

"Like, almost thirteen years."

"Dang, duncie."

"And you've been with Shane for, like, ten of those."

"Yep, yepyepyep. Ten. Years. Basically married."

"I—"

"I—"

"You go," said Max.

"No, you go."

"I forgot what I was going to say, rahhh," said Max, and Akiko rolled her eyes.

Behind them, Max could hear that the pétanque game had stopped; beer bottles snickthed open, which meant everyone was now gathered at the far picnic table.

"Remember there was this pool party?" said Akiko.

Max smiled into his knees.

"We were sitting with our legs in the water," she said.

"Shane threw you in."

"He's such a dumbass," said Akiko. "I lost an earring in that pool. I'm stuck with this one stupid earring in my dresser that I can never wear. But I keep it."

She laughed just once. Max noticed she had a dry spot on her upper lip.

"I think Shane wants to get married for real pretty soon," said Akiko.

"Oh, word?" said Max. He tried a happy grimace.

"I just think about how young you and I were back then, and how we didn't know anything, like we didn't know shit," said Akiko. "And now we're here, and look at us, we're all trying to change the world, really because of you, Max, and—I don't know—but I just really admire that so, so much, and it makes me so proud to be your, your, very best friend in the whole world."

Max kissed her.

Max saw her bed and the pillowcase lying there.

Max's left ear fell deaf for a moment. Then sound came ringing back into it.

"Maxie," said Akiko.

He touched her cheek, her ear, the scar above her left eye.

And now she was kissing him while the tall grass around them hissed once and long. He felt her fingers clasp around his, like some kind of miracle. They stayed like this and Max felt his entire chest thud with a vast low bass tone as the tip of her tongue melted into his mouth.

"Hey, dummies," called Shane, cresting the ridge now.

They sprang apart. Max released Akiko's hand—too fast, too fast—and scrambled to turn on the tablet. The poncho collapsed. Its warmth evaporated.

There Shane stood in a gap in the tall grass, not ten paces away. He held a chrome metal ball.

Say something, Max.

"You have to read the rest of this," said Akiko. Her face betrayed nothing. "It's heartbreaking."

She held up the glowing tablet: *See?* And Max felt his blood slow and stop as Akiko reflexively lied to Shane. He could feel her fear, strong as his own.

After this, no more.

But the kiss had happened. It had to mean something. It was a comet streaking across the sky that they and only they alone had seen.

In Max's mind, he rose from the pool that night long ago and led Akiko away before Shane could throw her into the glowing water. He took her to his house, gave her refuge from her family. He finally learned the story behind her scar.

And together they grew old and worked at a sunlit factory making artisanal coil springs.

Stupider and stupider, by the second.

"Tell me all about it later," said Shane. "Come play a round with us before it gets dark, honey bear."

Through the gap in the grass, Max could see Brayden and Pilot, waiting to play.

"Coming," said Akiko. She stood. She asked herself a question, then took out something from her pocket to glance at it: the magic eight ball key chain. She read its result.

What did it say?

She ambled away, with hips stiff from having sat too long, to where Shane stood waiting.

She gave Max a single glorious look back over her shoulder. Hair whipping in the wind.

Shane noticed that. He took her hand. He spoke to her while looking at Max.

"You're on my team," he said.

1.29

The campfire danced before them, creating underlit shadows that twitched upon their faces. Do not stare at her, thought Max. Only glance at her if and when she speaks.

For now, Max had to be satisfied with staring at her shoe. She wore them laceless. Easier to slip off when going indoors.

Easier to slip off.

"Mister Max?" said Pilot.

"Hey," said Max.

"You look like you're deep in thought," said Pilot.

Max waggled an empty beer bottle. "Mister Brayden, can you hook us up?"

"Sure, absolutely," said Brayden. He sprang to his feet and dealt out fresh icy bottles. "You got it."

"Thank you, Mister Brayden," said Max. "I don't suppose you have any ideas for our next hack, do you?"

Brayden took a quick swig. "Actually, I've been thinking. What if we hacked in and made everyone's selfie camera public? Like, you can watch anyone anywhere now, and everyone freaks the fuck out and turns off their phones, like, *Aaaaa*, and the internet legit becomes a ghost town. Wren stock would tank."

Shane lit up a joint. "That's not bad." He handed it to Brayden, who took a hit.

Pilot thought. "It is doable."

"I feel like people would hate us for that, though," said Akiko. "Version Zero has fans, but we're also on some pretty serious shit lists."

Max studied her laceless shoes.

"Okay, so," said Shane. "We're trying to make people see how fucked up the internet is, right?"

"Mhm," said Max.

"What if we built our own social network?" said Shane. "We promise no ads, a privacy guarantee, and trolls get shot on sight. Boom, done."

"Oh, baby," said Akiko. "That's a great idea, but it's so, so involved."

"Didn't Axial already try something similar?" said Max.

"Axial, and Boony, and Heynow, Trendship, ViReal, EarthTwo," said Brayden.

"Ah fuck," said Shane. He spat a sparkling stream of beer into the hissing fire.

"It really was a good idea, though, baby," said Akiko, giggling.

"Thank you, baby," said Shane.

Akiko stroked Shane's arm with the back of a finger, and Max looked back to her shoes. Better yet, his own shoes. Just to be extra safe.

Akiko spoke into the flames. "What about what *you* were saying?"

"Who?" said Shane.

"She means me," said Max.

Pilot leaned forward. "Do you have an idea?"

Max looked up and saw everyone waiting for him. Shane fanned Akiko's hair out and eyed him through a gap in the long strands.

"I guess I must have missed out on something," said Shane.

"It's just a thought, not even an idea," said Max, trying out a laugh. "I just think our hacks aren't moving the needle enough. We have to think bigger. Go beyond the technology."

"But the internet is technology," said Shane. "I mean, a technology. Technological."

"The problems of the internet aren't really technology based, though," said Max. "They're people based. We were on the right track with Trollout, but a dude died. That's not what we want, right?"

Max glanced around. Everyone waited.

"Plus, it wasn't our A-bomb. All it took was for Cal Peers to say *Oops sorry* and for users to think *Trolls suck, but they're not my problem*, and now account deletions are already slowing down. I mean, Wren made no changes in the end. Now everyone's wondering, *Who is Version Zero?*, which is not the point. The point is to keep the attention on the bad guys."

"Which bad guys?" said Pilot with a knowing smile.

"The CEOs themselves," said Max. "We live in the world they built. What if everyone knew what they really thought of their users?"

Max leaned forward to explain.

"What if we made their personal emails public? No amount of CEO face time would fix the damage to their public image. I know Wren had some doozies. It would be like that whole AE Motors scandal."

This made Shane sit up. He once worshipped cars made by Abschalteinrichtung—AE for short—until the company was caught systematically fudging emissions data in every onboard computer. "Those fucking emails, man," said Shane, flashing disgust. "Their CEO literally said, *The EPA can go fuck itself.* Fuck those guys."

"See?" said Max, pointing. "That's the reaction I want."

AE's sales tanked after the scandal. Their reputation went from mainstream-iconic to niche-boutique. They missed the electric car wave. They would likely miss the self-driving car wave, too. They were done. The rest of the automotive industry smugly rode their high horses like tin saints, but whatever: what mattered was that everyone had to walk the walk from that point on.

"The AE Motors scandal was uncovered by an environmental activist collective," said Max. "I want Version Zero to be exactly like that—activist, exposing evil, bringing assholes down using their own words."

"I dig that," said Shane, leaning back again.

Me and Shane are gonna be all right, thought Max. *Because after this, no more.*

No more pining.

Shane rifled a beer at Max and Max caught it, and Shane gave him a chin nod. It was a good sign. Max nodded back. He would not go after Akiko. He would not cause disaster. He would not break their bond.

Although, Max realized he could if he really wanted to.

Her hand gripping his. Her melting tongue. Her easy lie.

Sometimes you have to break a thing in order to fix it.

Max blinked back into now.

"Okay, so," said Akiko. "I'm thinking we could start with five or six targeted phishes at C- and E-level Wren execs spaced out over the next few weeks."

"No need," said Pilot.

"What?" said Akiko.

"There's no need," said Pilot, and all eyes turned to him.

And Pilot smiled that weird, knowing smile.

"Mister Max," he said. "You wanted the Big Five, yes?"

"Uh," said Max.

"Cal Peers, CEO of the social network Wren, 3 billion users.

"River Askew, CEO of the taxi and lodging service Airlift, 250 million users.

"Linda Belinda, CEO of the discussion forum Knowned, 300 million users.

"Jonas Friend, CEO of the computer giant Quartz, 600 million users.

"Hunter Mole, CEO of the retailer A2Z," said Pilot, "400 million users.

"Five people with data on almost half the world's population."

The campfire flames, if you closed your eyes, sounded like water.

The fire seemed to tilt.

Not just the fire, but the whole island.

The sticky note. The hit list.

"You read my phone again," said Max.

Pilot shrugged: *Guilty as charged.*

"It was just that one time," said Pilot. "I swear I have not looked around your phone since."

"You fucker," said Max, but oddly only half angry.

"It is an ambitious list," said Pilot. He tented his fingertips. "But not impossible."

1.30

Say we somehow get to each CEO," said Max. "Like Shane did with Cherry Lacroix?"

"Cherry Lacroix was a worker bee," said Akiko. "A million times easier to get to than a CEO."

"We just have to find each CEO's weakness and exploit it," said Max.

"A psychological backdoor," said Pilot.

"Right," said Max. He sat and thought. Nothing came to mind. He kept talking anyway, to keep momentum. "So. We somehow get to each CEO."

"I know River Askew hits the clubs," said Brayden.

"Which one is River Askew again?" said Shane.

"Pretty sure he's into Asian girls," said Brayden.

"Jesus," said Akiko, and she blew her cheeks up at the stars above.

Shane danced in his seat and jabbed Akiko with an elbow. "Work it."

Akiko punched him.

"Hey, I did it," said Shane. "Plus you're way hotter than me."

Akiko kissed the spot where she punched, and Max gazed at his shoes.

"We could get in close and hack into his phone," said Brayden, bouncing a knee with growing vigor. "Mister Pilot, you must have some tech for that?"

Pilot closed his eyes and nodded *Of course I do.* "First, we find the backdoors."

"This is gonna be a lot of work," said Max, mostly to himself. "And it'll get riskier each time we do it. Unless—duh—we wait until we have access to each of the Big Five, and then release their emails all at once?"

"That would be a motherhugging A-bomb right there," said Akiko.

"Eh," said Shane. "I don't know."

"You don't know what?" said Max.

"This is all sounding pretty impossible," said Shane with a twist of his mouth.

"That's the spirit," said Max.

Brayden stopped bouncing. "Debbie Downer."

"Mister Shane, I think at this point the impossible is precisely what our fans expect from Version Zero," said Pilot.

Shane opened another beer. "Dude. All the Big Five know each other. Any one of them has the slightest suspicion something's wrong, and one call is all it takes to say hey, Version Zero's up to something, everybody go to fucking DEFCON 1."

Max began to speak, but stopped. His mind sped through dozens of possible capers. None of them could defeat the simple defense of awareness. Shane was right.

"Shit," said Max.

"We could get to them through their kids," said Brayden. "Linda Belinda just had a baby, right? So maybe—"

"Brayden," said Akiko.

"We are not involving children," said Pilot.

Brayden shrank. "No kids, okay, cool."

Max poked the fire with a stick. He flopped another log onto the pile, sending embers billowing heavenward.

"Shane, you're right," said Max. "The Big Five's impossible."

"I didn't mean to shut your shit down," said Shane.

"It's okay. We'll just start over and come up with something else."

"Unless," said Pilot.

Max looked up. "Unless what."

"Shane, you're right in saying that the Big Five all know each other," said Pilot. "But do you know who else they know? And most importantly, trust? Ever since the very beginning, back when we were all tinkering in garages and college computer labs?"

Now Max was smiling. Everyone was.

"Do you know who they would just absolutely die to hear from after years of silence?" said Pilot with shimmering eyes.

"You," said Shane.

"Forget email leaks," said Pilot. "I would like to propose another idea."

1.31

I have a place," said Pilot. He splayed his fingers toward the fire. "It is across the ocean, high within the Balkan Mountains. There could be a conference. Very exclusive, very bogus. They would all agree to come. I am sure of it, for I have been in exile for three years, and their curiosity would get the best of them."

Max's mouth hung open. A little bird could fly in.

"There is no cell reception so high up in the Balkans, in such a remote spot. No internet. We could give the conference a ludicrous name."

"Disconnect," said Max.

"Duncie," said Akiko. "It's perfect."

"So bad it's good?" said Max.

Akiko answered with a guilty half smile.

"Disconnect," said Pilot, nodding. "We bill it as a back-to-basics retreat. A sort of digital Geneva Convention, where the righteous future of the internet will be debated and discussed without distraction. Something they could crow about later, to show how moral and civic-minded they are."

Max saw that the group had become animated. Brayden was bouncing again. Shane and Akiko whispered things to each other. And Pilot grinned and grinned.

"You can pull this off?" said Max, more as a statement than a question. Of course Pilot fucking Markham could pull this off.

Pilot wrapped an arm around Max. "They will come. We will barely have to do anything aside from establishing a private satellite connection. Just point a camera and let them dig their own graves. Leaked emails are one thing. Livestream video is something else entirely."

"This is so awesome," said Brayden, bursting now.

"There's a problem," said Max. "I don't have a passport."

Pilot laughed and laughed at that.

"So we go there," said Akiko, "hold this fake conference, and then just . . . ?"

"Sit back and enjoy the fireworks, I guess," said Max.

"After Disconnect, Version Zero may no longer need to exist," said Pilot. "We will have shaken them to the core. We can even part ways if you fear retribution."

Pilot leaned in and whispered into the fire. "This is what you wanted, Mister Max. This is exactly what you asked for."

Max watched the flames dancing in his eyes and knew the same flames were also dancing in his.

Pilot spoke so softly that everyone had to lean in. "Listen to me. I have three billion dollars," he said. "I have no need for any of it."

"What?" cried Shane.

"Fulfill your vision. Change history. When we return to civilization, your reward will be waiting for you to claim. Start a business if you wish. Start a charity."

"I'm in," said Akiko.

Everyone looked at Akiko.

"What, how could you not be in?" she said.

"Are you saying you're giving us money?" said Shane.

"It would be the only good investment I ever made," said Pilot. "A true angel investment." He looked at Max with wonder. "Mister Max. You inspired me when I thought such inspiration was no longer possible. Let me be your legacy. You are my son from another hon, so to speak."

Let me be your legacy was a weird way of putting things, but Max shrugged it off. He imagined Pilot retiring to this very island at some point, after their revolution was accomplished and done. He tried to picture him driving a golf cart in an aloha shirt and shorts, far away from Cal Peers and the Big Five and all of that.

"And you are my father from another mather," said Max.

"That doesn't really rhyme," said Brayden—but his smile was sad. Maybe it was hard for him, watching Max and Pilot grow closer before his very eyes. The boy probably craved a mentor. A father. What kind of parents left their high school son alone all summer while they traipsed off on vacation?

"We're all in this," said Max. "Right?" He reached out and snapped fingers with Brayden.

"Hell yeah I'm in," said Brayden, a little brighter now.

"No money for you, rich boy," said Pilot.

"Wait, what?" said Brayden.

"Joking again," said Pilot. "Got you."

"Cut it out," said Brayden.

"I'm in," said Shane.

From deep within Shane's embrace, Akiko stared at Max with something approaching pride. Hard to tell in the dim firelight. Nostalgia, maybe? Wistfulness for a legendary romance that could never be?

That last one was just Max making up wishful bullshit.

Max steadied himself. Were they really going to the Balkan Mountains, for real? Max had never left the country. Was there for real a big bag of money with the word MAX on it? One that could fund his very own company, and the one after that?

Everyone looked at Max, waiting.

"Let's get the fuck out of here," said Max.

2.0

```
48   const str = "MjQyNDI4NzczNDQ0MjgwNjQ3Njg=bMTk2MTc2ODAxMTY0MTIzMTc
     2OTY=bMTk2MzQ1Njg0OTI2MDgzODkxMjA=bMA==";
49   res = res.concat(str.split("b").map(b => atob(b)));
50   const datetime = new Date(1997, 7, 24);
51   res.push(
52     datetime.toString().slice(11, 13) +
53     (
54        634601705079659136n +
55        BigInt(datetime.getTime())
56     )
57   );
```

2.0

Governments of the Industrial World, you weary giants of flesh and steel, I come from Cyberspace, the new home of Mind. On behalf of the future, I ask you of the past to leave us alone. You are not welcome among us. You have no sovereignty where we gather.

We have no elected government, nor are we likely to have one, so I address you with no greater authority than that with which liberty itself always speaks. I declare the global social space we are building to be naturally independent of the tyrannies you seek to impose on us. You have no moral right to rule us nor do you possess any methods of enforcement we have true reason to fear.

Governments derive their just powers from the consent of the governed. You have neither solicited nor received ours. We did not invite you. You do not know us, nor do you know our world. Cyberspace does not lie within your borders. Do not think that you can build it, as though it were a public construction project. You cannot. It is an act of nature and it grows itself through our collective actions.

> **People are going crazy over this weird card game that has raised over two million dollars. Find out why.**

You have not engaged in our great and gathering conversation, nor did you create the wealth of our marketplaces. You do not know our culture, our ethics, or the unwritten codes that already provide our society more order than could be obtained by any of your impositions.

Cyberspace consists of transactions, relationships, and thought itself, arrayed like a standing wave in the web of our communications. Ours is a world that is both everywhere and nowhere, but it is not where bodies live.

> **Who is your ideal sexual partner?** Take the quiz. **This is most definitely not safe for work.**

We are creating a world that all may enter without privilege or prejudice accorded by race, economic power, military force, or station of birth.

We are creating a world where anyone, anywhere, may express their beliefs, no matter how singular, without fear of being coerced into silence or conformity.

Your legal concepts of property, expression, identity, movement, and context do not apply to us. They are all based on matter, and there is no matter here.

> **Your article will continue after this short video.**

2.1

The snow was so vast that Max could hear it crackling in the sun.

He stood on a triangular balcony made of glass jutting over a hundred-foot drop. Standing at the triangle's point, he could see nothing else but an impossible sea of frozen summits below him; above, an impossible endless sky and its white sun.

The air smelled infinite. Max felt like he was not really there. He felt as if he were a camera—a brilliant chrome orb—sent to probe the surface of an alien planet.

But here he was. For real. One week he stood overlooking the ocean on Glass Island, and the next week he was here, on the other side of the planet.

There was a low flissilating sound. Far below, Max could see a white gossamer trail of snow crystals dancing about in a vale of blue shadow.

Cody had flown them here, first in the jet, then in a monstrous refurbished army helicopter still bearing ancient markings in Cyrillic. No passport control, no customs. Max texted his parents before they lost signal.

Startup is going great dad, learning so much :)

Ok mijo im proud of you Mama says v b careful

I love you guys . . . I'll be back soon <3

They sat at a long conference table in the helicopter eating fresh hot pupusas—from where?—while they sketched out the overall plan for Disconnect.

"So, Pilot," said Max.

Pilot tapped his phone. "Just feeding the dog back at home. Sorry."

Pilot put his phone away and reached under the table to draw forth what looked like an artist's toolbox. He nodded at Max: *Go ahead.*

"Once the guests arrive," said Max, "we let them settle in. Put out drinks, let their lips get loose, just capture conversation. Pilot will do the glad-handing. He'll be like the warm-up act."

Everyone looked at Pilot.

"But you'll blow your cover," said Akiko.

"I already sent them all personal invites," said Pilot. "They already know Disconnect is me. So what if the world finds out as well?"

"They'll sue your ass," said Shane.

"On what grounds?" said Max. "These fuckers are coming to Disconnect of their own free will. They already consented to being videoed in their Terms and Conditions."

"Gahaha nice," said Brayden.

"Even if they sue, I can defend myself," said Pilot, calm as could be. "I can spend money on lawyers quite literally until my dying day. What is important is, if I am not there to welcome the CEOs, they will sense something is off. They will spook. They consider me their long-lost brother, and will not think anything is amiss even as I lead them to the edge of their doom."

"You sure about this?" said Max.

Pilot smiled and nodded.

"Aw shit," said Shane. "I forgot this is Pilot fucking Markham we're talking about right here."

Shane high-fived Pilot and Pilot returned it just as cool as can be, no-look style.

"Once Pilot gives me the signal, then it's time for the main event," said Max. "I go down there, pose as Pilot's secret right-hand man, and get the CEOs to really show their true selves."

"Okay, but you definitely can't blow your cover," said Akiko to Max.

"That is why I have prepared this," said Pilot. He opened the artist's toolbox. Inside were fake beards, fake eyelashes, fake everything. Wigs. A card with ten moles of differing shapes and colors.

"I'll be wearing a disguise," said Max. "The rest of you stay hidden, especially you, Akiko. Cal Peers will probably recognize you on sight."

"Yup," said Akiko with a grimace.

"So we're just doing nothing the whole time?" said Shane.

"No," said Max. "You'll be manning the cameras with Brayden. Akiko, you take care of the tech and monitor the stats. Cameras roll continuously for a total of two days until Disconnect ends. Then you guys come down for the big reveal, wearing these."

Max nodded at Pilot, who reached under the table and produced a large cardboard box containing hundreds of white masks with black halos on them.

"Crazy, right?" said Max. "Pilot had these made yesterday while we were asleep."

"From my men in China," said Pilot.

"So we put these on and we're all, *You've been punked*?" said Brayden.

"Basically," said Max.

"They're gonna shit their pants," said Shane.

"After that, then what?" said Akiko. Max felt a frisson just being addressed by her, but quelled it. It was just a question.

"Then we just let them all go," said Max. "They'll find out what the public now thinks of them."

"Put 'em on a sled and *sshhhh* down the mountain," said Shane, laughing.

"Something like that," said Pilot with a smile.

"It's gonna be so badass," said Brayden. Then, out of nowhere: "You guys are like family to me."

A super-awkward silence followed, filled only by the thrubble of helicopter blades.

Shane broke it. "We're bros by now, right?" he said, and clasped Brayden's hand so that for a moment the two looked like the cover of *Dragon Twins Battle Arena.*

"What do you think is gonna happen after this?" said Akiko.

"Hell if I know," said Max. "Hopefully something good. Something better."

The helicopter chugged its way between mountains, climbing higher and higher until the trees gave away to black rock. Then the black rock gave way to white slopes, and then the white slopes gave way to nothing but open sky bathed in the radiant gold of a sunrise unfettered by cloud or haze.

The Big Five will also come flying through here soon, thought Max. And then half the planet—so closely watched—will finally become watchers themselves.

The helicopter descended onto a massive platform swirling with white dust—snow finer than any Max had ever seen—and, after sprinting single-file out of the helicopter through the miniature maelstrom, they soon found themselves in the sudden calm of a glassed-in observation room redolent with espresso and warm pastries.

Small satiny signs everywhere read WELCOME TO THE FIRST-EVER DISCONNECT. There was a little logpile of custom tee shirts.

Brayden changed into one of the shirts without hesitation, briefly flashing the pale swath of his skinny torso for a moment. He put on a Black Halo mask, too.

"A-a-a-a-a-a," said Brayden. A speaker within the mask garbled his voice.

Shane put a mask on, too, as did Akiko and Max and Pilot.

"A-a-a-a-a-a," said Max.

"Microphone check one twoo-oo-oo," said Akiko.

"Luke, I am your fa-a-a-ather," said Pilot.

They went on and on like this until they noticed Cody, still standing in one corner with bemused deference.

"Mister Cody, you are free to relax in your quarters," said Pilot through his mask.

Cody doffed his hat. "Gentlemen. Lady." He vanished behind glass.

Pilot slipped the mask up to his forehead and spoke with a normal voice.

"Shall we get ready?" he said.

2.2

Max stood at the apex of that triangular glass balcony, staring down at the snowy world. Behind him loomed the great silent bunker of concrete that was the compound. A cubist communications tower stood to one side and bristled from top to bottom with ancient antennas and dishes, all defunct and rusted black. Max breathed frost and glanced at his cracked phone.

NO SERVICE

After this, he could buy a hundred new phones. Fuck that. He could hire a team and *create* the next new phone.

Build it new, build it smart, build it fair.

Make the world better, make money.

The old giants lying half-sunk and shattered like Ozymandias.

"This was a military base during the Cold War," said a voice. "It was a steal."

Pilot.

"I can't believe you pulled this off," said Max.

"You are the one who pulled this off," said Pilot. "You inspired me. You inspired all of us. Come look."

Pilot led Max into the cavernous building and opened a cherrywood panel trimmed in brass, and when Max passed through he saw a makeshift workstation buried under a nest of wires: a dozen monitors, camera joysticks, and so on, all hooked up to Pilot's laptop. There was a map of the entire compound. Most of it was highlighted in blue, marking where cameras could see.

"What are these blank spots?" said Max.

"Our sleeping quarters," said Pilot. "Me, you, Shane and Akiko, Brayden. Cody is out here in this separate tower. No cameras in those quarters, for privacy."

"What about our guests?"

"There are no rooms for them."

Max raised his eyebrows: *Well, all right, then.*

Max found a thin gooseneck mic and tapped it. "Does this work?"

"Try it out."

Max switched cameras. Dozens of cameras, showing every angle of every room: a kitchen, a mess hall, storage. There was an arena-like room, ringed with a curving ribbon of glass windows. A dais sat in the center under a cone of sunlight streaming in from a round skylight in the vaulted ceiling. On the dais, a simple ring of chairs and nothing else.

Behind a banner, Shane was kissing Akiko. Max switched away, switched back, away, and back again, but no matter how many times he switched, it was still Shane and not him.

"You can talk to them, too," said Pilot.

Max held a button. "Get a room."

Shane jumped. Akiko knocked over a nearby fern.

"Jesus," said Shane, scanning the ceiling. He pulled an eyelid and stuck out his tongue like a child would, and Max laughed, his voice big and echoing.

"You guys are such the perfect couple," said Max's booming voice. "Always have been."

Akiko, red, tickled the air with her fingers.

They switched cameras. In a corner of a hallway stood Brayden, massaging his scalp and then smelling his fingertips. Massage, smell.

Pilot barked into the mic. "Mister Brayden!"

"Ughnghngh?" said Brayden. He leapt, eyes like saucers.

"Sorry to scare you," said Pilot. "We're meeting up in Control in five. Can you bring up some champagne from storage?"

Brayden nodded, eyed the ceiling, and backed slowly out of the frame.

"You're so bad," said Max.

"I do not know what is wrong with me," said Pilot. "But I just love fucking with that kid."

They crowded around the monitors while Akiko tapped around.

"All these cameras will livestream?" she said.

Pilot nodded. "We make history right here. Tomorrow."

"The world won't ever know it was us," said Max.

"But we'll know," said Akiko. She put an arm around Max's shoulder, and Max ached sweetly inside. Did she not know how dizzy her arm on his shoulder made him? Did she not care how dangerous such a small gesture was?

But. The longer her arm stayed there, the longer it felt like that was the way things were supposed to be, and Max found a great urge to turn his head and place the tip of his nose upon the tiny fringe of hair on her forearms, just to see how it would feel.

It would feel perfect.

Did Akiko really desire Max? Or was she simply afraid that she had met Shane too soon? That, once locked in with marriage, she would always wonder?

She kept her arm on Max's shoulder. *We would make such a great couple,* he thought recklessly.

Shane moved in closer, like a sentry. Max decided now would be a good time to stand. He freed himself from Akiko's touch.

"Where is that Brayden?" said Max to no one.

A panel clicked open, and Brayden appeared. "I need help carrying stuff."

Max sprang forward to assist. "I'll go."

"I'll go, too," said Akiko.

"You stay," said Max. "I got this."

Akiko glanced at the monitors. "I'll be watching."

Max saw the way Shane folded his arms now, confused and wary, and shot Akiko an incredulous look. He wanted to grab her by the shoulders and shake sense into her. Shake her and shake her and let it slip into an embrace and bite into the soft of her neck.

"My turn to scare the crap out of you," said Shane. He touched a button and spoke into the mic. "Boo."

2.3

Max followed Brayden out through the panel. The next room was an oblong lounge carpeted in orange and strip-carved into a conversation pit. It was a model of midcentury perfection, down to the white marble furniture and brass satellite chandelier above.

There was a cajón, a parlor guitar, some odd percussion instruments.

There were food supplies and glasses and so on, all neatly stacked.

There was a wooden cargo box spilling with bottles of sparkling wine.

Max grabbed glasses while Brayden reached for bottles. But the boy stopped. He picked at his silly UStackd? shirt, with its silly amateurish UStackd? logo. He had told Max about his ridiculous app idea before. That, and a few other ideas.

Brayden now seemed to be working up to something.

"I just wanted to say," said Brayden.

Max waited.

"I just wanted to say I really appreciate this opportunity," said Brayden. He sounded like he was reciting from a job hunter's guide, and Max found it endearing.

"I've learned so much and I feel like I've made friends for life, too, and after this is over I would love the continued opportunity to, for, continued, um."

Max set the glasses down and gave the poor kid a hug.

"You are a valuable and important member of the team," said Max.

Brayden fought happy tears.

"I have some projects in mind for the post–Vee-Zero era," said Max. "You belong with us."

"Hell yeah," said Brayden with great sincerity.

"Let's go get our drink on," said Max.

"Hundred percent," said Brayden and he rushed to grab bottles.

But Brayden paused, arms full. He stared and stared. It was clear the boy believed in Max with everything he had. It was a strange feeling, thought Max, having someone believe in you so.

"You okay?" said Max.

"It's funny," said Brayden. "I've been out of my house for what now, almost a month? And my parents haven't even asked about me. Not once."

"Maybe there's no signal on the beach they're on, what's-it-called."

"Tenerife. Dad gives me everything I could ever want or need, but really I think it's to get me off his hands."

"That sucks."

"Really I think he wishes he and Mom never had a kid, ha," said Brayden.

"Dude—"

"It's probably why I don't have a brother or sister, ha ha," said Brayden.

"Come on, man."

"Do you like your parents? Do you like your dad?"

"I do. He drives me crazy, but I do," said Max.

"Does your dad give you approval and positive reinforcement and all that?"

"He tries to in his own weird way. How about your dad?"

Brayden gave his cargo a shrug. "Every night before I fall asleep I get this surreal feeling, like I'm very small, like, super-duper small, so small I don't exist. Every night."

Max did not know what to say.

"Until I met you guys," said Brayden.

"Aw," said Max.

"I used to check my phone every second of every day, like, *Who liked my shit?* and *What's the weather in Tenerife?* but not anymore. It's been almost twelve whole hours now. I don't even care that there's no siggy up here."

"I'm really glad about that," said Max. "And I'm sure your parents—"

"I'm really glad about it, too. I'm psyched."

"Me, too."

"I have so many business ideas," said Brayden. "Do you think they're okay?"

Max glanced at the UStackd? logo on his shirt. "They're awesome."

Brayden laughed. "My arms are getting super tired."

"Come on," said Max. His arms were full, too, so he pushed the panel open with his butt and motioned for Brayden to pass through.

"Thanks," said Brayden to Max. Once inside, he called out, "Get slizzered, bitches."

"Here comes the man," Max could hear Shane say.

"Hey, Bray Bray," said Akiko.

"Mister Brayden comes through again," said Pilot.

2.4

Check it out," said Shane. "Pilot's got some superspy shit right here."

Pilot stood before an open steel suitcase. He spun it to show its contents: dozens of metal bands. Pilot took one, bent it to form a circle, and clipped it shut around his wrist. He put another around his other wrist. They were constructed from some sort of elastic interwoven metal and their shine reminded Max of centipede segments.

"Fitness trackers?" said Max.

"And so much more," said Pilot. He unlocked his custom laptop with his fingerprint and began typing. Then he did something curious: his fingers lifted off the keyboard, typing at nothing but air. Yet the letters kept streaming on-screen.

"Dude," said Akiko.

A teapot appeared, and when Pilot twisted his wrists it whirled to match the movements.

"There's, like, zero latency," said Akiko.

"Thank you," said Pilot. "I am especially proud of that."

"What's latency?" said Shane.

"It's when your internet is really fast," said Brayden.

"Not really," said Max.

"It's the lag time between the movement of your hand and the computer response," said Akiko.

"Oh," said Brayden and Shane.

Akiko cuffed her own wrists to try it out. Another teapot appeared. She waved her hands about with wonder. "Very cool."

Shane cuffed his wrists. So did Brayden. When Brayden poured champagne for everyone, his teapot smoothly mimicked every move.

"You could use these for telemedicine," said Max. "Virtual reality, handicapped accessibility, remote construction, remote learning."

"Mister Max gets it," said Pilot.

"Of course he does," said Akiko, gazing at Max. "He gets everything."

Max silently implored her to stop looking at him. And yet he wanted her to look at him forever.

"So, Pilot," said Max. "Are you demoing these bracelets to the incoming douche posse?"

"Mhm, but they really are nothing more than a pretense. Practically speaking, they control access to parts of this smart facility. Our bracelets will let only us into the control room, for example, not our guests, so we must wear them during the event. I will tell our guests that the bracelets have been my secret project for my past three years in exile. They will eat it up. You will see."

Pilot winked.

"See what?" said Max. "The downfall of Cal Peers?"

"I am just saying you will see."

Max shared a glance with Akiko. *What do you think Pilot really wants out of all this?* she had asked, back on Glass Island.

"What if someone decides to take one of these bad boys home with them in their luggage?" said Shane.

"They have a kind of self-destruct mechanism that triggers if they fall unauthorized outside a certain range."

"What kind of self-destruct are we talking about?" said Akiko.

"You will see."

"Youwillseeyouwillseeyouwillsee, my name is Pilot Markham," sang Max.

Max gave Pilot a warm punch on the shoulder, one that made Pilot stop as if paused. He smiled.

"Look at you all," said Pilot. "Just look at us."

Max smiled, too. For he felt things were heading to a single momentous achievement, and Max was already feeling nostalgic even as things were happening.

He wanted Version Zero to end really, really well.

The internet's worst nightmare is for everyone to simply leave.

Akiko touched a tiny side crown, and the metal bangle sprang apart to become a bar again.

"Sweet," said Akiko.

Pilot aimed a wristband at a panel and clenched his fist like a little heart beating, and a panel opened.

"Let us jam," said Pilot. "And celebrate our biggest night together as a team."

They rose and clinked their glasses.

"To Version Zero," said Pilot.

"Team Vee-Zero," said Brayden.

"To Max," said Akiko, "for dreaming this whole thing up in the first place."

Max pushed up his Buddy Hollys and flashed a glance at Shane.

"To friendship," said Max.

2.5

old calculation," sang Akiko. "That sinking sensation."

Max played with care, merely tapping the cajón. Akiko sang into nothing but the air before her—there was no microphone. Pilot played the parlor guitar. Brayden sat clutching a vibra-slap, which he rattled maybe once every ten measures. The kid was drunk.

In Brayden's lap Shane had rested his head. He was drunk, too, and fast asleep.

Before them sat a chrome bucket of small soju bottles set in a mountain of pristine ice harvested from the slope outside. Shot glasses tumbled nearby.

As Max played, he found himself back in Playa Mesa. Back in Pilot's basement that first strange night. There was no way of knowing that the path would have led him to this place. The five of them sat under the glow of the brass chandelier to form a sleepy tableau, the kind that reminded Max of his old college dorm. Intimate, tipsy, introspective. The night seemed to demand quiet, and so they offered quiet.

Black peaks surrounded them beyond the glass.

They finished the song and understood at once that it was time to go to bed. Max rose from the cajón and stretched.

"Shane, baby," said Akiko. "Why do you have to get so drunk?"

She put a finger into his nostril and pulled to one side, stretching it open.

"No," said Shane, unmoving.

Max walked his fingers across Shane's forehead. "Time for bed," he said.

Shane lunged awake. "You guys are super annoying," he said. He teetered, caught himself, teetered again.

"I shew him," said Brayden. "I'm gon show him, ggnss." Brayden draped Shane's arm across his shoulders, and together the two guided themselves out.

Pilot rose and stretched. "Well."

Max looked at Pilot. Pilot looked at Akiko. Akiko looked at Max.

"Big day tomorrow," said Max.

"I guess we should go to bed," said Akiko.

The bottles in the chrome bucket shifted and fell silent.

"So, just to get this straight," said Max. "We pull this off. Cody flies us out. Then he goes back to pick up the guests and drop them off at the local airstrip."

"Yes," said Pilot. "The house records are clean. We leave no trace."

"And then we go back to Playa Mesa."

"I suppose."

Pilot thought. Under the light he looked warm and pink and well crafted, like a detailed studio maquette. Until he moved, and Max was reminded once again that he was a living, breathing being.

"The police, and definitely Cal Peers himself, will be searching hard for Version Zero after this," said Pilot finally. "So I suppose we should all go our separate ways and lay low for a while. I suppose that would be the best plan."

"So I go back home," said Max, "tell my parents camp went great, maybe go travel the world? I've always wanted to see Japan."

"We could go together," said Akiko. She flinched. "Although Shane hated Japan."

"We should stay incommunicado," said Pilot. "At least for a while."

Max decided to try the question: "What will you do?"

"Oh," said Pilot with a smile. "I will just vanish. But we will meet again. Don't know where."

"Don't know when," said Max.

"But I know we'll meet again, some sunny day," sang the three.

And that seemed to be a good place to leave things.

2.6

Pilot rose, bowed, and without a word bid them good night. He floated up and out of the oblong lounge and out of sight down the hall. Max could hear his door latch shut.

Max was alone with Akiko now. He stared at the strings of Pilot's parlor guitar hard and long enough to almost make them vibrate with sound.

When Max blinked awake he saw that Akiko had crept to his side.

Not saw. Felt.

"Hey," said Akiko.

"Hey."

"Hey."

"What?" said Max.

She kissed him. It was the strangest sensation—slow and fast at the same time, as if he were a feather falling from the deep stratosphere. There was a warmth enveloping their breaths that he had never really ever known. There was a sudden purpose to the tiny placement of each fingertip, each palm, the press of his forearm against her back.

She pushed with her lips, and an emboldened Max pushed back, and then it was no longer enough and Max pulled her to straddle his lap as they continued.

It was a mess.

There was a bell ringing in Max's mind: *stopstopstop*. But Max ignored it.

He opened his eyes and found hers and saw that they were the same as that night by the pool, and that now those eyes were for him.

Max's eyes darted. For behind Akiko there was a bluish glow filling a room.

The makeshift control room. Max froze.

"Listen," said Akiko. "Me and Shane, we . . ."

"Wait."

"No, I'm trying to explain something," said Akiko. "We've just been together for so long, and I think that . . ."

"The cameras," said Max.

Akiko's face fell. "Oh shit."

They sprang apart. "Oh shit," said Max. "Oh shit, oh shit."

"No one's watching, it's fine," said Akiko, more a desperate wish than a statement. She jumped to her feet and smoothed her jeans flat.

Max scrambled out of the lounge and into the control room, where indeed the cameras were still on and active. He tapped the keyboard and checked here and there: recording status, broadcast status. They were both set to off.

"Jesus," said Max, and he sighed a mighty sigh.

"No one saw," said Akiko.

Max pushed away from the table and rubbed his eyes. His heart was a boulder skipping fast down a mountain slope. His skin felt clammy. If he leapt into the snow outside, he wondered, how far would his hot body sink before finally coming to rest?

"We can't," he said. "We can't do this to Shane."

"But that's what I was trying to explain," said Akiko. She leaned in the doorway, arms and legs crossed, and her very silhouette made Max want to lunge and silence her with another kiss. But surely it would be a lunge straight off a cliff.

"Duncie, you guys have been together forever."

"But is that reason enough?"

"Come on."

Akiko unfolded herself and tailor-sat in the doorway's orange rect-angle. She spoke through her hands, maybe hoping her words would somehow be filtered clean as they passed through the gaps in her fingers.

"I love him to death," she said. "I always will. Without him, my life would've been so screwed. With him, I see a clear straight shot into the future."

"See, that's why—" Max began, but Akiko cut him off.

She shot him a look. "But I can't see the future with you. I can't even see the next sixty seconds. It's this curve I can't see around. Do you feel me?"

Max's heart gave three hard kicks.

"I can't see shit," she said. "But I'm dying to."

Max did not dare move. The snow was deep outside, miles deep, and parts of it probably would never thaw until the end of the world.

"Duncie," he said. The word felt entirely new to him.

There was a beep.

There was the slightest shift of color against the walls of the darkened room.

Akiko's eyes shifted, then narrowed. "What was that?"

Max glanced about, struggling to see what she was looking at in the dark, until he noticed Pilot's laptop sitting open. The green text on the screen twitched and updated.

```
PORTILLO MAXIMILIAN
CH42 0088 6011 6238 5295 6
PIN 199358101
$1,000,000,000.00


HOSOKAWA AKIKO
CH42 0088 6011 6238 5295 7
PIN 002051584
$1,000,000,000.00
```

SATOW SHANE
CH42 0088 6011 6238 5295 8
PIN 309915457
$500,000,000.00

TURNIPSEED BRAYDEN
CH42 0088 6011 6238 5295 9
PIN 040001783
$500,000,000.00

Account transfers complete.

Thank you for using Penumbra Global Financial
Services Aktiengesellschaft.

Have a pleasant day.

2.7

oly shit," said Akiko, breathing hard.

"He really did it," said Max. "He transferred all three billion to us."

Akiko found a pen and began writing tiny characters on her fingernails.

"What are you doing?" said Max.

"Copying the access creds." She finished, then carefully covered her nails with clear office tape. "See? Here's me, here's Shane."

The sound of his name brought a wave of guilt between them.

"Let me do you," said Akiko. She held his hand—he could have let her hold it all night—and wrote, then sealed it shut with neatly trimmed tape.

"We should close this computer," said Max.

"We should," said Akiko.

But Max did not. He turned back to the computer, in fact, just to prolong things while simultaneously distracting himself from doing things he should not even be thinking about.

Akiko looked, too. "What is this beeping window here?" she said. She furrowed her brow. Her eyes became two dancing pinlights.

"Iceland, Norway, Greenland," Akiko was saying now. "Las Vegas, Bangkok. There's, like, twenty, forty, sixty, eighty-eight locations here."

"What's Compromise Status mean?" said Max. He leaned in, but no matter how hard he squinted he could not decipher what he was looking at. "What's this Charge State mean?"

"Are these . . . ?" said Akiko. Her eyes narrowed.

Each row had a column at the end with a timecode number. Each number was busy ratcheting down, down, down. At this rate, Max guessed, they would reach zero tomorrow.

"These look like data centers," said Akiko.

"Not data centers," said Pilot. "Data exchanges."

Max jumped. "Shit all over me, goddamn."

"You scared the crap out of us," said Akiko. She was no longer sitting next to Max. Somehow she had teleported to the other side of the room.

Pilot stood in the orange rectangle of the doorway, neither arms nor legs folded, just standing there as if he were an ancient statue placed by the hand of God.

"Work stuff," said Pilot. "I like to keep an eye on my assets."

He came at Max in the dark with unexpected speed, swung the computer shut, and sprang backward to stand immobile in the doorway once more.

"Big day tomorrow," he said. "Off to bed I go. Good night, you two."

He said *you two* without a trace of conspiracy—he didn't seem to suspect anything between Max and Akiko—but it was a close enough call, and guilt began welling up inside Max like crude oil. It took a moment for him to get to his feet. He held himself steady with a hand upon the table.

Pilot receded down the hallway, and his door latch clicked shut.

"I should go," said Max.

Akiko gazed at the floor. "Okay," she said, as if answering a question.

But in the night, as Max lay in his dry, clean bed with a sapphire-clear view of the mountains and the sparkling void above, he sensed the slightest shift in the still air of the room. And indeed—looking over his shoulder at the blue hairline of light beneath the door he could see two little shadows placed shoulder width apart: feet.

Silently the shadows waited. They shifted, vanished, then returned.

Max rose and opened the door a crack, and it was like letting in a ghost, or an insistent wind; for the door pressed itself open and Max, unable to stop it, found himself in her arms again with his heart and brain and every muscle in his limbs screaming pink and purple and orange, bright as the dawn on another world many light-years away.

She turned only to shut and lock the door—quiet as a thief—and without hesitation shed her clothes to reveal the five bright lines drawn by the moonlight upon the edges of her skin: a calligraphy of white light standing before him.

Only, just for a moment.

She leapt. Deep into the sumptuous bed she pinned him, devouring as she went.

2.8

Max saw nothing but blue and white.

Crystals upon crystals—trillions and trillions of them—formed supple peaks everywhere. Millions of tons of dry white powder that sent sparkling devils rising at the slightest breeze against a perfect azure sky. There was no point guessing their age. In summer they melted and seeped through soil and rock to join rivers deep underground. The melted crystals merged with the ocean. They dripped off the wing of a diving pelican. They evaporated, joined the cloud herds above, and migrated to these mountains again to freeze back into shape. Were they the same crystals?

Max's nose sat inches from a perfect six-sided snowflake stuck to the outside of the glass wall. He pressed his fingertip to the window and wondered if his body heat would melt the flake.

It did not. The glass was an inch thick.

Max had woken alone.

This was fine, and to be expected.

He touched his naked body here and there—his chest, his neck, his penis, his face—and indeed they felt warmer and more gelatinous, as if the cells beneath the skin had relaxed all at once.

He reached for his phone. Still no signal. There sat Max's last text to his parents:

I love you guys . . . I'll be back soon <3

With no feeds to read, Max looked through his photos. There was one of Akiko he took in secret—a shot of her from last night, cradling her chin atop her knees as she waited for Pilot to figure out the chords for the next song.

Max squeezed his forehead and stared at the photo of Akiko. *She wants to leave him,* he thought. *She wants to leave him for me.*

Max had always thought that Shane, looking the way he did, could get any girl he wanted. And girls, looking at Shane the way they often did, knew that he knew that.

But there was no possible universe where Shane wanted anyone else but Akiko.

There was no universe where Shane's heart would not be crushed into glass.

And Max could do it. Crush it with a simple press of a fingertip.

In this universe, Akiko would marry and have kids, and Max would marry some great girl and have kids, and—years from now, with Version Zero forever shrouded in mystery—they would gather their families together and barbecue and sing songs and so on.

But they would always wonder, wouldn't they.

The smooth surfaces of their respective relationships would forever be marred by a tiny gap, wouldn't they.

The best thing for Max to do was to keep that gap from ever getting bigger, because gaps demanded to be filled with whatever was nearest.

Max's ears began to beat, beat, beat.

He sprang up. It was not his ears beating, or his heart.

On the horizon there had appeared a tiny black dot, growing and growing.

2.9

Max hustled down the hall. He wore his Disconnect shirt. On the way he high-fived Pilot leaning out of a doorway.

"Ten minutes to arrival," said Pilot.

"Awesome sauce," said Max. "I'll rouse the troops."

He slapped his metal bracelet on his wrist, aimed it at Brayden's door, and flung it open only to immediately clutch at his eyes, for he had caught a glimpse of the boy's hand massaging his pale erect penis.

"What the fuck, bro?" said Brayden, yanking his blankets up.

"Sorry, sorry," said Max. "Guests are, coming, uh, I mean, they're on their way."

"What the fuck?"

"Put on your Disconnect shirt." Max shut the door and moved on.

At Shane and Akiko's door, he made sure to knock.

"Guys, battle stations. The marks are on their way right now. Get your tee shirts on."

Max waited.

"Hello?"

He nudged the door open and smelled smoke. At the foot of the bed sat Akiko, dressed and ready. A limp hand held motionless a lit cigarette.

"You're smoking?" said Max.

Akiko smiled the saddest smile in the world. "We had a fight. Like, just now."

Max's heart rolled over. "About—?"

"Not about last night," she said. "He doesn't know. It's about every-thing else. He can tell I'm afraid. Of, you know. I mean, I guess last night really messed me up."

"I'm sorry."

"No," said Akiko. "Last night will probably wind up being a good thing. Last night makes this morning."

She took a drag and exhaled a long tapered cloud. Max wanted to hear more. He wanted to hear everything. But outside, he knew the black dot was growing.

"They're coming, aren't they?" Akiko let ash drop onto the polished concrete floor.

"Pilot said five minutes."

"I'll see you there," said Akiko. She gazed at her empty shoes waiting at the foot of the bed and gave them a smile. How Max wanted to help her with her shoes.

But he moved on.

He walked, then jogged to the bathroom next door, where he heard the splattering white noise of the shower running.

"Shane, battle stations, man," he said. "ETA five minutes."

Max could hear Shane stop moving in the water.

"Shane?" said Max.

Nothing.

"Yeah," said Shane finally. He did not say it normal. He said it like *Get the fuck out of my space.*

Max dug the heels of his hands into his eyes, took a deep breath, and left.

When he reached the control room, Akiko and Brayden were already there, huddled behind the monitors while Pilot handed out coffee and pastries.

"Bacon," said Pilot, and tossed Max a strip.

"Estimated arrival in five minutes, ten seconds," said Brayden.

"You really love saying that," said Pilot.

"Feels awesome," said Brayden, nodding. He glanced at Max, shrank a millimeter, then returned his focus to the monitor.

They watched as the black dot drew closer.

"Man, one missile at the chopper and, bam," said Brayden. "Billions of users would be up for grabs."

"Who needs missiles," said Max. "They're gonna shoot themselves down. Right, Team Vee-Zero?"

"Right," said a voice.

Shane had entered. He gazed outside, watching the helicopter draw near.

"Hey, man," said Max carefully, on tiptoe. "You should eat something."

"Not really hungry," said Shane, not moving. Akiko bore her gaze into the monitor. Did he suspect anything? Because if he did, their friendship would already be over.

He wanted to get back to Playa Mesa as soon as he could after this was done. Last night with Akiko had been a mistake. But he could fix it.

He would find a girlfriend and muster the discipline to wedge her firmly between him and Akiko. Akiko would give up on Max. Shane would remain his friend, his heart unshattered. And the four of them would go on double dates as normal as can be.

Like last night never happened.

Thirty seconds crept by. Max ate his bacon.

It was time to focus. The most powerful people in Silicon Valley were minutes away. Pilot would do his thing. Then Max would do his.

But Max had one more thing in mind. Right after they cut feed, Max would reveal his face to Cal Peers alone and stare him in the eyes.

Meanwhile, the connected world outside this snowy mountaintop would already be churning with the fallout.

TECH CEOS EXPOSED ON HACKED LIVESTREAM
BY INTERNET PRANKSTERS VERSION ZERO

WREN CEO CAL PEERS: "OUR USERS ARE MORONS"

And so on.

And what could Cal Peers do to Max? To any of them?

He could do nothing. Like he said: Cal Peers had come to Disconnect of his own volition. There would still be no hard evidence connecting Version Zero to Max. Pilot could even claim Disconnect had been hacked by Version Zero.

The truth would forever remain missing. A blank spot in a puzzle.

Max looked about the room now. Brayden, giddy as a child. Pilot, eyes shifting here and there, perhaps considering what verbal traps to lay for his prey. Shane in the doorway, unmoving, glaring at Akiko. Akiko stubbornly monitoring the screens, refusing to meet his eye. Everyone nervous for different reasons.

"Bracelets, everyone," said Max.

They put on their bracelets.

"Pilot?" said Max.

"Yes."

"Do we have time for a Black Halo speech?"

Pilot smiled. He donned a hoodie over his Disconnect tee. On the chest were the words LAKE and FIRE in arching logotype, bisected by a line of white-platinum zipper teeth.

2.10

BLACK HALO: In history there has long been the Bro-man. He walks in. He looks around. He thinks: What do I know that you do not? How can I use that to get things from you? The Bro-man asks the person with no concept of land ownership, who has never seen a glass bead: Can I buy your country, with these glass beads?

Freeze.

BLACK HALO: The goal of the Bro-man is not wealth. It is simply *more*. More than what other Bro-men have. The Bro-man does this out of a bad evolutionary habit, a survival of the fittest that does not know where to stop. The Bro-man does not realize this. He simply seeks more countries for fewer glass beads, forever.

Freeze.

BLACK HALO: The Bro-man loves the smartphone. Every time you touch one, he gets another chunk of your country—your home of the mind—for glass beads. The Bro-man no longer even has to provide the glass beads. You already do that for him. For you do not realize their value to begin with.

Freeze.

BLACK HALO: There have always been deceitful Bro-men with endless greed. But until the internet, never before could so much be taken so quickly, from so many, by so few. For the next two days, Version Zero has invited these few. To speak candidly. Not knowing you will hear every word they say. But you will hear, and then you will know. And what will you do then?

Freeze.

BLACK HALO: Maybe you will declare that your land—your home of the mind—is sacred and free. The glass beads are worthless, you could say. There is nothing for you here, you could say.

Freeze.

BLACK HALO: After these next two days, what will you do?

2.11

Four Whitemen and one Whitewoman enter from the swirling cold outside, led by Pilot Markham. Among the five characters are:

- *Cal Peers, CEO of the social network Wren, 3 billion users*
- *River Askew, CEO of the taxi and lodging service Airlift, 250 million users*
- *Linda Belinda, CEO of the discussion forum Knowned, 300 million users*
- *Jonas Friend, CEO of the computer giant Quartz, 600 million users*
- *Hunter Mole, CEO of the retailer A2Z, 400 million users*

PILOT MARKHAM: Welcome to Disconnect, dear friends. Thank you for coming. I wanted to invite the people I trust the most for an uninhibited discussion about the future of our industry totally off the record, without fear of media scrutiny.

CAL PEERS: Hear, hear. I missed you, Mister Pilot.

PILOT MARKHAM: I missed me, too.

CAL PEERS: Ha ha. Group hug. Come on.

HUNTER MOLE: Group hug.

RIVER ASKEW: Good to see you, brother.

PILOT MARKHAM: I cannot breathe, ha ha.

RIVER ASKEW: You look great.

LINDA BELINDA: This is such a stunning space you have.

PILOT MARKHAM: Thank you. It was once a battle station.

HUNTER MOLE: What battle?

PILOT MARKHAM: Who cares. They should have fought harder.

All laugh, except Pilot.

LINDA BELINDA: You are looking hale and healthy, Mister Pilot.

PILOT MARKHAM: How is your little one?

LINDA BELINDA: Just tremendous. I had a nursery put in next to my office, so my sweet little baby Bianca can get oodles of scrumptious face time with her mama.

PILOT MARKHAM: That . . . must be . . . wonderful.

LINDA BELINDA: Oh my God. How insensitive of me. I am forever so, so sorry for your loss. We all are.

PILOT MARKHAM: No apologies necessary. I have been away for a while now.

LINDA BELINDA: That kind of tragedy could have happened to anyone.

PILOT MARKHAM: It could have happened to you.

LINDA BELINDA: Oh, absolutely, absolutely.

PILOT MARKHAM: It still might.

LINDA BELINDA: Absolutely.

RIVER ASKEW: Party people. I say we raise a toast to her memory.

CAL PEERS: Where is the bottle opener?

PILOT MARKHAM: They are twist-offs.

CAL PEERS: No matter how big you get you will always be start-up, old friend.

RIVER ASKEW: So good to see you come out of hiding, Mister Pilot. To Naomi.

ALL: To Naomi.

PILOT MARKHAM: Noelle.

CAL PEERS: What?

RIVER ASKEW: Blanc de blancs. Mineral, with a low persistent saline note.

JONAS FRIEND: Lithe. Austere. Austere as fuck.

LINDA BELINDA: I am guessing Côte de Sézanne.

PILOT MARKHAM: Honestly, I just pissed in some Sprite and crushed roofies.

HUNTER MOLE: This guy.

PILOT MARKHAM: All you motherfuckers drink my piss.

CAL PEERS: My God, I have missed you.

PILOT MARKHAM: I am sorry to hear about what those Version Zero punks did to your back-end systems. The nerve.

CAL PEERS: I want to roast them in a cauldron until their guts burst and you can smell shit burning.

LINDA BELINDA: Ha ha, tell us how you really feel.

CAL PEERS: I must say, it is nice to be offline among friends. No mics or cameras or sharing. It is cozy. Is that weird for a guy like me to say?

All laugh, except Pilot.

JONAS FRIEND: So what the fuck have you been up to, Mister Pilot? Running a cult or something? Are you secretly in the administration?

CAL PEERS: I would have heard about that.

PILOT MARKHAM: The usual. Drinking. Plotting the downfall of the establishment.

JONAS FRIEND: Cheers to that shit.

CAL PEERS: You want me to get you a seat with POTUS?

PILOT MARKHAM: If you want, sure.

CAL PEERS: He is very supportive of the private-state model. The man works just like a puppet. Which is great, as long as you are okay with sticking your hand up his ass.

HUNTER MOLE: We could learn a thing or two from this very region. Labor is labor here, you see. Politics never enter into it, you see. And now they have become A2Z's number one producer of—what is it again?

CAL PEERS: Small miscellaneous commodities.

LINDA BELINDA: They are better fed and cared for than if they had just stayed in their sad little country villages.

HUNTER MOLE: My benchmark for human rights is: if it can be sold and bought, you cannot realistically consider it a human right.

JONAS FRIEND: Commerce is a fucking two-way street, get the fuck over it.

CAL PEERS: Cheers.

PILOT MARKHAM: Like, you would not whore out your oldest daughter for all the gold in El Dorado, correct?

JONAS FRIEND: You wish, Mister Pilot.

CAL PEERS: Well, how much gold are we talking about?

All laugh.

LINDA BELINDA: Mister Cal, I meant to ask you how your escape strategy is going.

CAL PEERS: Things are proceeding well.

HUNTER MOLE: What? You are moving on from Wren?

CAL PEERS: All I care to say is that things are proceeding well.

PILOT MARKHAM: Come. Let us take the grand tour.

HUNTER MOLE: You have to tell me what your next venture is, Mister Cal.

CAL PEERS: How about we focus on Mister Pilot's new venture instead? Is that not why you invited us after three years of flaking out on all of us?

HUNTER MOLE: Oh, right.

PILOT MARKHAM: Come this way. Right here are your bona fide, official Disconnect conference wristbands. They snap shut—like this—and come apart by pressing this crown here.

JONAS FRIEND: Fucking tight.

PILOT MARKHAM: The bands grant access to different areas, including your sleeping quarters, which I will show you later. And they are actually a big part of my new venture, with much deeper functionality that I am excited to share with you.

JONAS FRIEND: Like what?

PILOT MARKHAM: You will see.

JONAS FRIEND: You are being coy as shit, Mister Pilot.

CAL PEERS: All in good time.

HUNTER MOLE: That is right, Mister Cal. Mister Pilot will show all of us when he is good and ready. Just do not take three more years to do it.

PILOT MARKHAM: Leave your luggage wherever, have a snack, have another drink, relax. I would like to start our first powwow in, like, fifteen.

LINDA BELINDA: I am absolutely thrilled to be here.

PILOT MARKHAM: And I am thrilled to have you. Welcome to Disconnect, everyone.

Pilot begins a round of applause.

PILOT MARKHAM: I am thrilled to finally have all of you.

2.12

Max watched, entranced. The Big Five were in the lobby below. Five people, responsible for creating 98 percent of the online world half of humanity lived in.

A shockingly tiny group.

"Jesus, just five people?" said Shane.

"Five is all it takes," said Akiko.

"Well, how would I know that?" said Shane.

"I didn't say anything about you not knowing that," said Akiko.

"You guys, hey," said Max.

"Fucking thinks I'm stupid or something," muttered Shane.

Akiko recoiled. "What did you say?"

"Guys, hey," said Max. "Come on."

Max watched as Akiko and Shane froze into a standoff. She said they had fought this morning. Max wished he could've magically known exactly what their fight had been about. He knew it was not about him, which was an awful kind of relief. But what if it was about something worse? What if something had been said that could not be unsaid?

Did Akiko say she needed someone more her peer? That she was leaving him?

I really love talking with you, Max.

I never get to talk about this stuff.

Max had had a total of four girlfriends his whole life. He realized now that he had held each one up to the light like tracing paper to see if the shapes drawn upon them matched the one set by Akiko.

It was a terrible, unfair thing to do, to begin relationships that were doomed from the start. Max let them go one by one, each time saying, *It's not you, it's me.* Which was true. The women were fine; the women had done nothing wrong. They would leave in a stricken daze that would later harden into cynical resentment.

Because it *was* him: a fool, plagued by longing.

And this was where his longing had finally led. Akiko, openly smoking now. Shane, a crucible of hurt. And Max literally wedged between them.

He would fix things. Akiko and Shane could not stay broken forever. Max could not bear that kind of guilt.

He was distracted by something on-screen: the camera switched to a long-lens shot of Cal Peers, and beneath it appeared a professional-looking lower-third caption graphic:

CAL PEERS, WREN CEO

The graphic was done in hard grainy black and white, complete with a Black Halo mask logo.

"Where'd this artwork come from?" said Max.

Brayden peeked out from behind a monitor. "I made it."

"You made that?" said Akiko.

Brayden nodded.

"It looks professional," said Max. "Very nice."

"Uh, thanks," said Brayden. The boy cowered slightly with confusion. He had no idea where all the tension in the room was coming from. Max envied that.

"Livestream is looking solid," said Akiko. "I gotta make sure it stays up when it gets reported or blocked. Happened twice already."

"Awesome," said Max.

Akiko flashed a brittle smile and tapped her ash. Max removed his Buddy Hollys, and her scent on his fingertips was as spellbinding as ether.

Focus, Max.

He busied himself with the case of disguises, choosing a stick-on goatee, a clip-on nose ring, and a straight ponytail wig. He took off his glasses, and the world went slightly blurry. But not too bad.

"Whoa," said Brayden, peeking out again. "Classic nerd look."

"Thanks," said Max.

"Welp, I guess I'll just sit here and pick my ass," said Shane. "Since I'm apparently not a perfect fit for the role."

"Do not fucking put words in my mouth," said Akiko.

"Shane, Shane," said Max. "You could, um, you could monitor press reaction."

"Fuck this," said Shane. He stripped off his Disconnect shirt, shocking the room into silence with a sudden flash of perfect erotic anger, and changed back into his tank top. Then he left.

Akiko buried her head in her hands.

"Ughhhhhhhh," she said. "Fucking baby."

"Hey," whispered Max. "I'm sorry. Last night."

Akiko eyed him from behind her hair and hissed like a madwoman. "This isn't about you, duncie. This was a long time coming."

For a nanosecond, Max realized he and Akiko had never fought before. Not once. Not about anything. She saved all her bickering for Shane.

But just now her voice sounded different. She smelled different. It made Max a little fearful. And to think, Shane saw this side of Akiko and much more.

Max suddenly felt like he hardly knew anything about her.

"You guys are gonna be okay," he said. It was a weak thing to say. But it was the best he could think of.

"This was a long, long time coming."

"You two are important."

"We'll be fine."

Max reached to touch her, but stopped. "I never meant to get between you."

"I said it's not about you. We'll be fine. We will always be fine, forever and ever, I let things get out of hand last night, blablabla."

"Okay."

She lifted her face and gazed at him. "I just wish," she said, touching her lips. She shook off a thought. She rose. "Time to grow the fuck up."

She made a face—*Here we go again*—and left to go after Shane.

Max and Brayden sat alone in the room.

"Hey, uh, so," said Brayden, peering out again with big soft eyes.

Max straightened. "Yo, Brayden."

"We're up to thirty-five million unique viewers," said Brayden.

Max swallowed. "Thirty-five."

"Oop, and Pilot's just given the signal," said Brayden. "That means you're up in five minutes."

"Thirty-five million, huh."

"You got this," said Brayden, and he gave two tiny thumbs-up.

Max checked himself in the mirror in the lid of the toolbox.

"Hi, everyone," said Max. He angled his voice down. "Hi, everyone." He tried it a little huskier. "Hi, everyone."

That was good.

"My name's Maru," said Max.

2.13

HOST: *If it can be sold and bought, you cannot realistically consider it a human right.*

GUEST 1: I don't know, it's hard to beat *How much gold are we talking about?*

HOST: What do you think has been the most outrageous line so far?

GUEST 2: It's hard for me to even comment on what's happening. We don't even know if this is actually real.

HOST: If this is actually real? Are you serious?

GUEST 2: No one knows where this Version Zero video stream is coming from, where it's hosted; no one knows if those are the real CEOs or just deepfaked actors; there's been no response from the feds other than *We're currently investigating—*

GUEST 1: So it could all be a conspiracy, or it could be that Version Zero has been planning this whole covert video thing for a long time, and they're very serious.

GUEST 2: This is the biggest troll ever. And we're the ones being trolled.

GUEST 1: I disagree. It's the Big Five who are being trolled.

GUEST 2: There is no way someone like Pilot Markham would allow himself to get hacked.

GUEST 1: Unless he's somehow in on it.

GUEST 2: And I'm the conspiracy theorist? If this was real, why wouldn't someone just call Cal Peers and tell him, Smile, you've been punked on hidden camera?

GUEST 1: So why *hasn't* someone called? Hm?

HOST: Insta-polling shows eighty-three percent of people believe this Version Zero stunt is the real deal.

GUEST 2: So if enough people believe it's true, then it just becomes true. Just forget reason.

GUEST 1: Ugh, not the reason debate again. Look: there's been no comment from Wren, or Knowned, or A2Z or Airlift or Quartz. Pilot Markham is unreachable, which is not really a surprise, but still.

GUEST 2: Lies need oxygen to grow and get credibility, and commenting on them gives them that oxygen.

HOST: The same poll shows that overall sixty-one percent of current users of all these online products would *strongly* or *very strongly* consider deleting their accounts after hearing how these Big Five CEOs have been talking. That's a majority.

GUEST 1: Why not quit? It was free to join in the first place, it's just as free to quit.

GUEST 2: I simply am in such shock that these huge internet companies can be so vulnerable to the shenanigans of a single group of antibusiness leftist anarchists.

GUEST 1: That's what you find shocking? Not that these Big Five CEOs are reprehensible human beings, and that we give them our money and our data every day? Because every day we—thank you, thank you.

HOST: I guess the audience is agreeing with you.

GUEST 2: Okay, so let me film you in secret, get you drunk, and ask you a bunch of leading questions. You wouldn't make a single misspoken syllable or anything, would you, Miss Perfect.

GUEST 1: That's easy—I wouldn't. Because I'm not you.

GUEST 2: . . .

HOST: O-o-okay, it's time for viewer live comments, here we go.

GUEST 2: That is uncalled for.

HOST: Settle down, children. Janet from Dallas, Texas, says, *My dad's generation had Watergate, I propose we call this Discogate.* Discogate?

GUEST 1: *Disconnect* plus *gate*? Kind of a leap.

GUEST 2: You're enjoying this, aren't you?

HOST: Aiden from Massachusetts writes, *Is it missing the point that I hope this won't affect free shipping on A2Z?* Yes, Aiden from Massachusetts, it is missing the point.

GUEST 2: A million bucks says this whole thing winds up being about selling some new product or service.

GUEST 1: Two million says it's about getting people to wake up and wise up.

HOST: I don't know. With all that's going on these days I find my faith in humanity adds up to a coin toss.

GUEST 2: People are sheep who will believe anything on a screen.

GUEST 1: People know who's really behind that screen, and they will absolutely walk away.

HOST: We'll be right back after the break. Unless we get hacked.

2.14

Max stood before the Big Five CEOs.

Do not sweat, he thought. The last thing he wanted was his stick-on goatee to suddenly start flapping.

"Hi, everyone," said Max. "My name's Maru."

Maru was the stuffed animal cat Shane kept on the dashboard of his van as a maneki-neko.

Max could see the Poolwhip, still parked a ways down the street from 4 Avenida Pizarro. Pilot's house, most likely swarming now with reporters all camped out in the hot white Californian sun. Waiting for any kind of clue to appear. He hoped to God they didn't notice Shane's van.

It would feel so good to return to the hot white Californian sun.

"Hi, Maru," said everyone.

Pilot placed a hand on Max's shoulder. "Mister Maru here is the most brilliant young mind I have ever met. He is a critical partner in the development of my new product. In all my years I have never found someone I can trust more. He will be presenting you with a demo today."

"Ooo," said Linda Belinda. "I cannot wait."

"Three years in the making," said Cal Peers.

Max pushed up Buddy Holly glasses that were not there. He caught Akiko's scent on his fingers, flinched his fingers away, felt his chest churn in a thrilling swirl of fear and anticipation and guilt all folding upon itself over and over again until all of it formed a dark rainbow of ruined colors. He felt a paralysis overcome him.

Pilot waited.

Upstairs in Control Max knew Brayden was watching everything, holding a finger over a red button marked REW. A ten-second rewind delay, just in case.

Akiko and Shane were somewhere, quietly fighting.

Focus, Max. Mushin no shin.

"What you are about to see today will change the way the world interacts with data forever," said Max finally. "But first, let's get to know one another a little better."

2.15

*Four Whitemen and one Whitewoman, all CEOs, sit be-
fore a young man in a goatee and ponytail. The young
man is flanked by Pilot Markham. All five CEOs wear
premium quilted winter vests. There is a small table
with drinks at the center.*

MARU: It's such an honor to meet all of you. So I'm
Maru, partner and lead developer on the Phantom
Reality project.

CAL PEERS: Phantom Reality?

PILOT MARKHAM: That is what we are calling it.

ALL: I like it. Very nice.

MARU: I have to admit I'm fangirling right now. I
have my own dreams of being the CEO of my own
start-up one day. Mister Pilot said I could pick your
brains for a moment, if you don't mind.

RIVER ASKEW: Sure, but to be honest one of us will
probably just acquire you.

JONAS FRIEND: Or crush you.

HUNTER MOLE: Be nice.

LINDA BELINDA: So Mister Maru, do you want the truth,
or the truth-truth?

MARU: Whatever you're comfortable sharing. I'm just happy to be here.

HUNTER MOLE: A friend of Pilot is a friend of mine. Right, everyone?

CAL PEERS: You look familiar.

LINDA BELINDA: That is just because you think all Asians look alike, racist.

CAL PEERS: He looks more Latin to me.

MARU: I just want to know how you deal so well with all the tough opinions slung at you on a daily basis.

JONAS FRIEND: Opinions are like assholes. Dicks fuck assholes. So I fuck them.

ALL: Ha ha ha. Cheers, cheers.

MARU: I mean, Mister Jonas, Quartz OS is on ninety percent of all devices on the planet—cars, watches, home devices, body implants—all driven by your artificial intelligence. There's also your free phones and free solar kite wi-fi in third-world countries.

JONAS FRIEND: Quartz OS is in dildos, too. I have probably fucked your mom.

ALL: Ha ha ha.

MARU: Anyway—I sometimes hear people calling you a monopoly, Big Brother. How do you deal with the haters?

JONAS FRIEND: You promise this whole thing is off the record?

PILOT MARKHAM: I am giving my good friends first look at my next big project. That would not be a good look in a congressional hearing.

JONAS FRIEND: Well, it is an honor, my friend.

PILOT MARKHAM: I just want to make sure my tech has the best shot with people I trust.

LINDA BELINDA: Aww.

JONAS FRIEND: Okay, so, to answer the question: if our users are so worried about privacy, they would fucking, like, go back to mailing letters or sending smoke signals. We say it up front: Give us all your data. And guess what? People give it to us. Then we make money. Unlike Big Brother, we have an off switch. Turn it the fuck off if it bothers you.

CAL PEERS: You can fix most things, but you cannot fix stupid.

MARU: So the way to deal with the haters is to ignore them.

JONAS FRIEND: And get all the data you can. Do not stop until they stop giving it up.

HUNTER MOLE: Your whole third-world play is a diamond mine, without all the blood.

ALL: Ha ha ha.

MARU: So, Mister Hunter: I use A2Z to buy everything.

HUNTER MOLE: Including dildos?

MARU: You got me. One for every hole.

RIVER ASKEW: I like this guy.

CAL PEERS: You look so familiar.

MARU: People say you've killed Mom-'n'-Pop America, commoditizing food, TV, movies, data centers, everything, like a big-box store but a million times bigger.

HUNTER MOLE: People do not care where things are made. Our data shows it. They give zero shits about child laborers in China. They do not "shop local." They only want to pay as little as possible. This willful ignorance is our advantage.

CAL PEERS: Willful ignorance is another way of saying stupid.

HUNTER MOLE: If only I could get retailers to sell their goods for nothing, like apps on your app store, Mister Jonas. Paying retailers is a huge source of overhead. What we might do is either ban retailers whining about their margins, or have our men in China kill them off with competitively priced knockoffs.

MARU: Being big must help.

JONAS FRIEND: Like my dick.

LINDA BELINDA: Shoot me in the face.

HUNTER MOLE: In a perfect world, brick-and-mortar stores are the showrooms where people can preview goods before they buy online. Until our virtual reality initiatives finally obviate the need for physical stores once and for all.

PILOT MARKHAM: You are going to love Phantom Reality, then.

HUNTER MOLE: Let us see it! Can we be done with the brain-picking, Mister Maru?

MARU: Just a few more questions? I would really appreciate it.

PILOT MARKHAM: It's not like you have someplace to go.

RIVER ASKEW: Fine, fine.

PILOT MARKHAM: You are not going anywhere.

MARU: Mister River, how did you handle the Airlift murders?

RIVER ASKEW: My favorite topic, ha ha. Listen: You answer your door, you might die. Take a cab, you might die. Everything in life is a risk. Bad things can happen to anyone at any time.

MARU: But the killers used fake accounts with the intention of murdering people. Six people were killed before you shut them down.

RIVER ASKEW: My tech cannot be responsible for people's morals or lack thereof.

MARU: Guns don't kill people?

RIVER ASKEW: If you are dumb enough to get into a shady-looking cab, that is not my problem. Use your own car if you do not like Airlift. Get a traditional hotel.

MARU: This reminds me of Gorillagate in a way.

LINDA BELINDA: I do not like this.

MARU: Everyone told that actress the same thing: stop using Knowned. Especially after that girl was killed in that hit-and-run.

LINDA BELINDA: Mister Pilot, can we please move on?

PILOT MARKHAM: My apologies. He does not know.

MARU: Know what?

LINDA BELINDA: I cannot be expected to police every post and comment ever on Knowned. Harassment is going to happen on an anonymous, free service. That is the nature of free speech. We are all grown-ups.

MARU: How do you deal with Nazis? White supremacists?

LINDA BELINDA: You cannot, that is how. You cannot fix stupid.

MARU: That's a great line.

LINDA BELINDA: Cal Peers gets all the credit for that bit of wisdom.

RIVER ASKEW: More absinthe?

All drink.

MARU: Speaking of stupid, those Version Zero hooligans—

CAL PEERS: God, do not remind me.

MARU: —making that stink over the Soul Project—

CAL PEERS: Over something written, clear as day, in their Terms and Conditions? If you are smart, and the person next to you is stupid, and they have cash, the next thing to do is try to get them to hand over that cash, yes?

HUNTER MOLE: Every damn day.

MARU: So people are morons who don't deserve their money.

RIVER ASKEW: Not if they just keep giving it to us!

JONAS FRIEND: Dying is on them, not me.

CAL PEERS: I hear people talk about greed. There is no such thing as greed. We here are not motivated by money. We play a crucial role in society.

MARU: Which is?

CAL PEERS: The vast majority of humanity—ninety-nine point nine percent of it—simply waits out their lives like a cat tied to a stick driven into frozen winter shit. They are the Stupid.

LINDA BELINDA: Uh-oh, someone get Mister Cal a soapbox to stand on.

CAL PEERS: The Stupid go to work. They go to school.

Cogs in a machine. They celebrate their pathetic
goalposts of life: a new house, a new job, a new car.
Meanwhile we, the Smart, place these goalposts
wherever we want. We say fill out this form, they do
it. We ask, may we track you with your phone? They
say okay, and plus here is a thousand dollars for the
privilege.

We, the Smart, are the leading edge of human forward
evolution. That is our role. The role of the Stupid
is simply to be stupid. To provide the resources
needed to fuel our interests by continuing to give
birth to more Stupids willing to do whatever you
say—*even if it hurts them*. Nations for glass beads.

Of course Wren is a waste of time. The endeavors of
all of us here are wastes of time. But they are
essential experimentations we require as the
vanguard of human evolution. Evolution does not just
happen; it is a conscious choice. Someone needs to
decide where to take humanity next. That someone
is us.

All drink.

MARU: I think you just blew my mind.

JONAS FRIEND: Fuck that, I have a hard-on.

LINDA BELINDA: My lady lips got the drips.

MARU: Don't you ever wish you could say these things
out loud, on the record?

JONAS FRIEND: Like, every minute of every day.

CAL PEERS: The world is not ready for this kind of
honesty.

MARU: Thank you all so much for taking the time to
talk. It's really inspiring.

RIVER ASKEW: Mister Maru: Go as fast and hard as you can. Do not worry about laws or government. Just saturate the market before anyone has time to react. And give me a call when you do, ha ha.

JONAS FRIEND: And save the gorillas!

LINDA BELINDA: Too soon!

ALL: Ha ha ha.

CAL PEERS: You will go far, Mister Maru. Tech has a unique aura of legitimacy. We have addiction. We have artificial intelligence. Ours is the new magic.

PILOT MARKHAM: All you need is an eight-hundred-dollar device and yearly service contract and the surrender of all personal data to multinational corporations.

CAL PEERS: You are hilarious.

PILOT MARKHAM: Enough banter. Introducing Phantom Reality.

A long pause. Pilot Markham begins waving his bracelets like a mystic. A bottle sitting upon a nearby table begins to rise.

LINDA BELINDA: Wow. It is like Mister Pilot is using the Force.

PILOT MARKHAM: I can make one of these bottles float. If I twist my hand, it twists.

JONAS FRIEND: But if I wave my hand across the strings, hi-ya—oh, there are no strings. Holy fucking shit, how are you doing this?

CAL PEERS: It is some kind of hologram. Is it the table?

PILOT MARKHAM: Mister Cal gets it. You each get a bottle to play with. Go ahead, raise your wristbands and play around.

RIVER ASKEW: The fidelity is so convincing, Mister Pilot.

LINDA BELINDA: Incredible. Augmented reality without the need for goggles.

JONAS FRIEND: Goddamn, so this is what you have been up to for the last three years.

MARU: I think he likes it.

LINDA BELINDA: Imagine the partnership possibilities this technology offers.

PILOT MARKHAM: Is that not what good friends are for?

HUNTER MOLE: You are the best.

CAL PEERS: This is as big as the internet. You will change the world forever.

PILOT MARKHAM: Oh, we already have. Phantom, crash the bottles.

The bottles crash into a thousand virtual fragments.

ALL: Ha ha, whoa, wow.

2.16

Max gave Pilot a nod and left the arena. Once the doors closed behind him, he sprinted back up to Control. He ripped off his goatee. He flung his wig aside. He put his Buddy Hollys back on and pushed them up.

"How'd we do?" he said to Brayden.

"Dude," said Brayden. "We're trending so hard."

Brayden showed him a monitor full of text and charts.

"The *We have addiction* quote is trending," said Brayden. "Also this whole *All you need is* thing."

"Huh?" said Max.

"Like, *You, too, can have friends, all you need is an eight-hundred-dollar device and yearly service contract and the surrender of all personal data to multinational corporations.* Ha, they also did *You can find a soul mate, all you need is* and *You, too, can elect a president, all you need is.*"

"Trending is nice, but what about account deletions?"

"I don't know how to read that stuff."

"I'll do it," said a voice.

Akiko entered, followed by Shane. They looked haggard. They looked wrung out and red-eyed.

Had she told him? That was the last thing Max wanted. Not for his sake—for Shane's. He thought about all the times he and Shane had spent in the Poolwhip, air drumming or trading jokes or generally being stupid, and felt his eyes grow hot with budding tears. He could not fuck this up. He could not lose Shane.

Shane was an enormously talented and unique and loyal person who he had never fully appreciated. Max vowed to do better.

"You good?" said Max to Shane. He held out a fist, and to his relief Shane bumped it with his.

"Just a little jet-lagged, I think," said Shane. "What'd I miss?"

Max and Shane looked at the screens, which was much easier than looking at each other. There, Pilot and the CEOs continued to play with their wristbands.

Max's chest hurt. It was his heart, actually. He wondered how long it would hurt like this.

Not long, he told himself. Until then, just let it hurt.

He stared at the big red REW button at Brayden's workstation and wished he could press it and hold it down for a good long while.

Akiko sat next to Brayden and clicked around. "Account deletions are way up. Holy shit, Wren stock is down ten points and sinking."

On-screen, Cal Peers levitated a bottle and grinned.

"These fuckers have no clue," said Brayden.

"All their stocks are down," said Akiko. "Holy shit."

"No fucking clue," said Brayden.

On-screen, the CEOs spoke.

"The current administration is still majority anti–free market," said Hunter Mole. "Economic nationalism will kill my supply chain."

"Building the El No Paso is not about freedom," said Linda Belinda.

"That wall is a communistic act," said Cal Peers. "America is an outdated concept. Nations in general are outdated concepts."

And so on.

"It just keeps getting better and better," said Max.

"How long do we let it go on for?" said Akiko. She looked at him with a firm brow, all seriousness and all business, and Max knew she was trying to be good. To be just friends. She and Shane had come to some kind of reckoning and Max could see she was determined to stick by it.

But: Max had seen that brow soften, then tighten into a vee of ecstasy.

"Enough," muttered Max.

Everyone looked at Max. Had he said that too loud?

"I mean, I think we have enough here," said Max. "Enough material. It's time."

Max nodded at Brayden, who brought forth the box of Black Halo masks.

"Time for the big reveal," said Max.

2.17

A bar packed with young people, all watching dozens of television screens all showing the same thing: Cal Peers.

STUDENT 30: Did he just call us the Stupid?

ALL: Boo, fuck you!

STUDENT 12: Shut the fuck up, everybody.

STUDENT 30: He just fucking called all of us the Stupid.

STUDENT 58: Hey, yo, Mayra wants Spanish subtitles, can you get those?

BARKEEP: I think so. There.

STUDENT 18: Shhhh.

STUDENT 30: Are you fucking kidding me with this?

STUDENT 11: It is our role?

STUDENT 18: Shhh, stop fucking shouting.

STUDENT 19: Three IPAs.

BARKEEP: One sec.

STUDENT 30: Look at these motherfuckers.

STUDENT 42: Hey, we're a resource!

STUDENT 30: No way.

STUDENT 26: Eat a dick.

STUDENT 30: Fuck these fuckers.

STUDENT 42: Cal Peers just called Wren a waste of time.

STUDENT 30: This is the CEO, right?

STUDENT 26: Yes, this is the fucking CEO.

STUDENT 30: Whiteman?

STUDENT 47: Hell no.

STUDENT 42: Fuck you!

ALL: Fuck you!

STUDENT 26: We're watching you, you fucking fuck.

ALL: Boo, fuck you!

STUDENT 42: Everyone, look!

STUDENT 19: You're not livestreaming, are you?

STUDENT 42: Taylor deleted her Wren.

STUDENT 8: Again?

STUDENT 42: Ahem: *It is with deep gratitude to my millions of followers that I must do what is right in the face of this toxic culture that is causing more harm than good.* Sounds serious this time.

STUDENT 8: You know she'll just come back.

STUDENT 42: I don't know. Oprah's out, too.

STUDENT 8: Whoa.

STUDENT 42: So is Brad. Holy shit, so is Target.

STUDENT 26: As in the store.

STUDENT 42: As in the store.

ALL: . . .

STUDENT 8: Ariana's out.

STUDENT 30: Dude.

STUDENT 42: Let's all do it. Come on.

STUDENT 42: Come on, you'll live.

STUDENT 151: You guys, all of Brockton College just quit Wren.

STUDENT 42: Let's do it!

STUDENT 92: Delgado Beach represent!

STUDENT 42: Don't just delete the fucking app, I mean delete your whole account.

STUDENT 19: I'm in.

ALL: Fuck these assholes!

STUDENT 26: People lived without this shit just fine.

STUDENT 30: So do I just go to settings?

STUDENT 19: It goes account, settings, account settings, my account, my account settings, then scroll all the way down, hit the red DELETE MY ACCOUNT link, then a confirm. Let me know when you're at this screen right here.

STUDENT 30: Hold it up higher.

STUDENT 26: I'm ready.

STUDENT 19: On three, we all hit delete and yell "Delete," okay?

ALL: Ready, ready, ready.

STUDENT 19: One, two, three . . .

ALL: Delete!

Cheers all around.

ALL: Shots! Shots! Shots!

STUDENT 30: Okayokayokay, listen up, we're gonna do Knowned next.

More cheers.

STUDENT 42: Hold 'em up when you're ready.

ALL: . . .

STUDENT 19: One, two, three . . .

ALL: Delete!

2.18

Max slipped on the Black Halo mask. He aimed his wristband at the door—*Hadouken*—and opened it. He strolled down the hallway followed by Akiko and Shane, also in their masks. He opened another door and raised a fist at his squad: *Halt.*

He'd always wanted to raise a fist at his squad like that.

The three of them crouched behind a tall dead plant and listened. Voices floated up from the illuminated dais below.

"I disagree," said someone. Hunter Mole. "Mind has won over matter. The internet represents the purest marketplace in the history of mankind."

"But that purity is becoming tainted," said Cal Peers. "Government is interfering, obviously looking for a piece of the action. Look at Europe, look at America."

Max gritted his teeth. He couldn't wait to see Cal's face when he got down there.

Outside it was dusk but not night. Pilot explained that this far north the days never sank fully into darkness. The walls—and most of the ceiling—were glass, giving the impression that the entire room was simply a huge concrete disk improbably set atop a mountain.

All of this glassy openness reminded Max again of the Helix, back at Wren HQ.

Or the top floor of Pilot's house.

What was with these guys, and their urge to build Helixes?

"What is the poor entrepreneur to do?" sang Pilot.

"Well," began Cal Peers. He looked what could almost be interpreted as coy.

"Tell him," said Linda Belinda. "It is just so exciting."

"I have been working on my escape strategy," said Cal Peers. "There is an island northeast of Finland, unincorporated, absolutely pure and available for a steal. I have acquired it. I am calling it Helix 2."

"Barf," said Max aloud, then clamped a hand over his masked mouth. Akiko laughed silently. Shane didn't get it.

Max vowed to explain later.

"I will set up operations there. Trade exclusively in e-currencies. It will take governments decades to figure out how to regulate me. Decades of peace and quiet."

"To peace and quiet," said everyone.

Glasses clinked.

"Although I do think bootstrapping your own sovereignty might be overkill," said Linda Belinda. "A think tank could work just as well."

Everyone spoke at once, and quickly.

"Ha, like a Citizens for Internet Freedom or some such?"

"Regulate the people, not the tool?"

"We already publish self-help guides: Things You Can Do to blablabla."

"Advocate personal responsibility, sow doubt. It worked for tobacco."

Laughter all around.

Max rose. He nodded to Shane and Akiko to do the same. He took a deep breath and strode into the arena. He made his way down the dark staircase and headed into the cone of light illuminating the dais.

The three of them stood in their ghostly masks.

"Sow doubt," said Max to the room. His voice strangled by the digital filter. "I like it."

"You," said Cal Peers, squinting.

"No, you," said Max.

"Pilot," said Cal Peers. "What the hell is this?"

Pilot grinned so wide that he looked like a cartoon of glee. He composed himself.

"Everyone," said Pilot, beaming. "This is Version Zero."

White Costume Mask with Black Circle VZ01

sold by Taishan Manufacturing

#1 in Clothing, Shoes & Jewelry

105,116 customer reviews | 4,398 answered questions

Price: $12.95 + FREE same-day shipping

Back-ordered. Available in 5 days (vendor estimate).

PRODUCT DESCRIPTION:

- Show off your tech-savvy and revolutionary spirit with this stylish mask
- No. 1 trending costume design worldwide!
- Ergonomic precision molded plastic design comfortable for long-term wear indoors or outdoors
- Please notice this model does NOT include voice-changing function (see model VZ02)
- It is better for hand-wash care
- It is perfect for Dress Up, Cosplay, Pretend Play, Role Play, Public Gathering

PRE-PURCHASE NOW

We'll ship this item the moment it becomes available.

105,116 CUSTOMER REVIEWS

Ken Rothermund

★★★★★ **Definitely the best V-zero mask out there**

Stand fast all day against The Man without all the annoying face sweat. Love the quick-adjust headband. Paint and molding definitely top notch! Stay away from the cheap dollar store versions and get this one, the difference is obvious.

Wendy Rosenblum
★ ★ ★ ★ ★ **five star review!!!**
*Narrow eye slits are easy to protect from pepper spray by lowering the forehead pad
(included). Unlike cheap look-alikes this mask is solid enough to deflect a rubber bullet
or a swinging nightstick.*

beadfanatic
★ ★ ★ ★ ★ **all my friends are gone online**
all my friends are gone online

Nathan Coyle
★ ★ ★ ★ ★ **Hands down best quality Zero Nation mask! Worth the extra$$**
*Looks AWESOME. HEAVY mask almost ceramic, very high quality while still comfort-
able. Easy to breath and peripheral vision. Great for rallies, I scared the pants off my
brother on video chat!!!*

MORE REVIEWS

2.20

Cal Peers tried to peer around Max's mask. "I should have you arrested. I should arrange worse."

"A threat," said Max. "Try it."

Max wished he could see how the viewers were reacting at this moment. He would have to wait until Brayden filled him in afterward.

He smiled behind the mask. Then he imagined another Wren van, again parked outside his parents' house, and his smile flickered. Cal Peers couldn't legally do anything to them. Could he?

"Who are you?" said Cal Peers, squinting and squinting.

Max said nothing. He and Shane and Akiko stood in a rough triangle, faceless and mute as aliens.

"He is Version Zero," said Pilot. "As am I. We all are."

"Pilot," said Cal Peers. "What are you doing with these children?"

The other CEOs tried to talk, but Cal Peers silenced them with a hand. "How did you penetrate my systems?"

"It was trivial," said Akiko, her voice made low and gravelly by the mask. "We employed a dickfor."

"What the hell is a dickfor?" said Cal Peers.

Akiko barfed a single laugh, and the laugh was an infectious one, for now Shane was laughing and so was Max and Pilot, too, and the air filled with electronic phlegm. Max was particularly glad to see Akiko and Shane laughing together. They were meant to laugh.

Max hoped they had a good talk.

Max bet a good long talk could fix a good many things.

"What is a dickfor, goddammit?" said Cal Peers.

Max gasped for air and held his hands up in a call for order.

Cal Peers looked as if he wanted to lunge.

Come at me, thought Max.

"This isn't about any one person," said Max. "It's about all of you here."

"What do you want?" said Cal Peers.

Max glanced at Pilot, who served an open palm: *You have the floor.*

Max stepped forward, bumping fists with Pilot.

"I already have what I want," said Max.

Max realized he was making history in his own strange way. Giving the world a blunt view into a world they would never be able to unsee. He glanced up at a security camera suspended high in the arena, as if to say hi to Brayden. Good old Brayden, keeping watch from atop the pyramid panopticon.

Was Dad watching, too?

Was he huddled with Mom around their ancient laptop, thick as a phone book, set atop the wobbly dining table back home?

Might Dad put two and two together and figure out that it was Max with the great Pilot Markham? That it was Max doing all the talking?

Might Dad be proud? Or merely confused?

How is this a business? he might say.

Max wished he could speak to him across the wires and ether. *This is important,* he wanted to say. *And I am doing it. Tell me you are proud of me. Tell me you understand why it is important. Tell me*

you

get

it.

"This is kidnapping," said Jonas Friend.

"No, it isn't," said Max. "You came here, remember?"

"Do not hurt us," said Linda Belinda.

"No one is getting hurt," said Max. "In fact, there's the door. A chopper will be here soon."

Outside the glass a snow fog began to fill the world with formless white.

The five CEOs looked at one another with growing realization. Finally Cal Peers spoke.

"You have been filming this whole time," he said.

Max pointed out a camera, then another.

"No," said Cal Peers.

"Actually, yes," said Brayden. The boy's voice boomed throughout the space. "Wave hi to the world, everyone."

Max and Akiko and Shane waved hi.

"Hello, world," said Max.

"We're blowing up," said Brayden. "Fifty million viewers, tech stock indexes down almost seventy-five percent."

"Deletion count," said Max.

"We passed a quarter million a few minutes ago," said Brayden. "Mostly colleges at first, but now it's everywhere."

Max smiled. His mask was growing moist and hot, but he did not care. He would remove it soon, and the air against his skin would feel so cool and pure.

"No," said Cal Peers. "This is a hoax."

"Step on a chopper, fly 'til you get bars, and find out for yourself," said Max.

"Is a chopper there now?" said Hunter Mole.

"Soon," said Pilot.

"I am fucking out of here," said Jonas Friend.

"These are not coming off," said Linda Belinda, tugging at her wristbands.

Max straightened and addressed them all. "I'm curious about one last thing before you go."

"These will not come off," said Linda Belinda.

"Oh no," said Pilot with a grin.

"How much," said Max, "is enough?"

"She is right, these are locked," said Hunter Mole.

"How much money will it take for you to be satisfied?" said Max. "Or will you just keep searching for endless ways to get money for souls?"

"What the fuck," said Jonas Friend, tugging at his wristbands.

"Is a billion enough?" said Max, louder now. "A trillion?"

Cal Peers, who had been burning brighter and brighter through his pale skin, finally exploded. "You know nothing. It is not about one number."

Max smiled. He was close. He reeled him in with a finger: *Go on.*

"It is about having more than the nearest competitor," said Cal Peers. "It is about stepping on their necks and holding them down."

"Wow," said Akiko, eyebrows raised.

"I will hold you down, too," said Cal Peers. "Just wait."

Now Max raised his eyebrows.

Not Pilot, though. Pilot said nothing.

"Good-bye," said Max.

2.21

HOST: And so this new network of yours—

GUEST: Basic.

HOST: —right, so, Basic will offer the same social stuff everybody likes, just without all that spy advertising and fake news crap.

GUEST: Correct. We also recently announced our Basic phone, which has a minimalist, stripped-down function set and a black-and-white screen so that we can return to the enjoyment of life without all the distractions of traditional smartphones.

HOST: As someone in my sixties, I just find that so funny.

GUEST: Why?

HOST: Never mind. Tell me: How will Basic actually, ya know, make money?

GUEST: We have recently secured series B funding—

HOST: That's not making money, friend.

GUEST: I would like to finish, if that's okay.

HOST: Go ahead.

GUEST: You seem a bit agitated.

HOST: I think a lot of people are agitated! I think a lot of us are looking at our phones right about now and saying what the hell did we get ourselves into?

GUEST: My team understands that feeling one hundred percent. That's the whole reason we started Basic. We all worked as top engineers at the Big Five. We all started asking ourselves, what is it we're building, exactly?

HOST: What is *the purpose*?

GUEST: Exactly, what is the purpose? If we are building some new technology, and that technology is doing bad things, shouldn't we stop? Maybe build something else?

HOST: I admire what you kids are doing—I do—and in some ways it reminds me of my own generation of revolutionaries, but I gotta say you're up against some serious established infrastructure and inertia. Just plain old habit and laziness, if I'm being honest. Not to poop on your parade.

GUEST: We very much are aware of that, yes. But look: we believe that once we get enough first followers, we will reach a tipping point where there is a flood. And especially in this brand-new Vee-Zero era of online awareness—

HOST: Vee-Zero is short for Version Zero, for all you cave dwellers out there.

GUEST: We think we can all finally change things for the better for real this time.

Applause.

HOST: Now, my next questions are a little awkward, but . . .

GUEST: I know what you're going to say, but go ahead.

HOST: Your main investors also have sizable stakes in—wait for it—Wren.

GUEST: That is true.

HOST: And A2Z.

GUEST: Yes.

HOST: And Knowned, and many others.

GUEST: Yes. That's right. Yes.

HOST: How do you square that circle?

GUEST: How do we square the circle.

HOST: How do you keep your integrity as an ad-free, surveillance-free gazelle when you're drinking from the same pond as the panthers right over there?

GUEST: Well, like the gazelle we are also nimble? But more importantly, we have faith that people will choose what's good for them if offered a real alternative. We believe people are inherently good and wise.

HOST: And I want to believe that you believe.

2.22

Max watched the CEOs make the climb up the arena steps. He had done it. *They* had done it. The CEOs would return to a world of shit. Companies would crumble. A new generation would rise. And my God, Max would be there for it. He led once with Version Zero. He made a dent in the universe. And he could do it again, this time as Max.

His Benevolence, CEO Maximilian Portillo.

Cal Peers stopped in his ascent and turned around.

"Fourteen Mezcla Avenue," said Cal Peers.

Max glanced up upon hearing these words, and instantly regretted it. It was his parents' address back home.

Cal Peers sneered with glee now.

"Your father must be proud of you," said Cal Peers. "Ulises. Your mother Penelope, too."

Max's head emptied; his eyes flickered. But he held his gaze with Cal Peers. Brayden would edit that out with the big rewind button upstairs.

Maintain, thought Max.

Max continued to stare without a word. *Give him nothing.*

"Here is what is going to happen next," said Cal Peers. "We are going to leave here."

"Damn right," said River Askew.

"We are going to find that helicopter pilot of yours, and we are going to fly away from this place. This will all blow over, I promise you. People will normalize. I can look into this camera, right here, and order them to normalize, and they will, mark my words. People do not change."

Akiko began to say something, but Max stopped her with a touch.

Give them nothing.

"Come on," said Cal Peers to the others.

"You are no friend of mine," said Jonas Friend to Pilot. "Not anymore."

"You think you know someone," lamented Hunter Mole.

The CEOs began ascending the arena stairs.

"Just one more thing," said Pilot.

Everyone turned to him.

"Miz Linda," said Pilot. "You knew they were targeting my Noelle, did you not?"

Linda Belinda wrung her hands.

"The trolls, Miz Linda."

Linda Belinda began to speak, then tamped it down. She smoothed her bob; she draped her camel hair jacket on her forearm. She spoke with care. "Pilot, again: How could I have known what was going on? It could have happened to anyone. You cannot monitor everything that happens on Knowned."

"But it did not just happen to anyone," said Pilot. "It happened to my Noelle. It happened because she was right, and they were wrong, and they could not stand it."

Pilot raised his arms in a strange way, as if being controlled by a magical force, and Linda Belinda took an instinctive step back.

"Is that what this is all about?" she said. She began to flibulate with panic. She glanced at Cal Peers, and Max began wondering himself. Did Pilot set this whole thing up so he could get Linda Belinda to admit she did nothing to stop the death of his daughter?

Max was confused now. They were done. Version Zero had accomplished what it set out to do. They got the Big Five to expose themselves on video to the entire world, and now they were to release them to the media lion pit. All Max wanted to do was go back up to Control and watch the fireworks.

So why were they all still standing around?

"Did you never stop to think," said Pilot, "that in building Knowned the way you did, as a perfect faceless breeding ground for trolls, you had in effect built the gun? That by your silence and inaction, you had in effect pointed that gun? That all the trolls did was pull the trigger?"

"So this is about revenge," said Cal Peers. "Bravo, Pilot. You have your revenge. Shall we?" He climbed, and gestured for the others to do the same.

"You had access, too, goddammit," she shrieked. "As a cofounder and board member you had access. You could have seen those monsters coming. You talk about silence? Inaction? Where were you when they doxxed Noelle?"

Pilot cast his eyes down. "I was asleep."

"And you call yourself a father," said Linda Belinda, just in time for her wrists to explode in twin white garlands of magnesium razor sparks.

When the acrid ozone smoke cleared Max could see the two red stumps, and the blackened hands resting at her feet.

"Miz Linda," said River Askew. He glanced at his own wristbands.

"No one move," said Pilot, raising his arms to the room now. "Let her go."

Max found himself flung skyward, pinned to the ceiling of the arena, watching himself and the others from up above. This wasn't real. This wasn't happening. He looked at his own wristbands and with fingers gone numb tried pressing the tiny crowns on their sides.

Nothing.

He dared a look at Pilot. The man had become reptilian and blank. Slowly blinking. Tasting the inside of his own mouth. This was the same man who just days earlier had called Max his *legacy.*

It was not the same man.

Or was it?

Pilot looked at Max now. He seemed to be looking past him. He seemed to be looking past everything, the arena, the mountains, everything.

Looking at what?

"Help me," said Linda Belinda. She sat. "Help me," she said to everyone, ten or so times before falling into a slumber. Ribbons of red flowed from her arms. Her body finally relaxed. And the sour earth was released.

A foghorn sounded in Max's mind now. It was a foghorn heard in a foreign country, where the customs and rules were strange and such a horn could mean anything at all: tsunami, an air raid, a field goal, nuclear war.

I am not here to recruit you, Pilot had said. When Max first met him. *I am here to convince you to recruit me.*

Mister Max is making the world a better place, Pilot had said.

Mister Max gets it, Pilot had said.

This whole time, none of what Pilot had said meant anything. All Pilot needed was a few smart people to help with execution. Because this whole time, Pilot Markham had had a plan of his own.

Pilot was saying something now, but all Max could hear was the foghorn. Max had embraced this man, called him a friend, a *father from another mather,* laughed with this man, and oh my God Max had even wished—if but for a fleeting moment—that this man were his own father.

Pilot's mouth spoke, but Max heard none of it, because Max passed out.

3.0

```
58   res = res.concat(
59      [
60          "Mjg4NDIxOTU1MjI5NzAyMDYyMDg=",
61          "MTVkIGhlcnJpbmcgZ2V0IHJla3Q=",
62          "MTEwNTI5MDA1Mjk2MDU5NzY2MTM0",
63          "MjQyMzA1MjI2OTg2ODIzNjM5MDQ=",
64          "SG9wZSB5b3UgbGlrZSBSZWdleCE=",
65          "MTk1MjA0NjkyMDUyODYyMDQ0MDM=",
66          "MjE5MjQ2NjY0OTUzMjkxMjQzNTI=",
67          "MjYwMjg2MDQ4NjAyODMwNTUxMDI=",
68          "MTk2MzQ2MDI1OTM2MDc1MTUxMzY=",
69          "TG92ZSwgUGlsb3QuIDwzICA8MyA=",
70          "MzA0NTgyNTg0Mzk1NzM4OTU3OTM5"
71      ].filter(
72          i => i.match(/M[j|T].+[QUINOA][x12][DjTLMNOP]{2}
             [^aeiou]\*?.{1,5}[a-zA-Z5]+=/g)
73      ).map(atob)
74   ).map((i, j) => {
75      if(j > 5 && j < 12) {
```

3.0

The average college student spends <u>nine hours</u> a day on their smartphones. That's over half of a waking life! <u>Studies</u> have shown that all this screen time could be keeping us from being as happy as we should be. We at Quartz (<u>QRTZ</u>) think and write a lot about the connected lifestyle, and we've found ten simple things you can do to build a healthier relationship with your phone and finally quiet those <u>phantom buzzes</u> in your pants. You'll be fitter, happier, and more productive.

1. Buy an <u>egg timer</u>, set it for 5 minutes, and don't use your phone until that timer rings. Tomorrow, go for 10 minutes. Keep increasing this time period to see how far you can last. The key to using your phone wisely is to not use it.

2. Turn off data (<u>here's how</u>) on the weekends. It sounds totally insane, like not eating or drinking for Saturday and Sunday, but trust us: you can do it.

3. Keep a book in your bag to increase the likelihood that you will actually read it. <u>Bookmarks</u> are a handy way to keep your place.

4. Carry a <u>notebook</u> made traditionally with sheets of paper, and write ideas down with a <u>pen</u> when they strike. <u>Studies</u> say writing by hand is much more creative, because it uses muscles in your body.

5. Doodle, again using a pen and ink on paper. Studies show that doodling is fun and relaxing also by use of muscles.

6. Get bored! Studies show that boredom is not only totally acceptable behavior, it can even be a productive tool to foster creativity.

7. Do not sleep with your phone.

8. Don't forget to breathe. Studies have shown that people tend to hold their breath when scrolling.

9. Get a cellular-enabled Sparq™ smartwatch and leave the phone at home altogether! We've found it incredibly liberating.

10. Take comfort in the knowledge that the internet will still be waiting for you when you return.

3.1

The body of Linda Belinda lay unmoving before them.

"Control?" said Pilot.

Silence.

"Control?" said Pilot. "Control?"

Pilot eyed the ceiling and waited for Brayden's voice. Nothing came.

"I guess Control is busy," said Pilot.

No one said shit. Everyone stood at different levels of the arena steps, frozen in shock.

Max rose. He checked his forehead, his elbows and knees: no damage. The mask was still on his face, if a bit crooked. He must have crumpled rather than fallen, and only for a moment. When he had opened his eyes again it was all still there: Pilot, the CEOs, Shane and Akiko clinging to each other in their Black Halo masks, and finally the body of Linda Belinda, lying with her face mercifully obscured by a sheet of her bobbed hair.

It was all still happening.

Max heaved through his mask.

He pictured Brayden abandoning his station up in Control, sprinting down some corridor, and banging on the door to Cody's quarters. He hoped so.

Brayden was a good kid.

Max slowly turned his gaze to Pilot. The man was still staring past the walls.

"Pilot," said Max. "Whatever it is you think you might be doing here, you know it's not right, and we have to go now; everyone has to get on the helicopter and go because we're all done here."

Pilot aimed a wristband at the side of the arena and twisted a fist in the air. A portion of the steps retracted to reveal a storage chamber. Pilot reached into the floor panel, unfolded a black tarp, and covered Linda Belinda's body.

"You are a monster," said Cal Peers.

Pilot sighed. "I know. Now, everyone sit."

When no one moved, Pilot shouted. "Everyone sit!" And he pointed at Jonas Friend, whose wristbands began to crackle with electricity.

"No," said Jonas Friend.

"Then sit," said Pilot.

They moved back down to the dais and sat.

"Well, here we are," said Cal Peers. "Happy?"

"Pilot," said Shane. "Can we go? Come on, man."

"Please," said Akiko.

"One second," said Pilot. "I wanted you to sit in for this part of the agenda."

Akiko choked back a scream, and she buried herself into Shane's arms.

"Hey hey hey," said Pilot. "I am sorry I did not tell you about this part of the agenda beforehand. I just did not want to affect our velocity."

"Pilot," said Max. "We're done now. Everything's finished. Let's just go home."

"Oh, it is far from finished," said Pilot. "It will never be finished unless we take care of things right here once and for all. You know that."

Max's mind reeled. Everywhere his mind looked it found dead ends. How long had Pilot been planning this? He had enough foresight to develop and build his macabre wristbands for this moment. You didn't just find a place like this in the middle of the snowy nowhere in a few short weeks. You search. You make an untraceable purchase with ex-military brokers, maybe, in cash.

Goddammit, thought Max. Pilot Markham had been gone for three long years; plenty of time to stew with rage over the death of his daughter. Plenty of time to come up with his plan for all this.

And what was *all this*?

Pilot was going to kill the Big Five.

Is he going to kill us, too? thought Max. That would make no sense, if the bank transfers were to be believed. Or did he have something else planned for them? Were Max and his friends suddenly blood-bound for life with a sociopath?

Max wanted to take everyone home, scoop up his family, and bring them all to the safety of another planet.

But there was no going home. Unless Max could somehow convince Pilot to unlock the wristbands. Unless Max could tackle and restrain him before he could kill anyone else.

And then what? Drag the man, hog-tied, to the helicopter and stare at him for the six-hour flight back to the small airport? Then board the jet and stare at him some more for the even longer flight back to the United States?

The hours and days stretched before Max now at a vertiginous pitch. When was the last time he ate? *Bacon*, Pilot had said that morning by the pool so many days before, and Max had eaten the bacon. Max had eaten all the food he'd been given. The thought sickened him now.

Make it through this. Stay sharp.

"Okay," said Max. "Okay. What's next on the agenda?"

"You let us go right now, goddammit," said Hunter Mole.

"Hunter Mole, thank you for volunteering," said Pilot.

Hunter Mole whimpered.

"We will start with you," said Pilot.

3.2

Each of you remaining CEOs is a king ruling over its subjects," said Pilot. "Not in any real country, of course, but in your make-believe land of ones and zeros. As kings, you wield absolute control over your subjects. It is proven. Everyone now has some sort of device with which to receive and carry out your bidding."

Pilot turned his wristbands over and over again, as if admiring their sheen.

"But you have a problem on your hands now, correct?" said Pilot. "Your loyal subjects are holding a revolt as we speak. They will leave your castles in ruin. Unless you make a promise."

"Promise?" said Hunter Mole. "Promise for what?"

"To be better," said Pilot, irked by such a question.

"You are insane," said Hunter Mole.

"Dude," said Max. "Just give him an answer."

"What is your promise to be better?" said Pilot. "Answer that, each of you, and I will let you all go, you have my word."

"That question," said Hunter Mole, "is stupid."

"Goddammit," said Max.

Pilot raised his arms. "Stupid?"

Hunter Mole wiped his eyes again and again, but his face would not stop twitching. The silence stretched far enough that it snapped Pilot's patience. He stood and did a strange thing: he pointed at a camera along the top edge of the arena and closed a fist three times.

The camera exploded.

Glass shattered. Frigid wind came howling in.

"Is it still stupid?" said Pilot.

Max glanced with new horror around him. He knew there were dozens of cameras all over the facility. He did not know they could explode.

Hunter Mole's mouth moved fast as a rodent's and babbled a string of silent thoughts only he could possibly hear. Finally, audible words came tumbling out.

"I do not understand what you want. It is just business. We have shareholders, and we grow our user base with, with, with various customer retention tactics and strategic partnerships, and users are able to purchase things for the lowest possible price, but, but, I do not understand what this has to do with anything, or why you killed Linda. What in the name of God did you kill Linda for?"

"So," said Pilot. "The lowest possible price."

"Why did you kill her, goddammit?"

"Hunter," said Max.

"What would you price Miz Linda's life at?" said Pilot.

"Life is priceless, you sick fuck," said Hunter Mole.

Pilot clapped his hands. "Exactly. Life is priceless. That must be why you have never factored life as a cost. Squeeze your retailers, drive down prices, survive on investment cash until all the mom-and-pops are dead. This kind of behavior only works if you believe life is worthless, no?"

Hunter trembled. "I do not understand."

"Again: How much is a life worth?" said Pilot. "This time give me a smart answer."

Hunter recited from memory. "Budget officials have it at approximately eight million dollars, taking personal productivity and health costs and so on into consideration, but you cannot be saying that we should factor that amount per user in our business model."

Pilot rolled his eyes. "Jesus Christ, Hunter just does not get it."

Pilot made an X with his arms, and Hunter Mole screamed in a shower of sparks.

"No one touch him," said Pilot. "Let him go."

Hunter Mole fell to the ground, and the last thing his horrified eyes saw was the sight of his own hands laying atop one another.

"Fuck," said Max.

"You motherfucker," said Shane, and rose.

"Calm down," said Pilot. "I know this is new and unexpected for you. It is all part of a larger plan, trust me."

The reclusive J. D. Salinger of tech, in exile for over three years.

"Baby, please," said Akiko.

"We're gonna figure this out," said Max. "Okay?"

But it was not okay, and Max knew he would not figure anything out, because there was nothing *to* figure out. It was impossible and insane, like debating that Mad Hatter back at his table full of empty chairs, and Max felt his stomach twist at the possibility of dying here. They would not all die at once. Shane would have to watch Akiko die, or vice versa, or Max would have to watch either of them die.

How could my instincts have been so wrong? thought Max.

How could I have not seen this coming?

How could anyone?

Max thought he heard a noise from above—footsteps, moving fast— but did not dare flinch. What if it was Brayden?

Come on, Brayden.

"Mister Max?" said Pilot. He kept a wary eye on the CEOs while pointing at the body of Hunter Mole. With disbelief, Max understood what Pilot wanted. He wanted him to cover the body.

So Max did.

The mask was hot. He retched again but managed to hold it in.

I will let you all go, you have my word.

Max went over his current theory again: Pilot was not going to let any of the CEOs out of here alive. It was crazy. But there seemed to be no real definition of *crazy* anymore.

It is all part of a larger plan.

Max thought about Pilot's laptop, and the cryptic list of data servers listed within. Data exchanges, not servers. Whatever. It was not good. He must have some kind of massive cyberattack planned once the CEOs were all dead. Something that could take weeks for the world to recover from.

After that, Pilot would probably take Max and Akiko and Shane and Brayden somewhere else. God knew where. And they would have no choice but to go.

Unless.

Max took a breath and began formulating a to-do list.

- Jump Pilot.
- Restrain him somehow.
- Get his laptop.
- Stop whatever cyberattack he had planned. Somehow.

Max eyed the open floor panel and could see other items stored there: sponges, window cleaner, lassos of Ethernet network cables.

Ethernet cables, named after *aether,* or *heaven.* A divine name for what amounted to information plumbing. But if you wanted to fashion yourself as a god, Max guessed, giving your world godlike names was a way to start.

"Thank you," said Pilot to Max. "No one needs to see this sort of thing."

Now there were two black tarps hulking on the floor of the arena. Max rose and gave Shane as meaningful a glance as he could muster through the mesh in his mask: at the network cables, at him. Did he catch it?

Akiko did. She buried her face into Shane's neck, and Max could see her jaw moving just slightly beneath her mask, whispering.

"Who wants to go next?" said Pilot with a bright sigh.

3.3

Silence.

What Max needed was a moment of opportunity.

What would be a good moment of opportunity? And if that moment came, what signal would he give to Shane? Would he wait for Pilot to cross his forearms and then, while the sparks flew and the screams rose, tackle Pilot to the ground?

Max could not wait for another person to die. He would have to somehow make his own moment of opportunity.

But how?

"Mister River," said Pilot. "You are quiet as a mouse. What are you thinking?"

River Askew could only stare at Pilot, his white hands kneading his knees.

"What would you promise your loyal subjects, O great disruptor of the travel service sector?" said Pilot with a chuckle.

Oh my God, thought Max. Pilot was enjoying himself.

"I want to give you what you want," said River Askew. "Just tell me what it is, Mister Pilot."

Pilot's face darkened like a cellar door falling shut. "It is not about what I want, River. It is about what is right for humanity. Do not ask me what I want. No one can give me what I want, not ever."

"What," said River Askew, swallowing once, "what is it, that you want?"

"I want Noelle back."

"You want absolution. I understand that."

"You obviously do not understand," said Pilot with a sneer. "No one with your record could. Five murders in your cars. Dozens of rapes by drivers. Lodging lenders blocking minorities, using flats for prostitution. I could go on. You understand why I want you to clarify your wishes for your enterprise."

Pilot raised his arms, and hope began to leave River Askew's eyes.

"Now," said Pilot. "What do you promise?"

River Askew was too tremblesome to answer.

Max glanced at Shane, who glanced back. He hoped he was ready.

Max cleared his throat. "Pilot, Noelle's death was not your fault. You have to stop blaming yourself."

It was a risky tack to take. But maybe he would get Pilot riled up and monologuing. Maybe he would open a window for Shane to pounce.

"Of course it was my fault," said Pilot. "What do you think this is all about?"

"We need to let these guys go home, like we planned," said Max. He searched for a provocative next thing to say. He found it: "These CEOs are innocent."

"Five driver murders, five Noelles," said Pilot. "Jonas Friend there watches our every move with Milc phones made by child slave labor in China. And there is Cal Peers; who knows how many suicides and murders have been livestreamed on Wren without consequence. How much bullying and trolling and deceiving. They are hardly innocent. No one leaves until I am satisfied with a promise, any kind of promise, to fix the broken world they have built."

"How about I move my whole supply chain to the United States?" said Jonas Friend. "Would that make you happy?"

Pilot narrowed his eyes. "Jonas clearly does not get it."

Shane let go of Akiko, but did not make a move. Neither did Max. What if Pilot slipped their grasp?

Dammit, thought Max. Pilot had given them a good long stretch and they waited too long. Max needed to keep Pilot talking and distracted.

"What's it gonna take to satisfy you?" said Max. "Just kill everyone?"

"Do not give him ideas," said Cal Peers.

"These people," said Pilot, "are a cybernetic hive mind. They swoop in. They reduce the world to that which can be expressed only through their algorithms. They assimilate everyone and everything they touch."

Pilot was revving up. Max looked at Shane: *Get ready*.

"When you begin to believe that Wren equals society and that Knowned equals discourse and that your phone equals freedom of speech, then you, too, have become part of the cyborg collective."

Max nodded: *One, two, three*.

Suddenly the doors above the arena slid open. Max could hear a rhythmic sound, as in thwopthwopthwop, and knew at once it was a helicopter.

Fuck yeah, Brayden.

He saw Brayden's mad yellow crown of hair appear, and an object come lobbing down into the arena to explode in a giant asterisk of sweet foam.

A champagne bottle.

Pilot fell dripping wet from his seat.

Brayden stepped into the arena kick-pushing a cardboard box. He wore a Black Halo mask. He reached in and sent another bottle flying. It hit Pilot squarely in the back.

"The chopper's here," shouted Brayden through his mask.

"Now," said Max.

Shane lunged. He reached for Pilot, but Max, who was going for the Ethernet cables, slipped on a curve of glass made invisible by all the wet and knocked into him—a crucial, tragic misstep, one Max would never forget for the rest of his life, for Pilot was now able to stand and aim his forearms skyward to conjure a sickening scream from above.

Brayden.

"No," cried Akiko. She rushed up the stairs toward him.

"Motherfucker," said Shane. He fell upon Pilot like a bear gone wild with hunger; Shane, two-time district wrestling champion back in high school, pinning each of Pilot's limbs into a helpless X with ease.

"Get the rope," screamed Shane.

Max scrambled to grab two coils of networking cable.

Shane punched Pilot two times in the face—pop pop, hard as a nailgun—to render him limp.

"Chair, now," shouted Shane.

Max knew what to do. He and Shane began dragging Pilot to the chair through the wet broken glass, hoisting him into seated position, and tying him down. He tied his legs to the chair legs, his arms to the chair arms, his back to the chair back. He had never been this close to Pilot. He was a dead-heavy man, with dense rubber limbs falling into stubborn angles.

Through the sweat and heat of his mask Max could see the three surviving CEOs making their way up toward the exit.

Thanks for hanging out, assholes.

"Go check on Brayden," said Shane, and just as he said it they both knew it was loud enough for the cameras to hear, loud enough for the world to hear: *Brayden*. Max could see the queries flitting about online, searching for any connection to Pilot Markham.

Not that it would matter after the next few moments.

When Max reached Brayden he was in a bad way. The worst way. Akiko cradled the boy's head in her arms.

"Get this mask off me," whispered Brayden. "We should go."

"Okay," said Max. "Okay, man."

Max removed the mask. Brayden looked up into Akiko's hair.

"You smell good," said Brayden, and died.

Akiko's wail echoed through the arena.

Below, Shane slammed fist after fist into Pilot's face with the steady rhythm of a clockwork escapement.

"He was good," screamed Shane. "He was good."

3.4

M ax looked at Shane. Max looked at Akiko. Both stood frozen in a strange pose, staring with confounded wonder at their wristbands. Were they safe, with Pilot now restrained? Could they cut them off now, or would they explode if they tried?

River Askew was gone. Jonas Friend was gone. Cal Peers was gone.

Linda Belinda and Hunter Mole were still here, under black tarps.

Max looked at the ragged window raging with white wind and could picture all the other cameras concussing one after another to bring the whole arena ceiling crashing down.

The whole building.

Max found himself talking.

"What do we do with him?" said Max.

"We end this fucker," said Shane.

"Baby, you can't do that," said Akiko.

"But he fucking deserves it," said Shane.

"Unh," said Pilot. He opened an eye and cast it about. *Your CEOs are gone,* thought Max. And soon we will be gone, too. Except.

Except.

Max blinked behind his mask. In his mind there was a decision node fast approaching, and he swallowed it like a ball of black-green phlegm.

"We need to fly the fuck out of here," said Akiko. "We should just leave him."

"What if he escapes?" said Shane.

"Where's he gonna go?" said Akiko. "He's the world's public enemy number one."

The three of them looked at Pilot: this person, this man, now so alien, hunched in his chair with his chin touching a bib of spittle and red.

"I trusted you," said Max. "You took my trust and you used it."

"But we are of the same mind," said Pilot with a slow thick tongue. "Me. You. Same."

Max's gut twisted, because who the hell was he to talk about trust? He looked at Shane and Akiko and wanted to lash them together and catapult them to safety and apologize for everything: for all the wanting, for the betrayal.

Oh, he was a fine one to talk about trust, all right.

But was anyone, really?

No more talk. Max just had one thing left to do, and he would do it.

There were moments in life, so many of them, and it was only ever in hindsight that you could tell which were significant and which were not. There was no way, for instance, of telling whether you were seeing someone for the last time, forever and ever, infinity.

Max glanced down at something on Akiko's waist. It was a small black object.

A magic eight ball.

Akiko saw him see, and she tucked the eight ball into the small watch pocket in the front of her jeans with a gentle push of her thumb. It was a practiced gesture. Max thought she could probably just as deftly remove the magic eight ball from the pocket to obtain a quick fortune whenever she wanted. It was a gesture he was dying to see. But he knew he never would.

And he was okay with that now.

"We need to go," said Akiko.

"So we're seriously just gonna leave him," said Shane.

"Listen to your girlfriend," said Max.

Up the stairs they ran.

"Max," called Pilot.

*   *   *

Shane and Akiko sprinted into the cold sunlit vacuum outside and flung their masks aside. Max slid his own mask up onto his forehead and held it there against the whirling universe of crystal and snow. The massive transport helicopter was in full idle, ready to take off at a moment's notice.

The chopper's heavy steel sliding door sat open. Cody waved them in.

"Where's the others?" said Cody. "Where's Pilot?"

For a single insane moment Max wanted to quip, *He's a little tied up right now.*

"They're dead," said Max. It was easier than explaining what happened.

How could anyone explain what happened?

Cody's face fell. Frowning now, he helped them into the rumbling interior. He handed out headsets for them to put on before taking his seat up front and donning headphones of his own.

The other CEOs—River Askew, Jonas Friend, and Cal Peers—stared at their strange new compatriots-in-misery with faces gone slack with shock.

"So it *was* you," said Cal Peers in a monotone. His voice had been reduced to the nasally thin whine of a vintage radio broadcast. "Maximilian Portillo. And Akiko Hosokawa. And you, you drive that eyesore of a van."

Shane set his jaw and flexed.

Max drew the headset's mic closer to his mouth. "No one knew Pilot was gonna do what Pilot did."

"When we get out of this," said Cal Peers, "I plan on prosecuting the three of you to the fullest extent."

"Are you serious with that right now?" said Max.

"Can we fucking go already?" shouted Jonas Friend, so loud Max scrambled to dial down the volume on his headphones.

"When you get back to civilization," said Max, "you will step into a world of shit. All three of you. Because people know what's right and what's wrong. So yes, Cal Peers, this was about revenge. You'll see."

"People only see what they are shown," said Cal Peers. "People will see you and your friends, the terrorists perpetrating this heinous crime, and they will see nothing else."

"Except you're never gonna see us again," said Max.

Max glanced at Shane and Akiko, who startled at this notion.

"But they will see your parents," said Cal Peers. "They will see everything about them."

Max froze as the rotors idled.

"Don't you fucking dox them," said Max. "They didn't do shit."

"They are illegals, are they not?" said Cal Peers.

"There's no such thing as illegal people," said Max.

"I will put everything I have on Knowned," said Cal Peers. "For Linda Belinda. Thanks to you, her child no longer has a mother."

"Don't," was all Max could say.

"Don't fucking do it, man," said Shane, rising.

Cal Peers merely laughed once and stared.

"Excuse me, helicopter pilot," said River Askew. "May we take off now?"

The rotors whined in earnest now, and the whole transport labored to rise an inch off the ground.

All Max could do was hope any doxxing was vastly overshadowed by the storm of condemnation that would bury Cal Peers. He had no time to worry about this. Because he had something important to do.

He abruptly snapped his fingers at Shane and Akiko. "Look for pliers or something. Get these wristbands off." Pilot had said something about a self-destruct mechanism that triggered when the bands fell outside a certain range.

"Oh," said Akiko, her eyes still on Cal Peers. "Right."

You will see, Pilot had said.

Max did not want to see.

"Shut the door, shut the door," said Shane.

"I got it," said Max.

But instead of sliding the door shut, Max gave Shane a big slapping hug—his last hug ever—and turned to Akiko for a gentler embrace. A shoulder hug. Nothing too long. Nothing too weird. How he wanted to hold her face in his hands. But he didn't. He took a step back and hung from the open doorway. The helicopter rose another foot. The world tilted.

Akiko and Shane stood confused.

"What are you doing?" said Akiko.

"Be safe, duncies," said Max. "I love you guys."

"Max?" said Shane.

"They will tear your mother and father apart," said Cal Peers with a smile.

"Fucking try it," shouted Shane.

"I love you guys," said Max, and jumped out and away.

As Max stood on the whirling helipad, he watched as the chopper rose ten feet, then another.

Then the big machine paused. It wobbled.

When Max shielded his eyes against the brilliant sun, he could see a figure tumble from the doorway and hang perilously there.

Akiko.

Max clawed at his ears in horror.

Shane appeared. He reached for her with both strong arms. But someone within kicked at his head and neck. Shane retreated—just for a moment—and then there was just Akiko, kicking her legs in space.

Cal Peers came falling out.

He fell back-first, like an upended beetle. His legs struck the landing gear on the way down past Akiko, sending his limbs spinning. The helicopter bobbled. Cal Peers fell fifty, sixty feet to the helipad.

Above, Shane grabbed hold of Akiko and heaved her back in. Max could see him turn and cover his mouth in shock at the sight of Cal Peers's body below. He shouted something. *Is he dead?* perhaps, or maybe *Oh fuck*. Max would never know.

Max waved Shane away with big swings of his arms.

"Get out of here," he yelled.

But the helicopter ignored Max's command, and began to descend.

"Get the fuck out of here," yelled Max again.

The helicopter finally seemed to hear him, which was impossible, but Max liked the thought. The sliding door rammed shut. The helicopter drew a mighty arc away, away, away to disappear behind a ridge.

At Max's feet lay Cal Peers. Max drew his Black Halo mask back onto his face.

The man twitched once. Then he was still.

3.5

Akiko sat in the helicopter, warmed by the sun blazing in through the shifting portholes. Around her swirled a glittering cloud of frozen scintillae; beyond, the perfect day blazed on and on into a parallaxical infinity. She had no idea what time it was—the days were so long in this part of the world—and if,

if,

if,

if she were in another alternate universe, she would allow this day to stretch on and on and on while she lazed about with Shane in the warmth.

But this was this universe, and she was riding in a helicopter with Shane and three of the Big Five.

"They will tear your mother and father apart," Cal Peers had said.

"Fucking try it," shouted Shane.

"I love you guys," said Max, and jumped out the open door.

Max had not witnessed the rest of it, which was probably for the best.

"We have to go back for him," Shane had shouted.

Cody, the pilot, strained to look behind him. "We forgot someone?"

"Ignore him," said Cal Peers.

"Go, go, go," shouted River Askew.

"Just land for one second," said Akiko. "Please."

"He chose to leave," shouted Jonas Friend. "The whole place is going to explode."

"What the hell?" said Cody.

"Go the fuck with him if you want," shouted Cal Peers, and braced himself with both arms to give Akiko a hard kick.

Akiko swung out of the open doorway and dangled in space from a grab handle.

"No," shouted Shane. He dove to grasp for Akiko's arms.

"You, too," said Cal Peers. Akiko watched helplessly as he began kicking Shane everywhere he could: his head, between his shoulder blades.

But Shane was bigger than those kicks. He turned, caught Cal Peers's ankle with both hands, and shoved hard to flip the man onto his back. Both River Askew and Jonas Friend pressed themselves to the wall, as if to give them room to fight.

Akiko could not dare release her grasp in an attempt to climb back inside. What if she slipped?

Cal Peers, though supine, managed to score a hard jab kick at Shane's shin, sending him down to a knee. This gave Cal Peers enough time to get back on his feet and charge.

"Shane," screamed Akiko.

Her scream was unnecessary. Because Cal Peers did not know that Shane had taken aikido since he was nine, and that with just his fingertips, he could lightly grab and turn an oncoming opponent to alter their course by a few degrees.

A few degrees was all it took to send Cal Peers shoulder-first into the doorjamb and tumbling out of the cabin.

"We are landing right now," screamed Cody. He pushed a lever; the cabin began to dip.

Shane got low. He peered out the doorway. He covered his mouth at what he saw.

Then Shane blinked, gripped Akiko's wrists, and hauled her back into the cabin, where she scrambled away from the open doorway with eyes gone square with terror.

Shane crushed her in his arms. "You're okay, you're okay."

The helicopter stopped its descent. It began rising again. Akiko looked up.

Jonas Friend held something small and lime green in color: a box cutter blade, just an inch from Cody's neck. Jonas Friend was saying something. Without headphones Akiko couldn't hear what, but she didn't need to.

"No," said Akiko. No one heard her.

Jonas Friend touched the blade to the skin of Cody's neck, so Cody pulled the lever, and the helicopter rose. River Askew heaved the door shut. The air inside the cabin sealed. It stabilized. The roar of the wind and the rotors hushed to a murmur.

Akiko watched as the mountains outside sank to become nothing but brilliant blue sky.

River Askew shared a fierce look with Jonas Friend. He sat, fastened his harness. He eyed Shane and Akiko. Then he smiled.

"Enjoy this moment," said River Askew. "Before you rot in separate cells."

"He's the one who came at me," said Shane.

Akiko touched his arm. "Baby, don't say anything."

"Do you think anyone will believe anything you tell them?" said River Askew. "Think hard about who you just killed."

She could not bear to look at the man's face. So she slid, trembling, into what otherwise would have been a cozy little spot by the window with a spectacular view of the mountains gliding below them, if not for the sickening knowledge that she had been seconds away from plunging to her death—and that Shane had sent someone else down in her stead.

Shane, oh, Shane.

"It was self-defense," whispered Shane.

"I know," whispered Akiko.

"Could you remove the knife, please?" said Cody.

"Fly," said Jonas Friend.

They flew.

Shane held her. But she held him, too. Outside was endless beauty created by an alien god.

They flew and flew. For how long, Akiko couldn't tell. Adrenaline changed your perception of time, Akiko realized with melancholy interest.

For a few hundred seconds, Akiko kept her eyes on these two motherfucking monsters: Jonas Friend and River Askew, the last of the Big Five. So did Shane.

Twenty impossibly long minutes passed.

Everyone seemed to sag at once. The adrenaline ebbing. And the reality, coming at them as fast as the speeding horizon, of the chopper landing somewhere. Somewhere where there were people.

Max, oh, Max.

How quickly Max had shrunk to the size of an ant, alone on that helipad staring bewildered at the body of Cal Peers. A moment later and Max was no longer visible. They had sailed away from the sparkling white tor and cruised low over the endless mountains.

The terror of near death, she realized, had been a kind of punishment.

Akiko closed her eyes. She made a vow. She would keep her night with Max like a secret pressed into a book hidden beneath the floorboards. Maybe she would look at it from time to time in the dead of night. She would remember it with fondness and regret and joy and sickening guilt. Then she would put it back in its hiding place.

She pressed her wet face into Shane's chest and kept it there.

Max stayed behind.

Why?

Was it to stop whatever cyberattack Pilot had planned? Did he somehow know something about it that she did not? Maybe. Maybe not. Max himself said that hacks don't last, and he was right—the world would recover.

So why?

Akiko felt the wristbands on her wrists, and had an inkling. She imagined Pilot wriggling free of his restraints and, in a fit of command line fury, detonating their wristbands from afar. That must be what Max was going back to stop.

Or—what if the wristbands were on a timer? What if they detonated outside a certain distance from the facility?

What if, what if.

The cargo chopper would cut through the sky and land somewhere where there were people, people like police. Everything would come out.

All of it would come out, and the whole world would know. And there she would be. Her face, everywhere.

She thought back to that moment at Point Whittier when she had stared out at the ocean, stunned by Pilot's invitation forever ago. Had the trap already been set at that point? How long had Pilot been planning this bloodbath?

What if they hadn't answered his invitation?

What if they had just gotten jobs instead and lived normal lives like normal people?

What if?

All possible universes came crashing down, and in the end they were nothing more than glass. Only one remained intact.

She got up out of her seat and began rummaging through storage cabinets.

"What are you doing?" said Jonas Friend, still holding the blade at Cody's neck.

Akiko ignored him. She glanced at Shane, and Shane understood, flinging open locker after locker until he found a pair of specialized pliers. He grasped how it operated instantly, unlocking some kind of safety latch and rotating it into an open and ready position.

Shane always did like his tools.

"Baby, I think this will work," he said.

"It has to," said Akiko.

"Do not fucking try anything," said River Askew. He nodded at Jonas Friend, as if they were a couple of tough guys.

Akiko ignored them both. She held out her wrists.

"I should be wearing insulated gloves, but whatever," muttered Shane. It was a meaningless precaution, since Akiko herself had no insulation against the wristbands, but she said nothing. Now was not the time to correct him.

Now was the time to let Shane be Shane.

"Do it," she said.

He slid the tool's jaws under a wristband and crunched it down. Akiko expected it to spark, but nothing happened—the metal simply flattened, but held.

"Cut mine next," said River Askew.

"Stay the fuck back," said Akiko, keeping her eyes on Shane. He squeezed and squeezed, but the metal would not give. His hand slipped; the tool had pinched the flesh between his thumb and index finger, which now bled.

"I can't cut it," said Shane, sucking the wound.

"Oh, baby, your hand," said Akiko.

She found herself clutched in Shane's arms and closed her eyes to see his face staring back at her all underlit blue and white by the pool water agitated by the partygoers splashing around them. His thumb caressing her scar like it was sacred.

"Did you cut them?" said River Askew.

The bracelets would not come off. Maybe they would explode; maybe they would not. Either way, it didn't matter. The instant they touched ground on the other side of this nightmare, there would be questions.

Are you Version Zero?

How did you meet Pilot Markham?

And so on.

It was the end of her. It was the end of them.

"I love you," she told Shane, struggling against her own thundering heart.

"I love you, too, baby."

Maybe Max would be the one to get out of this whole thing safe.

Down the snowy slope, maybe, passing through villages that slowly grew in size until he reached a big city where he could dissolve into the crowd. Maybe he would come visit them in prison or whatever.

If they were lucky enough to make it to prison.

Separate cells, River Askew had said.

Wherever they wound up, she vowed to deny Max's involvement every time anyone mentioned his name, tit for tat. Every time. She would tell Shane to do the same. She was never going to give Max up.

Never gonna give you up

Never gonna let you down

Impossibly, Akiko found herself laughing. The two CEOs turned to look at her with incredulous eyes.

Shane released her to try once more with the tool, but he slipped yet again. The metal wristbands held.

"Fuck," he screamed.

"Baby, come here," said Akiko, and this time she held him. She wanted to rest. Rest forever and die there clutched tightly together.

"Give me that," said River Askew, approaching now.

Akiko kicked him hard and sent him back up against Jonas Friend, who exploded in a shower of sparks.

"What?" screamed Jonas Friend. A half second later it was River Askew's turn. Akiko watched as the magical trail of sparklers, pretty as small street fireworks, severed their hands clean off.

They waited for theirs to ignite as well, but nothing happened.

Akiko raised her wrists and stared at the bracelets with wonder. She pushed in the crown. The bracelets came free. Had they reached some trigger radius? Had Pilot marked them exempt from automatic detonation?

Why, Pilot?

The sparks that had swarmed the cockpit died in an instant, leaving the whole cabin steadily flooding with smoke. A harsh beeping filled Akiko's ears. She held her breath and watched as the two CEOs lay bleeding, dying, now dead.

The Big Five, all dead now.

In the last moment before the smoke obliterated her vision she saw Shane hold on to a chair arm. She did the same. Together they held tight as the world took a sickening pitch down.

"Goddammit," said Cody. "Am I bleeding?"

Cody's last word came out as a wet gurgle.

The rest of it was a strange, amazing dream in which gravity stopped working and Akiko's hair orbited her in resplendent liquid ribbons. Every part of her body drifted just an inch from where they should be: her arms from the armrests, her head from the headrest, her feet from the floor.

Then the chopper found ground. There were three hard bounces, like a triple jump colossal in scale, then a final long slide through an endless wall of pure snow that Akiko thought would never end. But it did end, and the world became a chattering storm of glass and groaning metal before falling utterly silent.

3.6

Max stared at the body of Cal Peers. The chopper was gone. All was silent. A perfect contour of snowslope next to the helipad had been ruined by a small avalanche triggered by the thundering helicopter, which had sent a shelf of glittering white tumbling down.

Max turned around to watch it go. It was beautiful.

The piece broke apart as it gathered speed, then hit a distant valley floor with such a sound that Max thought it might start a grand concerto of avalanches.

But the snow held.

No sound but footsteps.

Max glanced back just in time to be tackled to the ground with a sharp crack.

He felt cool air on his face. His mask was no longer there.

When Max opened his eyes, he saw the face of Cal Peers above him.

"Die," said Cal Peers, and he brought down both clasped fists onto Max's forehead.

The world fell sideways with a bounce, which Max realized was his head flopping to the right. There was a quick blackout as Cal Peers struck again, and the world became like a piece of negative film.

Cal Peers raised his fists for the next blow.

Max quickly flinched this time. Cal Peers's hands scored only a glancing blow. Max braced his arms and kicked—a mad sprint nowhere—and the man staggered back.

Max kicked at the ground now to put distance between them.

"You die here," said Cal Peers, rising to his feet.

Max felt his heart stop. CEOs tended to be very tall—and indeed, Cal Peers had more than a foot on him. Max could see this ending badly. Even if he fought as hard as he could, even if things devolved into slapping and kicking and biting, nothing could change the physics of a heavy person versus a light one.

Beyond the platform rail was nothing but open air for a hundred feet.

Max could see things ending very badly.

Ending alone, and cold, and silent.

Max did not want to die alone. He wanted to die surrounded by family and friends in a ranchito where it was always warm and full of talk.

He had enough time for a single dry swallow.

Cal Peers flung off his premium quilted winter vest and began a stumbling approach—injured, but too drunk with rage to notice his own limp.

Max could go back into the facility. There were things there. There were doors to slam and rooms to hide in, at the very least.

But he couldn't go there—Pilot was still strapped to a chair inside. A sitting duck. Cal would kill him, and then there would be no way to stop whatever cyberassault he had planned.

Everything that could go wrong had gone wrong in the wrongest way possible, but Max vowed to not let Pilot's final crime happen.

"I'm driving the fuck outta here," yelled Max, and he ran in the opposite direction.

Toward the cubist communications tower.

Max yelled *I'm driving the fuck outta here* to lure Cal Peers with the decoy promise of some sort of emergency vehicle, and it worked. Max had no idea if there was any such vehicle.

Max ran fast—nothing could change the physics of heavy and light bodies, and he darted across the narrow catwalk, sending exquisite chains of snow into the abyss, while Cal Peers lumbered forth.

Max flung open the tower door, then slammed it shut with the sound of a hundred steel timpani.

He found himself in an echoing steel vestibule painted green. All exposed conduits and steel mesh landings and structural beams, like a submarine balanced vertically on one end. There was a cot, and a dresser, a little fridge, a stove—Cody's quarters. No knives or anything useful.

The front door had no lock. Max looked for something to bar it with, found nothing.

The tower contained a single large spiral staircase climbing hundreds of feet up. Max did not want to go up. He spotted an iron service door, pulled it. It groaned for the first time in decades, but held firm.

"Fuck," said Max.

He looked back through the reinforced glass window slat and saw Cal Peers now just steps away.

"Fuck," said Max again and, *pong pong pong*, began climbing the metal stairs.

Max heard the door slam open; the timpani filled the air.

"Grahh," said Cal Peers, and took the stairs, *doom doom doom*.

Max's mind went blank. With curiosity he noticed that what they said was true—that the field of focus narrowed to a tiny circle during moments of extreme stress. He could've found a heavy something and flung it down, after all. Used his high position to his advantage. He could've kicked Cal Peers from above.

But all Max could think to do was run.

"Gnn," said Cal Peers, and something struck Max in the back hard enough to make him fall into the edge of a stairstep. It was a chunk of concrete, expertly thrown. Max tasted blood and, unbelievably, checked if all his teeth were intact.

They were.

Good thing you took the time out to check, Max.

Because now Cal Peers was right there behind him, snatching at an ankle. Max kicked and scrambled. His shoe came off in Cal Peers's hand.

Keep it, he thought. Then he leapt, taking the stairs two, three at a time.

The *doom doom doom* behind him paused. Something squeaked, then shattered. Then Cal Peers's footsteps resumed.

Max dared a glance: Cal Peers now held something in his hands.

A bat.

A broom.

An ax.

No, thought Max. How had he missed that? His field of vision finally opened up to reveal a three-ring binder filled with mummified papers. Max threw it.

The binder exploded on impact, split easily by the blade of Cal Peers.

Maybe there's another ax farther up, thought Max. *Maybe there's a working gun. Maybe there's a jetpack and I can fly away like Astro Boy.*

Max read *Astro Boy* for the first time by a Christmas tree when he was little.

He realized his entire life was beginning to flash by in his mind. This was bad.

"Stop," he said to his mind.

"First you," said Cal Peers, climbing and climbing. "Then Pilot, then your garbage parents, your garbage friends, everyone."

Max ran. He found a thermos, threw it. He found a folding chair on a landing.

Cal Peers batted the chair away, and it flapped to the ground far below like a shot bird.

doom doom doom

Max looked up and found a curved rectangle of light outlined above. He ran to it, this time making sure to scan with crazed eyes at everything, anything along the way—what he should've been doing all along.

And finally, he found it.

A small orange case with the clear pictogram of an emergency flare, captioned in Cyrillic. Yes. He unclipped it from the wall and kept going.

He reached the rectangle of light in record time—Cal Peers was at least ten seconds behind—and shoved the hatch open on shrieking hinges.

He emerged into pure light and cold. He stomped the hatch shut. The latch crumbled in his hands, but no matter. He walked as close to the opposite edge of the rooftop as he dared—it was so small, this rooftop—knelt, scrambled to load the flare gun, and aimed.

He could hear it: *doom doom doom doom*

The hatch bounced, then was silent. It bounced again.

Max freshened his grip.

The hatch burst open to reveal a triumphant ax-head shining in the sun.

Max knew how to do this. Look down the barrel with one eye, line it up—

Cal Peers stood tall on the rooftop now. A nice big target.

Max squeezed.

The flare ignited within the barrel for a disturbingly long instant before propelling itself out in a smoky line that ended at Cal Peers's armpit.

Cal Peers did not cry out. He danced. He hit himself over and over, for his shirt was on fire, and now his flesh, and for a moment Max thought how ironic it was that they were surrounded by a natural fire extinguisher—snow—but could not use any of it.

Max glanced at the ax on the ground. Cal Peers immediately clocked his intent and stepped on the handle: *Mine*. He tried to raise his arm, but winced. He seemed to accept this situation, like a cyborg would. *Left leg at 60 percent capability; left arm at 10 percent; dominant arm still fully functional.*

Cal Peers, as hurt as he was, knelt to get the ax. He looked like he had dipped his hand into a lake of hellfire. He clawed red streaks onto his pants to wipe them clean, prepared a one-handed backswing, and approached with renewed anger.

Goddammit.

There was no escape from that stupid ax except off the roof and far down, and Max did not know how deep the snow went. Perhaps it went for centuries.

He fumbled the second and final flare in. But the barrel was all wrong.

"You child," said Cal Peers. "You imbecile."

The cartridge was *backwards*, goddammit. Fucking *backwards*.

"You think you are so good," said Cal Peers, enjoying watching Max struggle with the gun. "There is no good. There is no evil."

Max pounded the cartridge in. Yes.

"There is only me versus you," said Cal Peers.

"Now there's just me, fucker," said Max.

Max aimed, fired, and went momentarily deaf.

The flare had not propelled itself. It had exploded with a sharp *pok* that repeated again and again across the mountains.

How old were these flares? Thirty years old? Forty? Max wanted to cry.

Max was indeed crying. His face was covered in wet.

All of this and for what, was all he could think.

Max wiped his face and found blood, not tears. His hand—oh God, his hand—was still there, sweet beautiful hand, but he could not move it. It felt numb, like when you hit a line drive with an aluminum bat, but a thousandfold. He raised his arm reflexively, expecting to be hacked in half by Cal Peers.

But Cal Peers was admiring the scenery.

Specifically, Cal Peers was admiring the millions of tons of snow now rushing at them, unlocked by the sound of the exploding flare.

There were no more cartridges for the gun. Max stood and prepared to fight.

Fight with what?

When Max was a kid, he hit his first fastball line drive with an alumi-num bat and marveled at the numbness in his hands while everyone screamed at him to run—

The rooftop jolted. Snow must have hit the base of the tower. Max regained his balance and dropped as low to the ground as he could.

Which—*of course, idiot*—Cal Peers took as an opportunity to charge anew. He raised the ax once again. Max crouched but stayed low, for now the tower was really bobbling. No—the tower was *leaning.*

Maybe the tower would go down, and they would both die. Wouldn't that be funny?

"We can't be here," said Max to no one. He found a curved pipe, hooked a foot into it, and waited.

Cal Peers spat in response. He took four good sprinting strides, but the fifth was no good. A wave of ice had sent a seismic spasm up the tower. Cal Peers fell to his side and knocked his lungs flat. And with the tower now at an almost rooftop angle, the tall man slid like a baseball player going for home.

Except he slid straight off the edge.

The ax drummed the rooftop and caught its neck in a pipe vent with a *king.*

Max looked up at a small sound.

"Help," wheezed Cal Peers. He gripped a thin rooftop antenna using his good arm. The antenna uprooted a bit with every attempt to pull himself up.

Max stared at this man, pleading openly. Max knew where this would go.

"Please help," said Cal Peers.

"Things You Can Do when you're holding on for dear life," mur-mured Max.

"What?" said Cal Peers, perplexed. The antenna came free in his hand.

Cal Peers vanished.

Thirty seconds later, the snow stopped thundering. It had completed its journey miles down the mountainside.

All was silent again, but for the steady *tic tic tic* of the straining tower.

Max pictured Cal Peers trapped under megatons of ice. Undiscovered for centuries of centuries. Maybe one day, far in the future, unlucky explorers would find his frost-blackened body and unwittingly wake the dormant virus of evil contained within, releasing it unto the world.

But for now, Max assured himself, the world was safe.

His evil was gone.

3.7

Max slid the mask over his face again.

Mister Black Halo.

The mask hurt. He wondered how bad his face looked. But he had no time to care about that right now. Inside, the cameras were still live. The world was no doubt still watching. They had no idea of all that had happened outside the complex.

Max had soldier-crawled his way across the leaning rooftop. He retrieved the ax from the metal vent. He tiptoed down the stairs inside the tower, as if he were nudging the entire structure by fractions of degrees with each step.

Finally he had reached the bottom of the tower, exited, and gingerly crossed the catwalk gone all twisted like a ribbon.

The ax was heavy.

No, Max was weak. He felt everything drained out of him. He dragged the ax behind him—a not unpleasant ceramic sound—and entered the main building.

"Pilot," said Max.

"Max," came Pilot's voice from below, as if he were greeting an old friend.

"I'm not playing," said Max. "There's gonna be serious consequences if—if—"

If what?

If Pilot did not take back the lives he had ended?

If Pilot ended more, beyond Max's reach?

"If what, Max?" said Pilot with a strange laugh.

Max turned and strode down the hall with purpose, the ax scratching a hairline into the shiny floor behind him.

"Tell me, Max," laughed Pilot. "What is that sound?"

Max walked and walked. He did not pick up the ax. He did not run. He did not want to see if the universe had some freak fatal trip-and-fall up its sleeve.

Iceland, thought Max.

Norway.

Greenland, Las Vegas, Bangkok.

He passed the sleeping quarters, pressed the mahogany panel with the brass clock, and entered the control room. There sat Pilot's strange laptop, looking like a blast shield fragment from an alien ship crash.

Compromise Status.

Charge State.

The timecodes, ratcheting down.

This was the thing. It had to be. He unplugged the laptop from its elaborate monitor moorings, disconnecting it from the array of cameras throughout the complex. The world now watched through one lens and one lens only: the tiny camera eye at the top of the laptop screen. Max did not dare close the lid, for fear of locking himself out.

He jogged back down to the arena.

He passed the body of Brayden Turnipseed, splayed now with limbs stiffening like roots searching for purchase. The boy had a fine mind, if a little chaotic and in need of direction. But to one degree or another, everyone's mind was chaotic. Everyone's mind was in need of direction.

Snuffing out a mind was like hiding a forest from the sun, forever keeping you from discovering what lived within.

Goddammit, Brayden, your young mind did not deserve this.

He had the absurd urge to cover him with a tarp as a meager show of respect in this godforsaken arena on this godforsaken mountaintop. How absolutely wretched.

But Max had no time even for that.

At the center of the arena was a dais, and upon that dais sat Pilot Markham. A thin line of blood ran from his nose where Shane had punched him.

Max knelt before the laptop and got to work without a word. He nudged the cursor around. He struggled to navigate the interface.

"Max," said Pilot.

Max just shook his head. Unbelievable, that this man would want to talk to him.

"I deeply regret what I did to Brayden," said Pilot.

Max clenched his fist hard for a second. He wanted to tell Pilot to shut up forever. He wanted to tell him to just die and cease existing. But he still needed Pilot. He hated that he still needed him.

"He was an immediate threat," said Pilot. "And I did what I had to do to maintain the agenda."

If only Max could shut him up forever and work in peace.

Max stood up, swung, and drove the heavy ax blade into Pilot's chest with a woody crack.

Max blinked awake. He had done no such thing, of course.

There Pilot sat with that stupid look on his face that begged: *Can we still be friends?*

"Brayden was not a bad person," said Pilot. "What I did was not a judgment of his character."

"Just," shouted Max, before forcing himself to calm, "tell me how to disable the wristbands."

Max glanced up to see Pilot looking hurt, and for an idiotic second Max felt bad. A leftover reflex between friends. Max had to remind himself that this person—this thing strapped to the chair—only bore a familiar face on the surface. Everything beneath was dark crimson and foreign.

"The wristbands have an out-of-range function," said Pilot. "They either detonate or disable, depending on the user setting. Akiko and Shane are set to safe, I promise you."

Max closed his eyes. "Just show me."

"Max, I promise you. Go to Phantom Reality, Groups, All Groups, Settings, Out-of-Range Settings. But you will need—"

"I'll need a password, I know."

Max was confronted with a password window, and typed it in:

NOELLEPHANT

"Oh," said Pilot.

He found the list of users. Akiko and Shane were indeed set to DISABLE. So was Max.

The others were not.

Max tried to change the three remaining CEOs from DETONATE to DISABLE, but could not. Almost idly, Max touched the crown of one wristband and startled to see it spring open. The other one came free just as easily.

"I would never hurt my friends," said Pilot.

Max squeezed his temples as hard as he could. *Keep moving.*

"Tell me how to stop the hack," said Max.

Pilot wiggled his fingers before regripping them, as if taunting Max. He smiled.

"I am not going to hack anyone."

"Bullshit. Is it a flood attack? Some kind of zero-day thing? Is it a power grid reboot loop?"

Max turned the laptop. Its little webcam was still broadcasting. He gave the world a clear view of Pilot, framed askew at a Dutch angle.

"What was that shit on your laptop?" said Max. "Those data centers."

"Data exchanges, not data centers," said Pilot, peeved. "But that is beside the point. I just—I just—"

Max raised the ax. "I'm about to swing this right into your face, man."

And without warning, Pilot burst into tears. It made Max stop. He lowered the ax.

"I would like to confess my crimes," said Pilot.

Max adjusted his grip. "You mean besides the three dead people right here?"

"They need to know the reason before everything goes dark," said Pilot. "They need to know why. Please."

"Whatever—everything goes dark, it'll all just come back online in a few days, because hacks don't last. I don't know if you want attention or what, but you're not getting it."

Pilot smiled. Max raged right at his face with the ax drawn and ready.

"You killed three people, asshole. Your daughter is dead. None of this is going to bring her back. Certainly not some hack."

Pilot laughed. "The funny thing is we are in violent agreement."

"Fuck you."

"Hacks do not last. That is why I want to destroy."

Max blinked.

"Destroy forever," said Pilot.

Max could only blink and blink. Words fled his mind. In their place was a dark shape revealing itself, and Max could only stare with terrified awe.

"When you are someone like me," said Pilot, "you can get any kind of friend you want. Not real friends, of course. What with their ludicrous ideologies. But anyway. They are better than any dumb hack."

"What are you talking about?" said Max.

Pilot spoke into the camera. "I am talking about a hundred tons of explosives placed for me all around the world by special friends. Hello, special friends. I am the one who hired you."

When Max was a kid, people had predicted mayhem for the year 2000. The Y2K bug, it had been called. Computers, unable to handle the double-zero year integer, would throw the world into chaos: planes falling from the sky, banking systems freezing, surgery rooms going dark in midincision. And in the end, of course, nothing of the sort happened.

But this was not that.

This was real.

"Bullshit," said Max. "You can't blow up the internet. It's physically impossible."

Pilot darkened. "Everyone says that! The hubris of that statement! That a man-made thing is somehow exempt from the laws of physics! As if we were gods!"

Pilot spat at the laptop camera. "The internet is not a clean little puffy cloud high above the icky-sticky mucky-muck of the physical world. It has a backbone, of cables and wires and chips and air-conditioned buildings surrounded by razor fences and cameras and guards. It is physical. It will be broken. Forever."

Max took a deep breath. He had to stay level. Pilot, he realized now, was a psychopath; but every psychopath has his logic.

"You can't do this," said Max. "It's going to fuck shit up so bad."

Pilot looked confused. "But you yourself said people would not change unless we had an A-bomb. I am giving you your A-bomb."

"I didn't mean it literally." Max was shouting.

"So you said one thing but meant another? I thought you had integrity. That is what I always liked about you."

Max blinked. "When I said *break something in order to fix it* I didn't mean *break the internet*. Whole systems depend on it. Markets and hospitals and fucking power grids—Pilot, you can't do this."

Pilot looked hurt.

"All I wanted was to fix what we have," said Max. "Not like what you're doing."

"But I thought you would love this," said Pilot.

The wrongness of this statement sent Max off balance. *I thought you would love this.* What had Max been to Pilot this whole time? A mirror? Some sort of moral proxy? It scared Max to his core to realize that when people saw one another, they all saw different things. They saw what they wanted to see, or what they wished to be, or what they wished to destroy, or this or that or the other and blablabla forever in infinite shattered permutations.

But no one ever could see things as they were for real.

So maybe that meant there was no such thing as *for real.*

And that was what scared Max, down to his very core.

Max looked at the tiny numbers under his taped thumbnail. He made a fist and squeezed it hard for a long moment.

I thought you would love this.

He navigated to the window with the list of data exchanges and their various countdowns and tried clicking one.

AUTHENTICATE

Easy. Max typed in the password: NOELLEPHANT. The window dismissed itself.

But another window appeared.

ADDITIONAL SECURITY REQUIRED

PLEASE PROVIDE FINGERPRINT ID

Fuck.

Max looked at Pilot. He slid the laptop under Pilot's bound hand. He wiped his hands on his pants and gripped the ax.

"Pilot, I'm gonna need your fingerprint now."

3.8

Pilot liked how this arena had turned out.

It had taken a full year to renovate the whole facility. It was a fine facility, and kept the elements out with an easy strength.

Now, with the window blown open above, it would take only a day or so to fill with snow. After that, nature would most likely move in to reclaim it.

Pilot pictured the arena as a cozy den for wolves to raise their young in, and warmed at the thought. How one little breach could change everything.

Max looked furious, holding his ax like that. It saddened Pilot. Of all things, he had not expected to infuriate Max. He had imagined the opposite happening in his mind so many times: revealing the big surprise endgame, Max hugging him and high-fiving him and telling him it was just what he wanted, too, but had been too nervous to explicitly suggest something so audacious.

They would return home, victorious and vindicated, and Max would perhaps move in—Pilot had plenty of room to spare, maybe Noelle's old room even, for by then Pilot would finally have the courage to clean it out and start fresh.

A brand-new start. A clean slate. A friend to trust until his dying day.

Things were not going that way.

He did not know how to make Max happy. He was not sure if he ever could again. His hunch about Max turned out to be a total failure of intuition.

How could my instincts have been so wrong? thought Pilot.

How could I not have seen this coming?

How could anyone?

That left only one thing to do, really.

Pilot turned to gaze at the laptop camera and addressed the world.

"Men like me are the cause of all the problems ever in the history of this country. Men like me always choose the path of greed and cruelty. The path of evil."

Max slammed the butt of the ax into the ground with a loud *king.*

"Pilot, unlock the laptop."

Pilot ignored him and shut his fist tight around his thumb.

"Men like me," continued Pilot, "are responsible for slavery, exploitation, genocide, rape, more than any other group in American history. For our thievery, we get statues in our name. We are the nation's worst terrorists, and we could stop it all tomorrow if we wanted to. But we do not. I, Pilot Markham, am one of those men."

"Pilot." Max tried to wrench his fist open, but Pilot held firm.

"We had a chance with the internet," said Pilot. He discovered tears flowing out of his eye ducts and savored the release. "A perfect utopia! And yet: we chose again the path of evil, this time unhampered by physical distance or time or visible identifiers—just anonymous, pure evil flowing freely to all corners of the world."

"Unlock it or I swear I will do it for you," said Max, shouting now. His sweat-slicked hands slipped and fumbled to no avail around Pilot's unyielding fist.

Pilot decided he had better wrap things up.

"Oh, what a glorious, gorgeous mess I have made," said Pilot through his tears. It felt so good to say all this. "Every invention unto a perversion, every touch unto blood, every daughter unto a lamb for slaughter. But now it is time to wipe the slate clean. Now it is time for you to place all your blame onto me, so that when I finally die that blame dies, too. Then you can rebuild, all together this time, as one."

It felt so good, to release like this before the whole world. Pilot could not wipe his tears, nor did he want to. His cheeks shone with wet.

Three years of planning in secret were coming to an end. The bombs would detonate; Pilot's soul would descend into the oblivion, where he would confront Noelle's killers forever, if such a thing as oblivion even existed.

The world—awakened by Pilot's death—will build it all new, build it smart, build it fair the next time around, and Pilot wished he could be there to see it.

But he accepted that he deserved no such privilege.

"This must end with my death," he said to Max. "If you have a shred of friendship remaining for me you will give me that."

Max raised the ax. He swung. Pilot closed his eyes to receive the blow.

King.

"I will never give you what you want," said Max.

At first Pilot thought Max had cut his hand free from its bonds, but when he looked down he saw that he had split it in half; the blade of the ax separated his index finger and thumb at a rude angle. Max worked the blade back and forth until the thumb came free.

The pain was unlike anything Pilot had felt before. Every cell in his body erupted in a chorus of red and juicy violet. Every pore opened as wide as it could and spewed all of it: fear, sweat, bile, blood.

Pilot screamed in pain, and it felt like singing.

Max wiped the thumb clean on his shirt.

"Kill me," said Pilot, screaming at the ceiling.

But Max dropped the ax. He muttered:

"You're not dying anytime soon, fucker."

Max headed for the laptop. He opened it. He put Pilot's thumb on the pad and watched the interface awaken.

"I'm stopping this countdown, and then I'm getting out of here, and the cops are gonna find you, and you're gonna go to jail forever," said

Max. He stared at Pilot's laptop. "They'll make a movie out of your stupid story. It'll probably entertain some people for a while, but then you'll be gone, just nothing."

Why was Max being so relentlessly cruel?

He was so hard to read with that damn Black Halo mask covering his face.

"You taught me so much," said Pilot, pleading now. "I want to teach the world, too."

"What the fuck are these menus?" muttered Max, clicking around.

Max was really going to do it. He was smart; it would take him no time to figure out how to stop it. Why?

"Please reconsider," screamed Pilot.

"Pipe the fuck down," said Max, not looking at him.

Pilot watched as Max found the main window. The one with the names of the data exchanges in cities across the globe. *Compromise Status. Charge State.*

Max's eyes widened at the sight of the timecode numbers. Only two minutes left. Away they ticked.

Max bore into the laptop screen and seemed to forget all about Pilot, which hurt.

"Just let it happen," said Pilot. "It will fix everything. You will see."

A calm overcame Pilot now. All pain had vanished. He saw things clearly: his hand was almost half its normal width now, well lubricated with blood, and so simple to draw through the crude knot of cable restraining it.

It was a tricky, messy affair untying the other hand without the benefit of a thumb, but he managed it, and after that it took mere seconds to free his feet.

Pilot rose and stood tall.

"My beloved friend Maximilian Portillo," he said.

Max stopped at the sound of his name spoken out loud for the entire world to hear. He looked at Pilot through his mask. Max looked and looked as if God himself were addressing him.

Oh, quit being so full of yourself, thought Pilot. You are no god.

Just make sure this life at least meant something.

"In the name of all that I have desecrated," said Pilot, "I now sacrifice myself for the sake of humanity. Let me become an eternal flame of remorse, and let Maximilian Portillo be forever known as the hero brave enough to carry this light out into the dark."

Pilot had written and rewritten these lines many times in his mind and hoped they were not too melodramatic. But a big moment deserved a big statement. He decided it was perfect.

Pilot positioned himself. He was framed correctly in the camera.

Good.

He raised his wristbands to his throat and struck his fists together thrice in a special gesture to ignite the sparks and send a torrent of blood whipping forth like a scarf in a gale—so curious the lack of pain, so thrilling the way his field of vision turned upside down, as his head no doubt flopped to one side like a broken stuffed animal billowing from a torn neck, never mended.

3.9

When Shane opened his eyes he found himself on his back, staring up at the sky through a bent window lined with ice.

Not ice. Safety glass. It was pretty.

A hand rested on Shane's neck. He held it, but it was cold, and it moved wrong.

Shane bolted upright and flung the severed hand out into the snow.

"Baby," said Akiko. Where was she? Shane wheeled around and saw her, rising from underneath a leather seat that had come unmoored from the undulating floor.

"Baby," he said. "Oh God, you're okay. Oh, baby bear, baby bear."

He examined her from every angle, touching and prodding and smoothing as he went. Finally he crushed her in his arms.

"Oh, my baby bear," he kept saying. "I almost lost you."

"I'm right here," she said. She hoisted her arms to embrace him, and her hands found their familiar purchase on his shoulder blades. She cupped her hands and clung. And the strength and ease of all their years were there waiting for him.

At their feet lay the men, all dead. Cody was dead, bled out from his neck gone ragged. Jonas Friend, River Askew. They lay covered by a blanket of glittering glass cubes.

"Baby?" said Akiko, full of worry. Shane realized he had been breathing hard, as if he were trying not to throw up.

She led him away from the bodies and into the blinding, serene snowscape, where the air was cold and dry and clean. Shane took huge gulps of it, then exhaled in long frosty jets. He did this ten times.

The helicopter had carved a gash a mile long. Shane gave silent thanks to Cody. A pilot's pilot, right up until the end. Executing a textbook crash landing even as the life gushed out of him.

"We have to go back for Max," said Shane.

"Baby, it's miles away."

"He's stuck there with that psycho. We have to get him before he does what he did to Brayden."

Shane began trudging up the slope, where the snow grew deeper and deeper until he was wading with his arms.

"Baby," said Akiko. "Hey."

Shane stopped. His face felt hot, so hot. He took two handfuls of the snow and pressed them to his steaming face.

"We have to get him," said Shane, weeping.

Arms reached to hold him from behind. Shane wheeled about and grasped Akiko.

"I thought I lost you," he said. "I thought I lost you."

"You never lost me. You saved me."

"You saved me," said Shane.

"I guess I owed you," said Akiko.

Shane squared his eyes. "Do you love me?"

Something in Akiko's face broke, and tears began trailing down. "I do."

There was guilt there. Shane saw it. Seeing it was enough. He did not need to hear an apology.

"And you're never going to leave me for someone else?"

"Never."

"Never ever?"

"Never ever ever."

Akiko nodded fast, shaking the tears free.

He kissed her, and it was the only warm spot in the world.

"We have to find help or something," said Akiko.

"Oh, baby," said Shane. "How do we do that without giving ourselves up?"

"We'll figure something out."

She suddenly seemed to remember something. She showed him her fingernails: two of them had tape on them, and under the tape were tiny handwritten numbers. She made a fist to protect them.

"What is that?" said Shane.

"We got paid," said Akiko. "Remember?"

Shane stared and stared at her fist. He opened her fingers and examined the numbers. And his heart convulsed with hope. For no one knew they were here. The only people who saw them without their masks lay dead behind them.

They would use the money slowly. Expand the pool business, buy a modest house, then upgrade to something bigger. Have two kids, a boy and a girl. Take five or ten years to do it.

There would be no rush.

Friends and family would come visit, congratulate him on his success, perhaps ask him how he did all this. Shane would have answers for that. Hard work and patience. A little bit of luck.

Perhaps people would ask him about his good friend Max, and he could honestly answer that he did not know, perhaps he was traveling, perhaps he was on a boat circling the globe.

For now, Shane prayed to God that, please, Max needed to live; that Shane did not care if anything had ever happened between him and Akiko; that none of that mattered anymore.

Please, God, just let Max finish whatever he needed to do and get away from Pilot alive and then please let everything be all right.

Shane couldn't wait to hear why Max had stayed behind. Akiko whispered something about a cyberattack. If it was as big as all that, that meant Max would be one of the biggest heroes ever.

Shane couldn't wait to see Max again.

Akiko shivered. It was freezing in the shade but hot in the sun—one of those types of days—and they moved to the sunny side of the wreck, where they discovered a back storage section spilling with emergency equipment: parkas, gloves, first aid kits, flares.

Shane held up a radio with a question on his face, but they both knew it was off-limits. The last thing Shane wanted was police swarming their position, asking questions. Akiko shook her head at it. He tossed the radio back into the metal cabinet with a clank.

They suited up. The days were longer in this part of the world. That would be advantageous.

Before him Shane saw the clear long slope of a piedmont, ten or so miles of white melting into black and then rows of green and russet brown, where a tiny thread of smoke rose from a building set among a little copse of trees. It was a walk they could make in a few hours. They filled their parka pockets with water pouches and ration bars.

Shane turned to take in the view. When he turned back to Akiko, he found her staring at something in her hands. A small, round, black thing, attached to a belt loop on her jeans.

The magic eight ball.

Together, they peered at its result:

OUTLOOK GOOD

Then Akiko unhooked the magic eight ball, gave it a squeeze, and let it fall into the snow. It bore a perfectly round, perfectly blue hole six inches deep.

"Let's drag our feet single file," said Shane. "So they don't know how many of us made it."

"Okay," said Akiko.

She took a step, and the dry snow barked in response.

Shane stretched his arm out behind him, and Akiko grasped it, and he led her carefully down the slope, step by step.

3.10

It was the smell.

Max stared at what once was Pilot Markham. His open neck had stopped bubbling. Its fringes were charred, like steak tips, and they smelled like steak tips. With equal parts fascination and revulsion Max realized he had not eaten anything substantial in hours. Anything that had been in his stomach he had vomited up long before he hacked Pilot's hand in half.

Pilot's hand in half.

Pilot's hand in half.

Max looked at his own hands. Opened and closed his fingers. His fingernails had tiny numbers on them. These numbers were protected by bits of tape.

Max blinked. He turned away from the body. The bodies.

Just a few hours ago Max had woken up alone in bed with an infinite view of heaven, dreaming of a girl. He had no idea what time it was. The days were long in this part of the world.

Pilot convulsed slowly six times, like a broken clockwork doll, and finally released his body with a long sigh.

Pilot was dead.

All the way from *I witnessed your moment musicaux, and I say bravo* to dead.

The world had just seen his mentor, the legendary Pilot Markham, eviscerate himself. Mom and Dad had seen it, too. Moments after Pilot had said his name out loud: *My beloved friend Maximilian Portillo.*

There was no explaining this. Max had wanted to change the world. He had wanted to open its eyes, to empower people to the forces that controlled them, and to realize they had the power, quite literally in the palms of their hands, to demand better.

Instead, he had delivered this.

This blood spectacle.

What in God's name was this that lay before him? A body, leaking red with its head dangling at a hellish angle, and no time to cover it up or anything. A man full of promises that turned out to be lies.

The king of all liars, deluded until the very end.

But was it a lie if you believed? Max had believed in Pilot. Pilot had believed in Max. What did that mean? Did it mean Max had a thin foul green vein of psychopathic malice threaded within his body, to match Pilot's?

Which led to the other question:

If Max had never met Pilot, would that thin green vein remain safely unexposed to air, forever, where it belonged?

Max did not get it.

He never would. He did not even have the bearings to feel betrayed by his mentor, so dizzy with shock was he. All he felt was that his life had just now become some kind of legendary mistake. He had just now written himself into the book of history with finger-blood on pages shaved from human skin. And his kidneys, his intestines, and his heart all flooded cold with a nauseating premonition:

He would never be able to face his friends or family again.

He turned to the laptop. It was still open and on. Beside it sat the severed thumb, which he swatted away with revulsion.

The mask was hot. He wanted to take it off. Did the mask even matter anymore, now that the world knew his name?

Max could no longer picture the world.

Down went the timecode numbers. Less than a minute left now. When Max blinked, he saw there were now forty seconds. Had he really sat with his eyes closed for ten whole seconds?

Forty seconds until global mayhem. Would markets tumble? Would planes fall out of the sky? Would cities go dark and trap millions in trains and elevators and jail cells all frozen shut? Max did not know and did not want to know.

He slapped himself. "Wake up, stoner," he said. "Fate of the world."

He reached a strange list of choices. *Dog. Cat. Horse. Bear. Dragon.*

Max saw the secret room upstairs at Pilot's house. He saw the dancing letters spelling NOELLE on the wall. The bed, the dresser, laden with plush toys, all little bears. The broken bear at his feet.

Max could see Noelle growing from a small child to a teen, realizing things about the world, burning with desire to fix those things. Now she is a young woman; now she opens her computer.

She starts a blog. It is easy.

Elsewhere in the world, the trolls also open their computers. They start a discussion thread. It is easy.

And just like that, she is doomed.

Max selected BEAR.

Nothing seemed to happen. The list was still there, the timecodes still spinning down.

Twenty seconds.

Max felt his forehead pricking with heat. Reflexively he flipped the mask up to wipe his face, and winced at the fact that he had just shown his face to the world. But it didn't matter anymore.

Hello, world, thought Max.

How Max wanted a long shower. A glass of cold water. A nap.

"Fifteen seconds," said Max to himself.

He looked harder. There, in the upper right corner of the list, had quietly appeared two tiny red words that had not been there before. Max moved the cursor over them: yes. They highlighted. They were active. All he had to do was click the button.

ABORT ALL

Max clicked, and the words changed:

REALLY TRULY?

Max rested his finger upon the button. But goddammit if there wasn't that voice in his head now:

Oh, what a glorious, gorgeous mess I have made.

Was he not right?

Every touch unto blood, every daughter unto a lamb for slaughter.

Steel into swords. Type into lies. Airplanes into bombs. Television into mind control.

The internet into—

The internet into—

Into what?

Place all your blame onto me.

There was a time before phones and feeds and screens everywhere. Of course there was. Max was very small then, but he remembered parts of it. A screen back then was quite a big deal. Those early ones had a slight squish to them that produced geely rainbow halos when pressed with a fingertip.

So weird, the world before screens.

Or was the world full of screens the weird one?

What would we lose, thought Max, compared to what we would gain? So much technology was required simply to make the world function in 2018. So much technology was required—so goddamn much!—to send something as banal as a hashtag. Don't text and drive. Fear of missing out. Virtual reality. Selfies and the Troll President and revenge porn.

All that.

Five seconds.

What did we gain with the world of screens? thought Max. We managed to live prior to them, didn't we?

Oh my God, thought Max.

Pilot was right.

Max blinked and blinked. He took a breath. He felt utterly calm but bursting with panic at the same time. Huge, but also very small, then huge again.

Max used to think the world simply stopped after death. But now he paused. Maybe Pilot was happy. Maybe he was with Noelle somewhere, on some kind of Glass Island of the mind. Someplace with no signal. She walked a llama fence now become infinitely long, and he held her hand to keep her from falling.

The laptop lens stared at Max.

Hi, Mom, hi, Dad.

Bye, Mom, bye, Dad.

This is what I did with my life. I hope you're proud of me.

Behind the lens the world chattered on and on about all that had happened, all that was happening, all that might happen next. *Who is Max* and *Who is Pilot* and so on. So much gibbleflabble and bluster, just this ever-boiling stew of sound.

"Why?" said Max.

He drew back his hands from the laptop and rested them in his lap.

The numbers counted down to zero. In each row flashed the words:

`IGNITION SUCCESS`

`DETONATING`

`SUCCESS`

`SUCCESS`

`SUCCESS`

`SUCCESS`

`SUCCESS`

`SUCCESS`

Across the world the eighty-eight concussions marched—sharp, towering hits to a drum herald cosmic in scale.

But here, all Max saw was a silent screen.

The laptop blinked. On it appeared the words:

`YOU ARE NOT CONNECTED TO THE INTERNET.`

3.11

Max took his long shower. He watched the blood marble the water and swirl away. He swabbed and bandaged his face, his hand.

He wrapped himself with a blanket and wandered. A mirror panel opened to the plush conversation pit where the instruments still sat waiting for players that would never return.

To one side of the pit was an egg-shaped fireplace. So Max started a fire.

From the sleeping quarters he gathered things—Shane's wallet, Akiko's bag—and put them in the fire to burn away. He put his phone in there, and it crackled apart. He put his mask in there, too, and it burned from the center of the black halo out.

A cherrywood panel swiveled open to lead him down a spiral staircase to a small garage where a large cuboid snowmobile sat. There were rucksacks full of survival gear and rations. There was a waterproof map.

He found a parka and donned it. He pressed a hard rubber button on the wall and watched the garage door scroll up, up, up, to reveal the frozen wonderland sparkling outside.

The vehicle started right away. In the back sat a dozen full canisters of petrol. He could travel for miles and miles, and he would.

At one point, he stopped the vehicle on a virgin slope and cut the engine. He stepped out onto the snow to look at the building he had just left. It was a spectacular work of architecture. A brutalist concrete relic from another time, perched on a forgotten mountain from a forgotten war.

If he still had his wristbands, would he be able to blow up the whole thing?

Or would the wristbands have detonated this far out?

Were Akiko and Shane okay?

He had to believe they were. The sky was dead now. Belief was all that remained.

Max aimed his hand at the building as if he were taking a photo with a phone. He touched his thumb to his palm and made the familiar old sound of the shutter's release.

"Chakee," said Max.

```
76          return BigInt(i) & BigInt(31775n << 50n);
77      }
78      return i;
79  }};
80  for (const i of res) {
81      const bin = BigInt(i).toString(2);
82      let ln = "";
83      for (const j of bin) ln += j == "0" ? " " : "#";
84      console.log(ln);
85  }
```

Hello, world.

Twenty days ago Pilot Markham launched a series of attacks that disabled the internet. He killed five prominent tech CEOs, a pilot, and a teenage boy before killing himself. You will find them in a remote place called Mount Szeitchk. All the deaths happened outside of my control. But I recognize they happened under my leadership as the creator of Version Zero.

You have to know that even though I could've stopped the Outage, I chose not to. I let those eighty-eight catastrophic explosions occur, because it was my hope that they would serve as our lights in the dark. Hope I was right.

I claim full responsibility. I've heard you call me a terrorist. I sympathize with your disgust. Every day I try to be the best human being I can, whatever that means.

For what it's worth, I've learned a thing or two about morality from all this. There is none. No good, no evil. There's only self-interest. Survival of the fittest, like a bad evolutionary habit humanity can't shake. I've thought and thought about why people do the things they do, and this is the best I can come up with. Sorry if it's less than satisfying.

But realize that for every selfish action, there's a selfless reaction battling to preserve the collective good. I've learned that when we stop looking at one another in the eyes, bad things happen. Terrible things.

We all look at each other now in a darkness lit only by the glow of eighty-eight fireballs. Let's remember this moment.

—Maximilian Portillo

The screens went dead.

The feeds tried and tried to refresh, but could not.

We wondered what to do next. Slowly it dawned on all of us that if the feeds were silent, that meant everything else had stopped working, too. So we checked our tablets and laptops and, later, our ATMs and fancy office phones, and were met with only blankness.

No planes fell out of the sky. The power blinked, but stayed on.

Cable news still works. Reporters gleefully showed the eighty-eight smoldering craters scattered around the planet. The backbone of the internet, shattered.

Pilot Markham and Maximilian Portillo have joined the canon of the greatest terrorists in history. Cameras swarmed Max's parents' house but found his mother and father mysteriously missing. Journalists scoured whatever they could still find about him online. Max was a bright student, a budding entrepreneur. Max had befriended one of the greatest innovators of our time, and he turned out to be a psychopath. So had Max, they said.

Max was this, Max was that, they said. There's a book coming out about him.

Max is the most wanted man on the planet.

How weird it was for Shane and me to watch the news, knowing what only we knew.

Technically, the internet has not been killed. It has been de-backboned. It has been shrunk. Sites physically hosted near you are still reachable, but without proper exchanges traffic effectively grinds to a halt. Imagine what nightmare gridlock would ensue if all the streets of your city suddenly became single-lane. The internet needs to be big in order to work properly.

Hundreds of thousands of workers remain furloughed to this day.

Silicon Valley, and all the Silicon wherevers, is a ghost town. On the other hand, television is surging. So are landline telephones, paper forms, paper newspapers, and paper everything else. People dig up old radios and typewriters. Vinyl and tape and music on chip is undergoing a renaissance. Record labels are rejoicing.

People are falling back onto what is now called the original internet, meaning the United States Postal Service. The Darknet is falling back into being the regular old black market.

And on the surface of things, everything looks and acts as it once did.

It's a mix of better and worse.

Trolls have retreated to where they belong: grousing in solitude under bridges. People no longer leave permanent trails of online fodder for them to exploit. It's harder to bully now.

The good parts have gone away, too. Marginalized folks lost their support networks in a blink. Protesting injustice takes much more work now.

It's a mix of better and worse.

But if I had to pick one, I would say *better*. Because we as a species had let out this genie called the internet, and it turned out we were ill-equipped to handle it—but unlike other times in history, we managed to stuff this one back into the bottle.

Or really, Max did.

Teens made zines again. People still made voice phone calls—that part of the smartphone still worked. Factories and power plants—although they at first scrambled with panic—actually now felt more secure without the possibility of online attack. Bankers and finance types freaked out, and would continue to freak out until today. But fuck those people.

For the ordinary person, the world slowed down. And it was kind of nice.

At first, dumb theories flopped around about who really caused the Outage. It was the Big Five, who faked their deaths as part of a hoax designed to pave the way for a totally privatized, pay-per-bit internet version 2.0.

But a few weeks in, a letter appeared in all the major newspapers everywhere.

The letter from Max to the world.

It was reprinted in every language. It was short. It offered no clues. Sometimes I read it again, and again, since my postcards have all gone blank.

The first postcard arrived in a sealed vellum envelope at my doorstep. No stamp. Max's square printed handwriting, writ small in watery blue fountain pen. It said:

Miami now. I thought you were dead. All them mans lying dead-ass-dead and I thought you were, too. I love you both and miss you. Please stay safe. Your new house is sick by the way. And congratulations on the bump.

Yes, I got pregnant. After we made it back, Shane and I just knew we had to. We waited a good long while, as if we needed to give our bodies time to stop jittering. We got married, too. Because what else could possibly be more important?

But also: *Your new house is sick.* That meant he saw the new house. Was he here? Did he hand-deliver the note? It makes my head spin, the thought of our paths coming so close but never touching. But this is the way it has to be.

The postcards kept arriving. They said things like:

Cuba now. Set up Mom and Dad in a mansion by the sea. Even a little fake ranchito there. Couldn't risk seeing them, but I did leave a long note to sorta kinda explain things. They still don't get it really. Parents, lol. Do we still say lol?

The postcards said less and less as the weeks passed.

A ranchito for me someday when I can stop moving around so much. A hangout just for us. Stupid. Anyway. Been thinking about morality. I'm going to write a letter to the world. Keep an eye out for it.

Later:

Budapest. Beautiful city. Don't forget to travel before the baby comes. Tell duncie to stop buying so much crap.

And still later:

Singapore. Police state. Never again.

And:

Korea. A wonderland.

That was the last one, from weeks ago. The ink on these blank post-cards vanished in twenty-four hours once exposed to air. But still, I feel the need to keep them. Safe and secure and hidden in my closet.

It's Day 394 of the Outage now.

There my apps sit on my phone, waiting for the information plumbing to start spouting data again.

We're still no closer to getting back online than we were on Zero Day, although the nerd elite keep trying. The nerds, frantically debating how to rebuild the internet in a genuinely decentralized, backbone-free way using personal data pods over a mix of network infrastructure—cable, broadcast wireless, copper, even peer-to-peer packet radios, how geeky is that—for better resiliency and redundancy and whatever. They talk about a return to the spirit of the early internet, like Arpanet, when there were no Big Five, no capitalist interests, no trolls, just a few hundred users who trusted each other.

For what is a civilization without trust?

Good luck, nerds.

Shane and I are headed to Japan for our babymoon. We're flying first class. It's still amazing to fly first class. I will never get used to it.

I stopped programming, of course. I haven't touched a computer in a long while.

The money lives in an island in the Caribbean. Satow Pool receives funding from an anonymous, autonomous angel investor. It funded our house. It funded our plane tickets.

We waited for the cops to stop coming before buying the house. We thought Max had been at start-up boot camp this whole time, we told them. We had no idea he was capable of such a thing.

Shane made me a mixtape for the flight and got two pairs of tiny wireless earbuds for my brand-new audiophile-quality music player that probably cost a fortune. It's stupid—Shane can be so stupid—but he says it's so we can enjoy music together the way it was meant to be heard. That makes him happy. And when he's happy, everything seems okay with the world.

It's a long flight to Japan. I used the time to finish writing down everything I remember in a thick leather notebook in permanent ink. For the things I don't remember, I'm forced to fictionalize from newspapers and magazines stuffed into the notebook's back gusset.

There's no shortage of press photos of the aftermath. The shattered windows, the bodies. The avalanche. Or that now-famous comms tower, leaning at its perilous angle. It's become this iconic visual shorthand for the Outage.

I started writing this after I knew I was going to have a baby. It didn't seem fair that the world would never know the true story about what happened. My urge is to wait until my daughter gets old enough, and then tell her the legend of Max and Pilot in a backyard tent by flashlight.

But the truth is I don't know what I'll do with this notebook now that I'm finished. I can tell Shane's not comfortable with it, and he's right to be. I've fashioned a kind of bomb. But Shane also knows it's something I needed to do, for reasons that will hopefully reveal themselves one day.

Maybe it doesn't even matter. Maybe Max's story will no longer be relevant in the distant future. Just a historical footnote among others much worse, and much bloodier. Maybe, after hearing the whole thing, my daughter will just say *Wow, Mom* and resume the joyful business of being alive.

I know I should probably burn it. But no way. I insist that this story should be shared—

—*must* be shared—

—even if there's no one but me to read it.

None of what I'm saying makes much sense. Or does it, in its own strange way? It has to. It has to. Why else would I have such an urge to write everything down?

Shane opens the chrome case for the brand-new audiophile-quality earbuds as if he's proposing to me all over again.

"Superspy shit right here," he says.

And we kiss.

I stand under the temple gate and wait for Shane to set up his shot with his outrageous camera and its foot-long lens. I stand at profile, squinting sidelong in the bright morning light. I rest a hand on my belly. I am here visiting my father, who now lives outside Tokyo in a seaside suburb.

I used to hate him for never standing up to my mother. But now I don't think about any of that crap from the past. I just let myself miss him, and I let myself be excited to see him for the first time in a long time.

"Hurry up, baby bear," I say.

I am at a large intersection that plays music when it's safe to cross. The music plays, and the crossing surges with hundreds of people before emptying again like a tide. Then the music stops. The music, I later learn, is the old folk tune "Toryanse," performed in a robotic square-waveform drone.

The intersection has street vendors for everything: fried octopus, ice cream, toys, balloons. I hear hawkers, children whining, someone on a megaphone shouting about a sale or something. I can only understand bits and pieces. My Japanese sucks.

And then, in between rivers of foot traffic, I see him.

Our eyes lock. He looks thinner. Sharper. But those are the same Buddy Holly glasses. The same bad posture. It is Max, standing and staring. I watch as he lifts something to his lips—a vaporizer—and exhales a long curling stream of smoke into the sharp morning air.

Shane peers out from behind his lens. "What's wrong?"

All I can do is raise my hand and point. Am I really seeing what I am seeing? I want to shout *Max*, but you can't just shout such a thing in a place as crowded as this.

For we are we, and he is he.

A bus goes by, and then another, and when the intersection is finally clear of cars Max is gone but for the smoke. In his place, there on the sidewalk, rests a small stuffed animal.

Once again the intersection floods with people. I join the fray.

"Baby," cries Shane. He jogs to catch up.

I keep pace, eyes on the toy.

"What is it?" says Shane.

We reach the other side, and I pick it up. It is a teddy bear done in the unbearably cute Japanese style. The tag on its ear bears the handwritten words:

Congrats, duncies

Shane looks at me. I look at Shane.

The ink will vanish within the next twenty-four hours. The crosswalk music plays.

Going in is easy / Returning is scary
But while it is scary
You may go in / You may pass through

ACKNOWLEDGMENTS

Before I was able to write full time, I worked in the tech industry for twenty-odd years—all the way from the early days of the World Wide Web to around 2016, two years before Max's adventure begins. So, in a way, you could say *Version Zero* was a very long time in the making. This story represents many of my obsessive ruminations about the impact of networked computers on human society that have been overgrowing in my head. The fact that you are holding my book in your hands right now is an absolute honor.

There's no way this novel could have happened without Joelle Hobeika, Sara Banks, Josh Bank, and everyone at Alloy Entertainment, who steadfastly believed in this book as it sprawled out over the years before being trimmed back into the tidy form you see today.

It also could not have happened without Josh Getzler and Jonathan Cobb at HG Literary, champions from the start, and of course the terrifyingly perceptive and wise Mark Tavani, Executive Editor at Penguin Putnam. This book also owes its very existence to Putnam President Ivan Held and Publisher Sally Kim—thank you from the bottom of my heart. Major respect also to Editorial Assistant Danielle Dieterich as well as the copyeditors who put up with my made-up words (eighteen total—can you catch 'em all?).

Thanks to early readers and best buddies Nathan Cernosek, Patrick Coyle, and especially Andrew Dodge, for our IPA-fueled *What if?* discussions about the internet.

Thanks to Eric Yoon (yoonicode.com), my genius nephew who created the Easter egg code found on each act break. Yes! An Easter egg!

Thanks also to Penny, *goodayscooday, fadina,* and *halafa.*

Biggest, most heartfelt thanks to superstar wife Nicola Yoon. Only she knows in intimate detail all the thrilling ups and heartbreaking downs involved in writing this book. Throughout it all she kept me off the cliff, and kept me going. *Version Zero* would have died in a drawer without her.

I must finally mention the The Rubicon Project, PhishMe (now Cofense), and all the dozens of startups I worked with over the years as a user experience expert, for exposing me firsthand to all the fascinating behind-the-scenes insight on how our internet sausage is made. The people working at these companies are good folks with brilliant minds and curious spirits who at heart just want to make cool stuff. Like all of us, they work under larger forces that bend every technology, however seemingly insignificant, to the will of late-stage capitalism. There are no tech stories—only human stories.